T0129215

Best friends since their schooldays, Henrietta, Harriet, and Hero are wise and witty young ladies, embarking on the sometimes bumpy road to happily-ever-after, each in her own brilliant way . . .

Hero Whitby has harbored long-buried fears since a devastating attack by two young men of the privileged class. Now, while her peers aspire to husband-hunting, Hero pursues her passion to be a doctor, working alongside her father, a respected Devonshire physician. But when a badly beaten stranger is carried in to his practice, Hero is stunned by her reaction. Over three days of tending to the man, along with her instinct to heal, she finds herself intensely drawn to him . . .

Robbed and left for dead by highwaymen, Alexander Sterne has no memory of his past as a soldier in Wellington's army—or as a carousing playboy. But as he becomes aware of his surroundings and the plight of the locals, Alex realizes only he can break the corrupt hold of an evil land steward. And when Hero's tender kiss awakens him from sleep—and restores his identity—he knows that he must regain not only his strength but a newfound compassion . . . which can only be ignited by Hero and a meeting of hearts that may heal them both . . .

IT ONLY TAKES A KISS

She lifted her head to gaze into Adam's eyes—those blue eyes that never failed to mesmerize her. There was a long pause, then he lowered his mouth to hers in what she later supposed had been meant as a casual congratulatory kiss.

It quickly turned into something else.

Her arms slipped up around his neck and she pressed her body against his, needing to be closer, ever closer. For the minutest fraction of a second, some analytical part of her brain told her this was not real, that it was happening merely as an aftermath of the tension she had felt earlier. She ignored that and gave herself up to the sheer passion of the moment...

Books by Wilma Counts

An Earl Like No Other
The Memory of Your Kiss
My Fair Lord
It Only Takes A Kiss

Published by Kensington Publishing Corporation

It Only Takes a Kiss

Wilma Counts

LYRICAL PRESS
Kensington Publishing Corp.
www.kensingtonbooks.com

First Electronic Edition: October 2018
eISBN-13: 978-1-60183-909-1
eISBN-10: 1-60183-909-X

First Print Edition: October 2018
ISBN-13: 978-1-60183-910-7
ISBN-10: 1-60183-910-3

Printed in the United States of America

For Marty Hutton
who loves Cornwall
and managed to do her job
despite my babbling
about my characters

Prologue

The Duchess of Thornleigh was worried about one of her sons—she had three, as well as two daughters, and she worried about all of them from time to time, but she had convinced herself that this time her concern was more than justified. Never one to suffer in silence, she unloaded her worries on her husband.

"I vow, Alfred, ever since his return from the Continent, Alex has seemed out of sorts," she said as she swept from her dressing room into the master bedchamber of Thornleigh House, the duke's London residence. She sank onto a couch beside the duke, who had been calmly reading a travel book as he waited for her. She had not bothered to tie the sashes of a maroon silk robe that she wore over a pink nightgown, also silk.

Her husband was not at all surprised that his energetic wife had started in the middle of a conversation. "What is it this time?" He put his book aside and draped an arm over her shoulder.

"No one thing in particular," she said with a sigh. "It is just that I often catch him sort of staring into space. He is out every night. He is gambling too much and drinking too much. And there are women too. Not *a* woman. Women—plural, and of a certain sort. I know I am not supposed to know these things, but they are common knowledge below stairs—"

"The man is thirty years old," her husband admonished. "He is entitled to live as he pleases."

"He is thirty-one," she corrected. "But the point is, he is behaving as he did when he was a twenty-year-old."

"Well, not *exactly* as he did then, but—"

She rushed on. "And I have it on good authority that he rides that black beast of his like a madman, returning it to the stables in a high degree of lather."

"Now, now, my dear." He squeezed her shoulder. "You must not put yourself into a lather too. *Our* son returned to us. Wellington lost thousands at Waterloo, you know."

"I do know. And my heart grieves for those other mothers. But Baxter tells me—"

"Servants' gossip, my love," he chided.

She waved a dismissive hand. "Baxter tells me the servants talk about terrible nightmares in which he seems to relive horrifying scenes of battle."

"I know. Jasper told me."

"And you accuse *me* of listening to servants?" She reached to brush a lock of silvery gray hair off his brow. "Your valet and my maid are caring people. Besides, they have known Alex since he was in short coats."

"I know, my dear. I am worried about him too. He needs purpose—something to absorb all that pent-up energy. I can hardly buy him another commission, can I? Or threaten to cut off his allowance—when his income exceeds anything I might give him."

"If my brother were not already dead, I should be sorely tempted to kill him for making Alex his heir," she muttered.

"Alex needs to take more interest in his inheritance."

"He needs a *wife*," she said vehemently, "but he refuses most invitations to affairs of polite society where he might meet eligible ladies. Instead, he prefers to spend much of his time at his club with other returned soldiers."

"I will speak to him—again. But he has been home only a few months. Ten years and more is a long time to be away."

"He was never like this when he had occasional leaves during those years. Then, he had changed a little—matured—but not truly changed. Not like this."

"He always knew he was going back to it. He is not going back this time."

"Thank goodness."

"The point is, my love, he needs time to work into this new life."

"Alfred! He has had seven months already."

He kissed her cheek. "Stop fretting, Elizabeth. I will speak to him. But he is his own man now. There is not much more I can do. I keep hoping he will turn his attention to that neglected property in Cornwall, but..." His voice trailed off, then brightened. "Now—let's talk about something else—like our trip."

She laid her head on his shoulder. "I am not even sure we should go—not with Alex in such straits."

He gave her a shake. "Oh, no, my dear! You are not changing your mind at this late date! You have nagged at me for years about wanting to see Rome and Florence and go the opera at La Scala. Now that the Corsican monster is firmly ensconced on St. Helena, we are going. Period. End of discussion."

"I do not nag. But Alex—"

"Is a big boy. He can take care of himself. He has managed to do so for over a decade with little help from us. But—just in case—I have asked Finneston to look in on him now and then." The Marquis of Finneston was the duke's heir, and Alex's older brother.

He pulled her close and said, "When we get to Florence, I don't want you to go comparing my attributes to those of Michelangelo's David. Remember, David was a young man in his prime."

She snuggled even closer. "I've no quarrel with your 'attributes,' my darling."

Chapter 1

May 1816

The persistent pounding finally filtered through the fog of sleep. No, it was not a ship's carpenter pounding on the deck of a pirate's galleon—though just why Miss Hero Whitby, daughter of a country doctor, would ever be a captive on a pirate ship, watching a handsome pirate captain swashbuckle his way through formidable enemies, was quite beyond her. Must have been something in her younger brother's last missive from school. Jonathan had always loved pirate stories. Either that, or the letter she'd received recently from Lady Henrietta Parker—no, Lady Bodwyn now.

Hero smiled at recalling how her friend Retta sang the praises of her new husband and of the married state in general. She was amused because the so-called "Three H's" at Miss Pringle's school—Henrietta, Harriet, and Hero—had long considered themselves firmly "on the shelf." Such romantic effusions were distinctly out of character for any of the H's. Hero knew that a woman in her midtwenties was expected to be dismayed by her unmarried state, but it was a fact of her own life that Hero regretted not at all, handsome pirate captains notwithstanding.

Reluctantly giving up the comfort of dreamland and pleasant musings, she tossed aside the covers and forced herself fully awake.

"I'm coming," she muttered, pulling an old woolen robe over her flannel nightgown, her feet seeking fleece-lined slippers. She turned up the wick on the oil lamp next to her bed and glanced at the clock. Five o'clock in the morning! She carried the lamp into the hall, where she heard her father's door open.

"I'll see to it, Papa. You need your rest—and stay off that gouty foot."

"Hmpf!" he grunted in response. "'Twas not I who spent all day and much of the evening yesterday seeing Mrs. Humphrey through the birth of her seventh child—or was it the eighth?"

"Her eighth—another boy," Hero called over her shoulder as she started down the stairs.

"Don't know why that woman can't figure out where all those babies come from," Dr. Whitby growled in an undertone, then raised his voice to call, "I'll be there shortly."

The knocking was louder as she reached the entrance hall; it was now accompanied by a gruff male voice yelling, "Hey, Doc!"

Stewart, the Whitbys' handyman who served variously as butler, gardener, and coachman, was already opening the door.

"Need the doc," the voice said.

"What is it, Mr. Jacobs?" Hero asked. She had recognized him immediately as a local fisherman.

"Got a man hurt bad, Miss Hero. Me 'n' my boy was jus' going to the boat 'n' we saw him a-layin' on the side o' the road. Got him in the back of the wagon."

"But he *is* alive?" she asked.

"Oh, ya. Moanin' like the devil he is, but don't say nothin' that makes sense."

"Stewart, get the litter and help Mr. Jacobs and his son bring the man into the surgery. I will meet you there."

"Yes, ma'am."

Before going to the surgery herself, she approached the door of Mrs. Hutchins, who had a bed-sitting room on the ground floor just off the kitchen in the rear of the building. Mrs. Hutchins had served the Whitby family as housekeeper and cook since before Hero was born. The door opened even as Hero raised her hand to knock. Mrs. Hutchins, several inches shorter than Hero and some four stone heavier, was tying the sash of her robe.

"I heard the commotion, Miss Hero. I'll get hot water goin' right away. Should still be some warm in the tank on the cooker."

Hero hurried to the surgery, saying a brief prayer of thanksgiving that a decade earlier, when her father had built his new surgery, he had also seen fit to install a fancy cast-iron cooker to replace the old-fashioned kitchen fireplace. Arriving at the surgery, she lighted a spill from the lamp she carried and lit the side lamps in the surgery and one hanging directly over a long rectangular table in the middle of the room. As she had on many previous occasions, she fleetingly marveled at the medical facility her father had designed for the community he served: Besides the surgical room, there was a room with two beds, an office, and an examination room for run-of-the-mill illnesses and mishaps. Visiting medical colleagues never failed to show approval—and envy—of the facility, however much they may have been surprised at finding Dr. Whitby had a female assistant. She lit the fire in the fireplace, then exchanged her wool robe for a lighter, apron-like garment that would allow freer movement. As she checked to see that everything was in order, she heard the three men grunting and muttering with their burden. The two Jacobs men lifted the litter even with the table as Stewart and Hero maneuvered the patient onto the table. He groaned and flailed his hands feebly, but he did not really fight them. Finally, he was in position to be examined.

"He's a big 'un," the elder Jacobs man said. "Don't know how long he musta laid there in the cold afore we come along."

"Pa 'n' me think robbers spooked his horse 'n' made off with it 'n' any valuables," said the son, a broad-shouldered lad in his late teens.

"But they musta been interrupted," his father noted. "Didn't have time ta git his boots."

Hero glanced briefly at the man's boots—shiny and black—but concentrated her attention on the rest of him. Mr. Jacobs was right: He was a big man. Hero estimated more than six feet and maybe thirteen or fourteen stone. Dark brown hair, matted with blood above one ear. Streaks of blood on his face, smeared where he had apparently swiped his face with his arm. A torn white linen shirt showing splotches of dirt and bloodstains, especially on one sleeve. No coat, which might have held a wallet and some means of identification. Well-fitted buckskin pantaloons. The pantaloons. Something wrong there. Blood had stained through the leather and there was a sharp angle in the right thigh just above the knee. Good God! Bone. She'd seen broken legs before, but not like this. She ran her hands along a firm torso. He flinched at her touch and moaned anew.

"Broken ribs. Get his clothes off," she ordered.

"But, miss—" the older Jacobs man protested.

"Do as she says," her father said, limping into the room with his cane and taking in the situation at a glance.

"Do it carefully," Hero said. "Mrs. Hutchins will have a fit if we totally destroy his clothing."

Her father supervised the disrobing, ensuring that Stewart cut the garments along the seams, as Hero turned her attention to the man's head wound. As usual, the head injury had bled profusely, but there was only a small laceration and a bump the size of large egg above his left ear. She ruthlessly destroyed the handiwork of some stylish hairdresser or valet and cut away the hair around the wound, which she then washed thoroughly. She also wiped away the streaks of blood on his face, glad to see no fresh flow of blood. "Hmm. Not too bad, I think. Do have a look, Papa."

Her father limped the few steps to where she stood. "He could have a concussion. No telling how long he's been unconscious. Just put a loose bandage on that, then help me see to his leg. It's a bad break and if gangrene sets in, he will lose the leg."

"We'll jus' be goin' now," the elder fisherman said. "Gotta catch the tide just right, ye know."

"Of course," Hero said, tying the ends of the bandage around the patient's head. "He will be all right now. You likely saved his life."

"We'll check back wit' ye later."

The Jacobs men left and Hero immediately mentally kicked herself for letting them go. The leg had not been set yet.

The man was naked now except for a towel Dr. Whitby had thrown across his groin. Hero smiled to herself. It was not as though she had never seen a naked man before, but her father always tried to be protective of his daughter's modesty.

"He looks to be in good physical shape," Dr. Whitby said, "in spite of all these scars." He pointed at a scar on the man's side that ran to his back and a long scar on the thigh of the leg that had not been broken. Hero noted two others on his face, one from his nose to his left jaw and another that slashed through the outer edge of his right eyebrow, but she also noted that neither of these diminished his looks appreciably. His face and neck, as well as his hands—though bloodied—were deeply tanned; his torso from the neck down slightly less so. She could not help noticing that, cleaned up, this would be one very attractive man.

"I would say our sleeping giant either is or has been a soldier," her father continued. "Come look at this leg, Hero. You will have some needlework to do here."

Hero looked and was dismayed to see that her father was right. She hated sewing pieces of human flesh back together, though the Good Lord knew she had done so often enough. A jagged section of the man's femur jutted from a six-inch slash above his right knee.

"You will need to clean that out thoroughly," her father said. "See that there are no small bits floating about to cause infection."

"Yes, Papa," she said patiently.

"Sorry, my dear. I sometimes forget that you know as much as I do by now."

"I sincerely doubt that, Papa, but I do remember how to clean a wound."

"Stewart, you help her set the leg. There should be some boards and strips of cloth for a splint in the closet."

"Yes, sir."

Mrs. Hutchins and a maid shuffled in carrying buckets of hot water.

The maid Dorcas—Mrs. Hutchins's pretty sixteen-year-old niece— stared at the body on the table. She emitted a long sigh. "That there is a real good-lookin' feller."

"Never you mind, missy," her aunt said. "You just set them buckets down and get on back to the kitchen. Refill that tank and then you get started on the bread. It ain't gonna make itself."

"Yes, ma'am." Dorcas backed out of the room slowly, keeping her eyes on the supine figure on the table. Mrs. Hutchins made a shushing noise and waved the girl on her way.

With the help of her father and Stewart—and silently glad the patient was still unconscious—Hero carefully placed several strips of cloth and a flat length of wood under his injured leg. These would form the basis of the splint to keep the broken bone in place.

Stewart had brought in a stool for Dr. Whitby, who watched with great interest while Hero cleaned the surface of the wound and began probing for bits of shattered bone, which could cause problems later. The patient groaned and flinched from time to time. Stewart stood at the head of the table, ready to grab the man's shoulders if necessary to keep him in place as Hero worked. It was yet another task the handyman performed occasionally. Dr. Whitby, acting as his daughter's assistant, kept mopping the fresh blood away. In recent years, that had been more and more the way of things. Whereas Hero had once been his apprentice in all but name, the roles had been reversed as her father's stamina had weakened and he now experienced occasional tremors in his once steady-as-a-rock hands.

"I think that's it." Hero stood back for a moment while her father mopped at the slowing trickle of blood. "Now, to set this bone. Mrs. Hutchins, if you will hold his shoulders down to keep him from thrashing about, and, Mr. Stewart, if you will take hold of his foot and ankle and pull when I tell you to—"

Hero gripped the patient's leg around his upper thigh to hold it steady; Stewart gripped his ankle and pulled, and Dr. Whitby guided the bone into place, then held another, shorter, flat length of wood against the inside of the leg as Hero stitched together the edges of the wound on his outer thigh. The patient had groaned and tried to thrash about as they repositioned the bone, but Mrs. Hutchins was a strong woman and prevented undue movement. The final step was to bandage the wound, then place a third length of wood along the outside of the leg and tie the strips of cloth that would hold the splint in place.

Hero stepped away from the table slightly and arched her back. "What time is it?"

Her father extracted his watch from a pocket. "Almost nine."

"Oh, dear. And we've still his ribs to see to. Papa, why don't you go and get your foot elevated?" The fact that he offered no protest told her volumes about his degree of pain and lack of stamina.

She ran her hands along the injured man's rib cage—bare, this time. His skin was warm—not feverish yet, just warm. As she leaned close, she caught a whiff of cedar and spice. His shaving soap? As she ran her hands over his ribs, she felt and saw some old scars. It occurred to her that if her father's conjecture was right—and she thought it was—this man had been through more than one campaign. She thought of her brother Michael, two years her senior, still with the British Army of Occupation in Belgium. As a medical man, Michael would not have been directly involved in that awful battle at Waterloo nearly ten months ago, but he would have seen the results firsthand.

She abandoned these musings and turned to the task at hand: binding broken ribs. With the help of Mrs. Hutchins and Mr. Stewart, she managed to get two wide bands of cloth under the man's rib cage despite his incoherent protests. She then tied them tightly. Stewart wheeled one of the beds in from the adjoining room. That was another of her father's brilliant innovations: wheels on patient beds. Stewart blocked the wheels with small wedges of wood and, trying to cause the man as little discomfort as possible, the three of them transferred him from the table to the bed and wheeled the bed back to its customary location next door. They also put side rails in place to prevent the patient's rolling out of bed. The wheels were again blocked, and he was covered with warm blankets. The transfer process had not been easy because of his size and his state of unconsciousness. His mutterings had decreased significantly and Hero thought he might have drifted into real sleep.

"I'll sit wit' his lordship while ye get a bit o' rest," Mrs. Hutchins announced. The older woman, nominally a servant in the doctor's household, had years ago taken a motherly interest in her employer's motherless children.

"'His lordship'? What makes you think he deserves such an exalted address?"

"Well, he ain't no fisherman or farmer with that fine linen shirt an' them boots."

"You may have a point there," Hero said, "though he could just as well be a member of the gentry as the aristocracy. However, I'd rather you see to breakfast—late as it is. Stewart, will you watch 'his lordship' for a few minutes as I freshen up?"

Twenty minutes later, Hero had hurriedly changed into a comfortable day dress and serviceable shoes and rebraided her hair, arranging the braids in a crown on top of her head. She also grabbed a bit of breakfast, choosing to sit at one end of the kitchen worktable rather than sit alone in the dining room, when Mrs. Hutchins told her that her father had already broken his fast and gone about whatever business called him today. Hero always loved the warmth and the spicy smell of the kitchen.

Taking with her a bucket of hot water, she reported back to the hospital rooms, where she found not Mr. Stewart, but her father sitting on a chair beside the patient's bed. She sighed. She should have known.

"How is he?" she asked, setting down her steaming bucket and reaching to feel the pulse at the base of his neck.

"Quiet. Getting a bit feverish, though. Have to watch that."

"Mrs. Hutchins is calling him 'his lordship' until we have a real name for him."

"Is she now? We could use someone of that rank in this area. Someone to put Willard Teague and his bully boys from the docks of Bristol in their place."

"I know, Papa. But you know as well as I do that the only person who could wield such authority is the absentee owner of the Abbey. Ever since Sir Benjamin died—"

"Now, now, daughter. Don't you be working yourself into a tizzy over that man's absence," her father cautioned mildly.

"I won't," she promised, idly fussing with the bedding covering their patient, "but it is such a shame. That whole estate—the farms, the mine— people are really hurting. Our neighbors! Diana says their roof needs repair. The roof, Papa! He's responsible."

"Never mind, my dear. Your sister knows well enough she and her family need never go without a roof over their heads."

"Papa, that is not the point and you know it. Sir Benjamin has been dead for what?—eight years now—and the biggest landholding in the area continues to go downhill. Tenant farmers like Diana's Milton and those miners—they are all victims of an owner who puts none of his gains back into his holdings. How on earth could anyone with a shred of conscience allow people to suffer so?"

"No tizzy, remember?" His voice softened. "Of course you are right. But we cannot do much about Weyburn Abbey if the current owner continues to ignore it." He pointed at their patient. "Best stick to what we *can* do—like see to this poor fellow." He rose and hobbled on his cane to the door. "Keep an eye on him. Let me know if his temperature rises."

Hero placed a hand on the patient's forehead. "Not bad at the moment. And, Papa, you should be in the drawing room with your foot elevated!"

"I'll go as soon as I see to Jupiter. Perkins says that gash above his left foreleg is not healing well and Jupiter will not allow anyone in the stable to touch it."

"You be careful now," she said automatically. She worried about her father's doing too much, but she hadn't the heart—let alone the authority—to force her stubborn parent to slow down. *Maybe when Michael comes home*, she mused.

She poured clean water into a bowl, dipped a clean cloth into it, and, parting the patient's lips, dribbled a bit of liquid into his mouth. She was pleased to see his throat move as he swallowed.

"We must see that you get enough water," she said to the inert figure.

Leaving open the door between the surgery and the room where he lay, Hero set about putting the surgery back in order. Mr. Stewart had already swept the floor and restored the litter to its proper place, upright in a corner. She washed the instruments they had used and the surgical table, then placed a clean sheet on it, noting that Mr. Stewart had already taken the soiled one, along with the patient's clothing, out to the washhouse.

She looked around for something else to do, but all seemed in order. Again, she forced a bit of water into him, then took the chair her father had vacated and just sat there watching that rather disturbingly handsome man breathe. She chastised herself for not thinking of bringing a book or her knitting. One of his hands lay at his side outside the blanket. Noting that the nails were mostly free of dirt, she lifted the hand in her own. It was much larger than hers, with long, well-shaped fingers. Suddenly, he seemed to grip her hand, and he mumbled something; it sounded to her like "Damnation, Ollie!" Then he loosened his hold and fell silent again.

"Well," she murmured, putting his arm and hand back under the covers, "there's *something* going on in that mind of yours. Let's hope you wake up sooner rather than later."

She dozed off, resting her head on her arms folded on the edge of the bed. She was startled awake when Stewart touched her shoulder.

"Doc says I should relieve you, Miss Hero. Says you should have a proper nap."

"Oh. Oh, all right." She yawned and showed Stewart how to dribble water into the patient. "Don't hesitate to ring for me if you need to," she said, gesturing at the bellpull at the head of the bed.

"Yes, ma'am."

Chapter 2

She had a nap, albeit a short one. Then she returned to the side of her patient. Beginning to think of the process as not unlike watering a plant to keep it alive, she gave him a bit of water, then set about making up a schedule of two-hour shifts for herself and others of the household to watch over him—with strict instructions to call her immediately in the event of any changes. Out of worry for her father's health, she would have left him off the schedule, but she knew he would feel slighted if she did not include him. As would Mrs. Hutchins, who, besides having her household duties, was of an age with Hero's father. Dorcas was thrilled to be asked to help watch over "such a fine-lookin' feller"—until she had been at it for about fifteen minutes and discovered watching another person breathe and moistening his lips occasionally was not such a thrill after all. A young footman shared Dorcas's lack of enthusiasm for the task, but both performed it without too much protest.

Shortly before supper, the Whitby household received a visit from Samuel Porter, the blacksmith and mayor of the town of Weyburn.

"Heard you got yourselves a new patient," announced Porter, a man whose physique fitted—or resulted from—his profession. Hero's age, he was of medium height, but had shoulders as wide as the door. Hero had helped in the delivery of two of his four children; each time the strongest man in the town—who had been through the process before—hovered anxiously outside the bedroom where his wife, knowing he was there, tried to control her cries of pain. Hero had grown up with both of them and had always envied the closeness between Sam Porter and his Susie.

"Yes, we have a new patient," Dr. Whitby said as the visitor was shown into the library, where the doctor sat with his foot propped on a footstool and Hero had been reading about blows to the human head in one of her brother Michael's medical books.

"Know who he is yet?" Porter asked, still clutching his cap in his hand.

"Haven't a clue," the doctor replied. "Hero, take Sam out to have a look. See if he knows him."

Hero led the way to the hospital rooms, asking about Susie and the Porter children as she did so. Dorcas sat at the patient's side with a pile of assorted cloths on a small stool near her chair, needle and thread in her hand. She looked up with a smile, welcoming the interruption.

"I hate mending," she announced without preamble, "but Aunt Mary says I 'might as well do something useful while I'm here.'" She imitated her aunt's speech, then added in her own youthful tone, "Hello, Mr. Porter."

Porter nodded at the girl. "Dorcas." He stepped nearer the bed and studied the patient, then said, "I never saw him before, but Wellman said some feller rode through town yesterday—late afternoon. Well dressed, Wellman said. Asked directions to the Abbey, but didn't say anything else."

Wellman, the town's butcher, owned the town's mercantile store, which also held the post office. Hero knew that Bertie Wellman would have been disappointed that a new face in town did not stop to supply him with more information.

"Maybe he *is* a lord then." Dorcas was obviously excited at the prospect. "The owner, maybe."

"Don't mean to dash your hopes, Dorcas," Porter said, "but the man who owns the Abbey is a real nob—son of a duke. Those sorts travel in fancy carriages with outriders and all."

"I s'pose you're right," she said glumly.

"And besides that," Hero said, "Papa thinks this man was a soldier."

"Well, *some* nobs is also soldiers," Dorcas said, sounding defensive.

"The main seat of the Duke of Thornleigh is way up north in Yorkshire," Porter explained. "I doubt any member of that family would be traveling down here on horseback. Alone." Porter put his cap back on his head and turned to Hero. "I gotta get goin'. Susie will have supper on the table already. Let me know if you find out who he is."

Hero had no sooner seen Porter on his way than two more visitors arrived at the Whitby gate. The elder Jacobs man jumped down from the wagon as his son sat holding the reins of their horse. The father handed Hero a package wrapped in newspaper.

"Cod. Good fishin' today, Miss Hero."

"Let me pay you for this," she said.

"Now, Miss Hero, you know well as I do it ain't bin a year since you saved my Aggie. The deal was I'd keep you supplied with fish for a year."

"Well, thank you," she said, acquiescing.

"So, how's our man a-doin'?"

"He's still unconscious."

"Did Porter know 'im? Saw Sam leavin' as we drove up."

"No. Still no clues. Though Mr. Wellman is said to have spoken with a stranger riding through yesterday afternoon. Asked directions to the Abbey."

"Hmm. That's not necessarily good news, now, is it? Could be he has business with Teague."

"Now, Pa," the younger Jacobs cautioned. "You promised not to be sayin' anything openly against Mr. Teague. 'Tain't safe."

"I can surely speak freely with Miss Hero."

The son merely shrugged.

The Jacobs men took their leave and Hero took the fish into the kitchen.

"More fish, eh?" Mrs. Hutchins commented. "It's good at least *some* of your patients pays you in real money. Just put it on the table there. I'll have Davey take it out to the well house when he comes in for supper." Davey, twin brother of the teenage Dorcas, helped out in the Whitby stable, but also functioned as an extra footman, doing odd jobs for Stewart, mostly outside.

Concerned that her patient remained unconscious, Hero had checked on him throughout the afternoon and evening, seeing little change in all those hours. Before retiring for the night, she reiterated that the "night watchers" should notify her immediately of any change. Thus it was that half after two the next morning she answered a soft knock at her bedroom door to find a nervous Stewart standing there.

"I went to relieve Mrs. Hutchins and the two of us think maybe you'd better come to see to his lordship. He's moanin' to beat all an' he's thrashin' about some."

"I'll be right there," she said. She donned her robe and slippers and made her way downstairs behind Stewart, both of them wary of waking her father. She found Mrs. Hutchins standing over the patient, patting his shoulder and murmuring softly to him.

"Oh, good. You're here," Mrs. Hutchins said to Hero. "He's not conscious by any means, but he keeps talking—doesn't make sense, mind you—an' he's also moving his arms an' that good leg of his. Tryin' to move the other one too. Tosses the cover off as fast I can put it back."

Hero put a hand on his forehead. "Hmm. His temperature is up." She checked the bandage on his head wound. "That bump seems a bit smaller than it was. Let's look at the leg. Bring the lamp closer, please."

Mrs. Hutchins gasped when Hero lifted the edge of the blanket and they saw an angry red splash of color on either side of the bandage. Hero removed the bandage and inspected her stitchery. She dipped a cloth in a basin of clean water that Stewart held close; she gently washed around the wound. Almost as if he were aware of what she was doing, the patient's moans lessened to long, shuddering breaths and the leg was still as she worked.

"We'll just leave this uncovered for a bit, shall we?" she said to herself more than to anyone else. She wet another cloth and wiped his face, neck, and shoulders; he seemed to calm even more. Mr. Stewart set the basin aside and she dipped the corner of yet another cloth in the bowl of water from which they had been keeping his mouth moistened. Again, she was glad to see him swallowing and even spontaneously licking his lips. "Like that, do you?" she asked softly, leaning closer. He turned his face toward the sound of her voice.

"Would you look at *that*?" Mrs. Hutchins murmured as she put the lamp on a nightstand near the bed. "That's the first I've seen him really respond to anything."

"It's a hopeful sign," Hero said. "I'll sit with him now. You two go and rest. The sun will be up before we know it."

With only token protests, the two did as she bade them. Hero placed a clean bandage on the leg wound, then dipped a cloth in the cool water and wiped his brow, his neck, his chest to the edge of the bandage on his ribs, his arms, and his uninjured leg. Tucking the blanket around him, she settled herself in the bedside chair. At least she had had sense enough to leave her knitting here earlier. She reached for the basket under the edge of the bed and inspected her work to pick up the pattern again.

About an hour later her patient began to mutter and thrash about, especially tossing his head from side to side. At first the sounds were soft grunts and moans, but they grew in both frequency and volume. And they became more distinguishable as words or names.

"On your right, Ollie!"

"Over there, Fitz!"

"Stand your ground, men!"

"Hold your fire!"

"Look out, Ollie! Ah, God, Ollie—No! Olliiiiie…" This cry ended on a sob, and an immediate, firm, "No time. Mourn later."

"Fitz! Take over. There! That cannon!"

Hero quickly set aside her knitting and said to herself, *Well, that confirms Papa's theory about your being a soldier.* She moved her chair nearer his head and grabbed the hand nearest her to keep him from flailing it about. "You are safe now," she said softly, holding his hand in both of hers. "Everyone is safe. Shhh."

He quieted. When the hand she held relaxed, she thought he had lapsed into real sleep again. Nevertheless, she gave him a bit of water and straightened the blanket covering him. She gazed at him, admiring the regular features of his face, taking in the fading scent of what she had assumed earlier to be his shaving soap, and listening with pleasure to the sound of his regular breathing. She was puzzled by her own sense of protectiveness about this particular patient, especially given the possibility that he might be a lord, as Mrs. Hutchins had suggested. At best, Miss Hero Whitby extended only passing indifference to male members of that element of society. She had long since got over her fear—indeed, her intense dislike—of such men. Still, there were residuals of those feelings that had once dominated her attitude to them.

Nevertheless, this man occupied her thoughts far more than she liked to acknowledge, even to herself. Had he been the first injured man she had ever treated, she could have understood this feeling better. But she knew if she lost him or if he lost his leg—gangrene was still a possibility—that it would be a *personal* loss for her, a *personal* failure. What was it about *this* man that moved her so?

The next day passed pretty much as the first one had, with one significant exception. In the early afternoon Dr. Whitby and his daughter received a visitor who was greeted with a degree of reservation and indifference rather than enthusiasm.

"Mr. Teague," the doctor said politely, as the man was ushered into the library by Mrs. Hutchins, who had answered the door. The doctor gestured to a barrel-shaped chair for the visitor near the one he himself occupied, with his foot, as usual, propped on a footstool.

Hero rose from the couch where she had been sitting while she and her father discussed their concern over the fact that their patient was still unconscious. "May we offer you some tea or lemonade?" she asked.

"I would welcome a cup of tea." Teague stood near the chair indicated as Hero stepped out to find Mrs. Hutchins waiting at the library door for the order of a tea tray.

Hero returned and seated herself as Teague too sat down. Teague was a man of medium height, and, approaching his late thirties, was still in reasonably good shape, though in a very few years he would be "portly" at best. He was known to be something of a dandy and was dressed as he probably thought a country squire should dress: in a tweed jacket, brown wool knee pants, and highly polished brown boots. He had a full head of blond hair, which he combed in an attempt to emulate a man of fashion. She knew that he fancied himself something of a ladies' man and that, indeed, a number of local women found him attractive. He sat back in his chair with one leg crossed over the other and his fingers laced across his midriff. He looked around the book-lined room as though he were evaluating its contents. "My Lettie would have loved this room," he offered conversationally.

Hero merely raised an eyebrow, knowing full well that the late Letitia Teague had probably never read a book more challenging than a cheap gothic novel once she left the local dame school. But then the poor woman undoubtedly welcomed any diversion from the petty tyranny of such a husband. Mrs. Teague had died giving birth to her fourth child barely ten months after delivering her third. Four babies in six years had just worn the poor woman out. "I knew 'twas too soon," she had said on visiting the Whitbys well into her last pregnancy, "but Willard is a hard man to say no to." The Whitby father and daughter had then exchanged a look of disgust over a bruise on the woman's face.

Mrs. Hutchins brought in the tea tray and set it on a low table in front of Hero. With her back to their visitor, the housekeeper gave Hero a knowing glance and then departed, according him only a nod in passing.

"Doesn't say much, does she?" the visitor observed.

Hero busied herself pouring the tea. "Milk? Or lemon?" she asked him, adding milk as he requested, fixing cups for herself and her father, then serving the tea and a plate of biscuits.

"Was there a particular reason for this visit?" Dr. Whitby asked when they had all settled back in their seats.

Teague placed his cup and saucer on a small table near his elbow and sat more erect with his hands on his knees.

"Well, sir, there's actually two reasons I've seen fit to call today." He gave Hero an oblique look and turned his attention to her father. "My Lettie's been gone for well over a year and I've come to ask your permission to call on Miss Whitby."

Hero gasped, nearly choking on her tea.

Scarcely noting her reaction, Teague went on. "I know such a request would ordinarily be addressed to the father of a young miss in private, but as Miss Whitby has been of age these several years, it seems only fair she should know my intentions right up front, so to speak."

"Well, now," Dr. Whitby said slowly, setting aside his own tea, "my daughter is of age, as you pointed out, and has a mind of her own, as I am sure you know very well."

"Yes, sir. But I'm something of an old-fashioned man, and I thought to gain her father's permission." Teague's ingratiating tone belied almost everything Hero knew of the man who was famous for demanding his own way and causing woe to those who crossed him on even the most insignificant matters. He went on, his tone more firm. "A man needs a woman, don't you know—a helpmeet as the good book says. And there's not a woman alive but what needs the guiding hand of a man."

With the fingers of one hand on his forehead and his palm shading his expression from the visitor, Whitby gazed at his daughter, his eyes fairly dancing. Hero glanced away, afraid she would burst into laughter. She allowed a moment of silence, then innocently offered "More tea?" as a way of leaving a response to this preposterous statement to her father, who did, indeed, rise to the occasion.

"As I said, Mr. Teague, my daughter is her own person. I would not presume to tell her whom to befriend. Didn't do that with her sister; won't do so with her."

"Her sister? That'd be Mrs. Tamblin, Milton Tamblin's wife?" he asked just as though he, as steward of Weyburn Abbey, did not know very well all the Abbey's farmers.

Neither Hero nor her father responded to this, so Teague blundered on. "The Tamblins have one of Weyburn Abbey's tenant farms. Couple of miles from my cottage. I always think it's nice to have family members close by."

"Even better if said family members have a roof that does not leak," Hero said before she could stop herself.

"Well, now, that's a problem that could be remedied easy enough, Miss Whitby."

Her father apparently decided to rescue her, for he said, "You said there were two reasons for your visit."

"Ah, yes. The other is this matter of the man I hear you are doctoring. As I am sort of unofficially a deputy to the magistrate in this area, I thought I should check on any stranger, don't you see?"

Hero snorted inwardly. *You mean,* she thought, *that you have that poor old man bullied into letting you exert undue authority regardless of whether a matter is of any real concern to you.* What she said was, "The man is still unconscious."

Teague continued to address her father. "You got any idea who he is yet?"

"No, we have not," Dr. Whitby said in what Hero recognized as his "professional" voice. "He came to us in rather bad shape, and he is likely to be incapacitated for some time. Broken bones take time to heal."

"Maybe he has family that should be notified," Teague said.

"My daughter and I will handle that issue as soon as he comes to."

"I… uh…see. Well, let me have a look at him. Might be I know who he is as I get around so much in the county."

"As you wish," the doctor said. "Hero?"

She rose and led the way down to the entrance hall, where she picked up Teague's hat from a side table and handed it to him. "This way, please. Please do not try to talk to him. He moans some, but nothing he says makes much sense at all. He is probably asleep."

Teague followed her—too close, she thought, and, as they approached the medical rooms, he made an ostentatious show of opening the door for her and "accidentally" brushing her breast as he did so. She quickly stepped away from him and he chuckled. "Taming a woman like you could be a lot of fun."

"I beg your pardon," she said coldly. "The patient is in the next room."

She crossed the surgery and opened the door to the other room, glad to see that the watcher of the moment was Stewart, who greeted the visitor politely but without enthusiasm. "Mr. Teague."

Teague merely nodded.

"No change, Miss Hero," Stewart said. "He called out them same names again, but don't make no sense."

"Names?" Teague said sharply. "What names?"

"Someone named Ollie an' another'n named Fitz. We think they's fellow soldiers," Stewart explained.

"How d'you know he's a soldier?" Teague asked.

"We do not know that he is, or was," Hero said, "but he has some scars that would indicate that sort of life."

"I see. Well, let me get a look at him."

Hero pulled the blanket away from the patient's chin so his face showed to better advantage, feeling as she did so that she was somehow allowing Teague to invade the man's privacy.

Teague stared long and hard at the figure on the bed, then turned away. "I never saw him before," he said brusquely. "Let me know if you find out who he is." He slammed his hat on his head and left abruptly.

"I didn't wanta say nothin' in front of Teague," Stewart said, "but seems to me he ain't a-sleepin' so deeply as he was afore."

"Hmm. I'll keep watch until suppertime. You need to get at that herb garden while it is still daylight. Get Davey to help you."

"Yes, ma'am."

After supper that evening, as was their custom, Dr. Whitby and his daughter shared cups of tea and whatever had passed that day.

"You were right, Papa," Hero said as she handed him his cup of tea prepared exactly as he liked it: milk and just a little sugar. He reached for the cup. "Fathers are always right, my dear, but about what this time?"

"Our patient must have been a soldier." She told him about the man's unconscious ramblings.

"Hmm." Her father's expression turned serious. "When he becomes conscious, we should probably watch him quite closely. Maybe try to get him to talk about what happened."

"Before the Jacobs men found him, you mean?"

"That too, if he remembers it. Sometimes the most recent memories are the hardest to retrieve."

Hero shifted in her seat across from him. "You mean get him to talk about his experiences in the war?"

"Only so far as he wishes to share those. Sometimes a soldier's worst wounds don't show."

She nodded thoughtfully. "How'd you come to know that, Papa?"

"My cousin James was a few years older than I. He served in America. He came back from his duties there pretty broken up. He'd seen action against both the natives and the colonists. I think it eventually killed him."

"I thought he died in a riding accident."

"He did. But it was probably deliberate. We all knew no horse could take that fence."

She sucked in her breath, appalled. "It was suicide?"

"Mm-hm. Probably. As I say, some wounds just don't show much." He stood and placed his cup back on the tea tray. "It is something to consider." He paused. "With Michael too, maybe—when he comes home."

"Michael?" She set her own cup on the tray and looked up to hold her father's worried gaze.

He nodded. "Michael was a battlefield surgeon. He has done and seen things you and I cannot even imagine."

"You are really worried about him?"

"Maybe not *worried* precisely, but you are the one who noted the change in tone of his last letters. It's something to think about."

"I'm sure Michael will be all right," she said, recalling her brother's laughing eyes as he described some experience from his years in medical school in Edinburgh.

"No doubt he will be," her father said. "And right now we have this fellow to concern ourselves with. I'll go and check on him now, then I'm off to bed." He paused at the door and Hero watched the twinkle return to his eyes. "Now. About this development with Teague. I feel I should tell you I would not welcome him as a son-in-law."

Hero gave an unladylike snort. "There is little danger of that! Where on earth might he have come up with such a preposterous idea?"

"Hard to tell with a man like Teague. He sees things as he wants to—and the devil with anyone else. You be careful around him, Hero."

"I will—and thank you, Papa." She twisted in her seat to turn up the wick of a lamp on a side table and picked up the book she had laid aside earlier in the day.

Chapter 3

Having taken the last of the night shifts with the still unconscious patient, Hero slept late the next morning. She woke to a small hand patting her shoulder and a slobbery kiss on her cheek.

"C'mon, Auntie H'ro. Wake up. You promised..." a childish voice implored.

Hero opened one eye to gaze fondly at the small four-year-old girl badgering her. "Mm. What did I promise? I do not remember any promise." She pretended to snuggle back into her bedcovers.

"Riding!" the child squealed. "'Member?"

"Ah, yes. But was it Annabelle or Tootie who was to ride with me?" Tootie, Annabelle's imaginary friend, had joined the household a few months ago. Hero recognized Tootie's existence as fulfilling a lonely child's need for a companion in an environment dominated by adults.

"Bofe of us! And Bitsy too." Annabelle pushed a black-and-white kitten into Hero's line of vision.

The maid Clara Henson, charged with the care of the little girl, burst into the room. "Oh, Miss Hero, I am so sorry. I turned away for two seconds and she was gone just that quick!"

"Never mind, Clara. I did promise Annabelle we would go riding."

"An' Tootie. An' Bitsy," Annabelle insisted.

"Oh, but how can they ride?" Hero asked. "Sandy is but one small pony."

"I'll hold Bitsy, an' Tootie can sit ahind me," Annabelle said.

"That will work for Tootie, but perhaps we should leave Bitsy in the barn to visit with her brothers and sisters."

"Awright. Long as Tootie can come."

"Of course," Hero said, swinging her legs out of bed.

Although strangers sometimes initially mistook the child as being Hero's daughter, the truth was Annabelle was a ward—of sorts. As one of two midwives in the town and surrounding area, Hero had helped to deliver the child whose mother, a young woman known only as Barbara, had unfortunately died giving birth. At the time, Barbara had been one of four young women or girls then lodging in the home of Weyburn's other midwife, the widowed Sally Knowlton. For years Mrs. Knowlton had taken in young women and girls who were "in trouble." The whole town knew of the situation, and occasionally someone made a snooty remark, but mostly these "fallen women" were tolerated or ignored, since they pretty much stuck to the grounds of the Knowlton home. The young mothers were of two sorts: either daughters of upper class, even aristocratic families, or servants who had been seduced—or, in some cases, raped—by males in such households. The babes were most often placed with foster families.

Hero found it deplorable that always it was the women—and their babes—who paid the price for a situation that, after all, required two in the beginning. The men—or their parents—merely paid money to cover it up, but women and children paid the full price emotionally and socially. Hero simply hadn't much time for the men of England's social elite. She had known some fine men—her father and brothers, for instance—but her own experience, coupled with that of "Mrs. Knowlton's waifs," had shaped her view profoundly.

With the death of Barbara, her babe was first placed with a local farmer's wife to wet nurse. When it came time to place the child in foster care, Hero could not bear to see that happen. So Annabelle entered the Whitby household and proceeded to steal everyone's heart.

"Please take her down to the kitchen, Clara, while I dress for our ride. And please tell Mrs. Hutchins I'd like some toast and coffee."

"Yes, ma'am."

"Ya-ay." Annabelle danced out of the room, still clutching Bitsy to her chest.

Annabelle chatted throughout the ride. She praised the antics of her pets and other animals on the property; she asked dozens of questions beginning with *how* or *why*; and she retold the plots of her favorite tales from the Bible and other bedtime stories. Hero, preoccupied with the problem of her still unresponsive patient, only half listened, but managed to participate appropriately. Once again, she was impressed with the extraordinary depth and breadth of the little girl's sponge-like mind. She was also amused to hear sage-like pronouncements, some of which she recognized as having originally come from herself. Hero smiled at hearing Annabelle admonish

Tootie, "We must treat our animals with respect 'cause they give us so much of themselves."

Afterwards, as they left the stable, Hero said to Annabelle, "I want to check on my patient in the clinic."

Having retrieved her precious Bitsy, Annabelle slipped a small hand into Hero's and skipped beside her. "Can I come too?"

"May I?" Hero corrected.

"May I?"

"Yes, but you must be very quiet. The man is sleeping. And do not touch anything."

Davey, the youngest male servant of the Whitby household, rose from where he had been sitting beside the patient's bed.

"Any change?" Hero asked, moving to the head of the bed. She felt the man's forehead for temperature and the hollow at the base of his neck for pulse.

"Not much as I can see," Davey replied. "Ever' once in a while he cries out, but then he jus' mumbles."

"I am worried that he has remained unconscious for so long," Hero said.

"Is the man sleeping, Auntie H'ro?" Annabelle asked, standing on tiptoe to gaze at his face.

"Sort of, darling. And we need to have him wake up to get well."

"Kiss him," the little girl said.

Davey grinned at this idea and Hero said, "Wha-a-t?"

"Well," Annabelle said, sounding very practical, "that is how the prince woke Sleeping Beauty."

"Ah. So it is." Hero took the child's hand and led her toward the door. "What works in storybooks does not always work in real life."

"But maybe—sometimes—it does?" Annabelle looked up at Hero, who hadn't the heart to simply squelch the child's eagerness to help.

"I suppose it does—sometimes…"

"Well, then?"

Hero shared an amused glance with Davey and said to him, "Continue trying to get water into him—or maybe some of that broth. He needs nourishment too. I showed you how to dip the corner of a cloth into liquid and then dribble it on his lips. Sometimes you need to part the lips slightly."

"Yes, ma'am."

Hero watched as Davey demonstrated that he had mastered this process, then she tugged Annabelle's hand and said, "Come along, my little miss. Let's you and I find a snack."

"Bread and jam!" The child's attention was now firmly diverted.

"And perhaps some cheese and apple juice."

They sat at the kitchen worktable for this repast as Annabelle regaled Mrs. Hutchins and the kitchen staff with a full, detailed account of her morning. Hero was going over in her mind yet again what she might do to bring the patient around.

Later in the day, Hero relieved Dorcas early from her stint at the patient's bedside.

"He still don't say nothin' that makes any sense," Dorcas said.

"At least he is *trying* to communicate with us," Hero said. "That is a good sign."

As Dorcas left, Hero set about what was now routine for her: seeing that the patient got water and lately some broth as well, then wiping his brow, his face, and exposed limbs with a damp cloth. Eyes closed, he turned his head and emitted soft groans or grunts.

"I do so wish you'd wake up," she said. She stood gazing at him, taking in the clean lines of his features. He truly was extraordinarily handsome, despite three days' growth of beard. His body reminded her of the Greek statues she had seen in Lord Elgin's collection in London. *What else might we possibly do?* she wondered. She smiled at remembering Annabelle's suggestion. *Maybe...No. That is ridiculous. Fairy tales, indeed!*

She sat and took up her knitting, but that ridiculous idea would not leave her alone. *Should have brought my book*, she told herself. But it occurred to her that yet another method of stimulation just might—possibly—work. 'Twas worth a try, was it not?

Dismissing the idea as patently silly, she noticed he was turning his head rather vigorously and groaning. She stood to give him more water, then she caressed his face and patted his shoulder, trying to calm him. His beard was just long enough now to be soft rather than bristly. The cedary-spicy smell was still there, but very faint.

"Shhh." She bent near his ear and murmured, "You are safe. Everything is all right now." But his movements increased.

Later, she would chastise herself as several kinds of fool, but suddenly— impulsively—she kissed him!

His lips were dry and warm, and, surprisingly—perhaps instinctively— they responded to the touch of hers. She quickly drew back. His eyes fluttered open and she gazed into their clear but unfocused blue depths. He moaned softly and his eyes closed again, but he seemed quieter now.

Oh, good grief. Whatever possessed me to do that? She stifled a groan of her own and sat back down again. He began to try to thrash around, but they had bound him tightly to the bed to prevent his further injuring himself. She caressed his arm and shoulder, murmuring to him as she did Annabelle when the child was ill. Then she sat and held his hand. Finally, he seemed to sleep again, and, when Stewart came to relieve her, the patient had been quiet for at least half an hour.

Some two hours later, Hero was in the stillroom with Mrs. Hutchins, sorting dried herbs and putting them in labeled jars.

"We are very low on willow bark," Hero observed. "So useful for ordinary pain, you know."

"You have plenty of laudanum, though," the housekeeper said, replacing a container on the highest shelf.

"Good. If our patient ever wakes up, he will likely need it."

The stillroom was located near the kitchen and the servants' hall, just off a hallway that contained a system of bells to notify servants when they were needed elsewhere on the premises. Ordinarily, a given bell sounded once or twice. Now, however, one of them clanged repeatedly and erratically. Mrs. Hutchins, closest to the door, looked out to check the source.

"Goodness. It's the clinic, Miss Hero."

Hero dropped a handful of dill and hurried out. Dorcas was the watcher of the moment and Dorcas was in a panic. The maid frantically clutched the bellpull at the head of the patient's bed with one hand as she tried ineffectually to control the man's moving about by pressing her hand to his shoulder. A strap across his waist and another across his chest under his shoulders held him on the bed. Another stabilized his injured leg.

"Oh, thank God, you're here," Dorcas said. "I think he's wakin' up. He keeps movin' about and he talks real loud sometimes."

"Go and find Stewart," Hero said calmly. She wished her father were here, but he was making house calls in town this afternoon. She took Dorcas's place near the man's head and shoulders. He was moaning fiercely, moving his head side to side and up and down, trying to lurch up. Pain and the straps restrained him.

"God damn it," he said clearly and then emitted a fine sampling of curses in English and at least two other languages. She recognized French and thought another was Spanish. He waved one arm around and kicked out with his uninjured and unconfined leg.

"Shh." Hero placed one hand on his brow and patted his nearest shoulder comfortingly with the other. "Please try to be calm."

His gaze focused on her face and the body movements seemed less frantic. "Who—? Where—?" The words ended on a groan. He closed his eyes tightly against a wave of pain.

"You have been injured," she said. "Rather badly, I'm afraid. But you need to lie still."

Stewart was suddenly at her side. "How can I help, Miss Hero?"

"Hand me that cold cloth and try to keep him from kicking that bad leg," she said in the same steady voice. She placed the cloth on the patient's brow and continued to speak softly to him. "You've a broken leg and possibly some broken ribs, as well as a nasty bump and cut on your head."

His eyes were open now and focused in the direction of her voice. "Did we hold them, Ollie?" His voice sounded fuzzy to Hero.

"You held them," she assured him.

His gaze was clear and held hers now. "You're not Ollie." He sighed. "Of course you're not. Ollie's dead. So are they all. All dead." He was silent for a moment, then asked quite lucidly, "Where am I? How did I get here?"

Hero exchanged a look of triumph with Stewart. "You are a patient in Dr. Whitby's clinic in Cornwall."

"Cornwall." His brow wrinkled in question.

"Actually on the border of Cornwall and Devon. The town of Weyburn."

"Weyburn," he repeated without apparent recognition. His expression deepened.

"You have been seriously injured, but you will be all right now, I'm sure."

"How—?"

"We think you were set upon and robbed and beaten on your way to Weyburn Abbey. Three days ago."

"Abbey," he repeated dully.

"In Cornwall," she said, trying to trigger his memory with familiar place names. "Can you tell me your name? We should notify your family."

He moaned incoherently and seemed to be trying to think. "Thirsty," he mumbled.

"Of course." She gestured for Stewart to hand her a cup of water and removed the damp cloth from his forehead. She slipped her arm under his neck to help him raise his head enough to swallow the liquid. His hair was matted and perspiration gathered on his forehead. His skin felt warm against her arm. She could still discern a now faint whiff of his shaving soap blended with a smell that was—well—just him. He gulped the water and turned away, his eyes closed. She placed the cup on the nightstand.

"Sir?" Hero said firmly. "Are you still awake?"

His eyes fluttered open. "Mm. Yes. Pain. Hurt all over."

"I know. I will give you something for the pain. But first—please—tell me who you are."

"Who?" he repeated dumbly, his eyes closing again.

"Yes. Who are you?" She raised her voice slightly.

"I…uh…I…" He opened his eyes. His gaze darted around, panicked. "I…I don't know. I. Do. Not. Know. How can I not know my own name?"

She patted his shoulder reassuringly. "Never mind. It will come to you. Temporary amnesia sometimes accompanies a severe blow to the head." She said this with a false sense of confidence, for she had only yesterday read it in one of her brother Michael's medical books.

"Amnesia." He seemed to understand the term.

"The head wound," she said. "Do you remember what happened? You arrived in our clinic three days ago with a quite appalling bump on your head. Also broken—or very badly bruised—ribs, and your right leg is broken about five inches above the knee."

"The femur," he said almost tonelessly.

"Why, yes," she said, surprised, for few patients would know the term. She tried to be encouraging. "See, your memory is still there. Do you remember how you got these injuries?"

He lay very still for a moment, his eyes closed, the muscles along his jaw clenched.

"Sir?" she prompted.

"No." His voice was hoarse and it was clear to Hero that he was putting up a valiant fight against pain. "I…I do not know. Not Waterloo…"

"No. Not Waterloo."

Just then Mrs. Hutchins bustled in carrying a tray. "I've brought some fresh broth for his lordship."

"Thank you," Hero said as Stewart brought a small table close for Mrs. Hutchins to set the tray on, then went back to his post near the patient's feet. Hero noticed the tray also held a small bottle of laudanum. "You did say you'd have need of that too." Mrs. Hutchins stepped back and put her hands on her hips. "So? How's his lordship doing?"

At the sound of this new voice, a frown creased the man's brow and he turned his head to gaze in that direction, but pain abruptly stopped the movement. "Ugh."

Hero, still standing near his head, touched his shoulder. "Don't move. Let me help you up a bit. Those pillows, please, Mrs. Hutchins." She gestured to a sideboard.

As Hero leaned over him, he grabbed her hand and whispered fiercely, "Get these damned restraints off me." In a less intense tone, he added, "Please."

"Now that you are conscious and aware, we can do that," she said.

"The wrapping around my chest too."

"But, sir. That is standard treatment for broken ribs."

"I've had broken ribs before. They will mend on their own."

Seizing on this, she said, "When? Do you recall when?"

He closed his eyes again. She could almost hear him trying to remember. After a moment, he opened his eyes again and seemed to grope for a right answer. "Spain? Yes. Spain. Badajoz."

"Oh, good. Very good." Hero shared a smile with Stewart and Mrs. Hutchins. "Now. Do you remember who you are?"

There was long pause as he seemed to be trying to come up with an answer. "N-no. How...why can I not..."

She touched his arm. "Never mind. It will come to you. For now, we will get those straps off and maybe get some soup into you." Hero loosened the strap under his shoulders and motioned for Mr. Stewart to deal with the one across his waist. "Is that better?"

He nodded.

"We must keep that leg stabilized, though," she said. Hero helped him raise his head and shoulders; Mrs. Hutchins removed the soiled pillow, put it aside, and pushed two others into place. Hero held the bowl of broth close and tried to spoon some into his mouth.

He turned away, wincing at the pain of doing so. "I'm not hungry. The pain—"

"You have had hardly any nourishment for three days."

"I am *not* hungry." He sounded testy and grunted in pain. "Leave me alone."

"If you will eat at least half of this broth, I will give you something for the pain."

He glared at her, but opened his mouth as she offered the spoon again. Mrs. Hutchins clucked in approval as he did so.

Finally he said, "That's it. I cannot do any more."

Hero prepared the laudanum in a glass of water and held his head up as he drank it. As she released him, he lay back and said, "You're a hard woman, Mrs....Miss..."

"Miss Whitby." She could see that the medication was already taking effect. She removed one of the pillows under his head. "We shall leave the rails in place, though," she said, even as she observed that he was already lost to them in genuine sleep.

Chapter 4

He was awake. Had been for at least two hours now, watching as dawn slowly drove the gray from the room, racking his brain, trying to recall... anything—anything of immediate significance. To little avail. He could remember snatches of battles—isolated but vivid scenes. Badajoz: Collins shot in the face as he climbed a siege ladder; Pamplona: the thunderous sound of an exploding munitions depot; Vitoria: Wellington furiously threatening to hang the next looter he caught; Toulouse: a battle that need never have been fought—and so many dead lying there on a muddy field. Finally, Waterloo: Ollie and Fitz both dead—again a muddy field of battle. *Why was death always so dirty?*

He even dredged up scenes of life in London after Toulouse. And, a year later, after Waterloo as well. Being congratulated in gentlemen's clubs. *Congratulations, back-slapping goodwill—for killing people?* Flirting women in gaily colored gowns at balls. Fawning hostesses. Drinking. Gambling. Whoring. Anything to forget broken bodies, countless dead with their staring, accusing eyes: *Why am I dead while you live?* Broken lives—including his own.

Fragments. Only fragments. But fragments from a distant past. Someone else's distant past. Months—even years ago. *Why—why—can I not remember here and now? Three days? I've been trussed up like a Christmas goose for three days? That was what the woman said, was it not? The woman with cool, soothing hands and smelling of lilacs. And the other woman—older—had referred to him as "his lordship." How is it that I have no such recollection? Surely one could recall being a lord! Why...why can I not conjure up a name? My own name, for God's sake!*

She said not to worry. It is all right. It will come back. But it is not *coming back.*

He ticked off letters of the alphabet, trying to find one—even one—that might trigger a name. Nothing. He did it again. Still nothing.

Not to worry indeed. Easy enough for her to say.

As though he had conjured her up, suddenly there she was, carrying a heavily laden bed tray.

"Good! You are awake. I thought you might be. Good morning. I have brought you some breakfast. Real food: buttered eggs, bacon, toast, and coffee."

He gazed at her, really seeing her for the first time. Earlier impressions had come through a haze of pain. He noted dark brown hair with light streaks of reddish gold, braided and coiled into a crown. She had hazel eyes, a profusion of freckles, and a cheerful demeanor as evidenced by an engaging smile that showed slightly uneven teeth, which he thought added to her charm.

"I may be able to do justice to such fare this morning," he said.

She set the tray on a table. "I'll remove the strap keeping your injured leg stable, then perhaps you can pull yourself to a sitting position. Use the rails on the side of the bed."

This task, accomplished with a great deal of pain in his chest and his leg, was not easy, but he managed it without crying out. She placed extra pillows behind his back, set the tray carefully across his legs, and lifted the cover from the plate of food. The smell alone set his mouth to watering.

"I'll be back soon to get these things." She gestured at the tray. Then she was gone, taking with her some of the sunniness of the morning. He ate in solitude, noting familiar tastes and textures in the food. *I remember these well enough. Why can I not grasp my own name and why—or how—I came to be in...ah, yes...Cornwall, bordering Devon. I must have had a reason...*

Twenty minutes later she returned as promised, but she was not alone. Two men accompanied her. She removed the tray and set it aside, then introduced her companions. The older man was her father, Dr. Charles Whitby, who must once have been a tall man but was now stooped by age. His gray hair was tied back with a leather thong. The other man, with dark brown hair, was half the age of the doctor; Miss Whitby introduced him as "Mr. Stewart, our butler, our chief of sundry other duties, and our friend."

The patient thought this was a decidedly unusual introduction of a servant, but who was he to judge customs in the countryside of Cornwall? Stewart carried two steaming buckets of water.

"Well, lad," the doctor said affably, "my daughter tells me you are having a bit of a memory problem."

"Yes, sir. Some things I recall well enough, but—"

"Temporary memory loss is not unusual with a severe blow to the head. Give yourself a few days to get back to normal."

"But meanwhile," Miss Whitby said, "what shall we call you? We cannot continue to call you 'the patient' or 'the man'—both those are too indifferent."

"Hmm. Last night the lady referred to me as 'his lordship.' Did she know something I am not remembering?"

"No," Miss Whitby replied. "Mrs. Hutchins was merely judging by the fine workmanship of your clothing and your riding boots. They look expensive."

"I see." He tried to recall what he had been wearing, but came up with nothing.

"Sir," she prompted, "what shall we call you other than 'the injured man'?"

He thought for a moment. "How about *Adam*? Does it not mean 'man'?"

She smiled and clapped her hands. "Of course it does. Perfect! And a surname?"

Again, he took time to think about it. "Perhaps *Wainwright*?" *Where on earth had that come from?*

"Adam Wainwright." She paused in thought. "Adam Wainwright sounds fine to me. Papa?"

The doctor nodded. "Adam Wainwright. Seems adequate." He paused and gazed at each of the others in turn. "But I think we'd best put it out that that *is* his name, that he woke up and that's who he is—not just something we're calling him."

The man in the bed nodded his immediate understanding of the doctor's reasoning, but the daughter asked, "Why?"

Her father explained. "Because the fellows who did this to him might not have picked a random traveler. Might be they knew—or thought they knew—who they were dealing with."

"That's a bit frightening," she said. "You're suggesting they might try again."

"They *could*. But not likely, if they think they got the wrong man the first time." Dr. Whitby addressed his patient. "Now that you are fully awake, Mr. Wainwright, I assume you can be of some assistance in protecting yourself. I also assume that you have some expertise in the use of firearms."

"Yes, sir, I do."

"I shall bring you one of my pistols. Keep it under your pillow, just in case."

"Thank you, sir. I had not got that far in my thinking. Still trying to deal with more basic issues." Adam paused, then said, "So. I think I have not yet been properly introduced to you, Miss Whitby."

"Hero," her father said. "Hero Gwendolyn Whitby. My daughter did most of the patchwork on you, lad."

"Hero." Adam turned the name over, tasting the two syllables. "I would venture to say that her efforts were, indeed, heroic, but I doubt that is the explanation for such an unusual name."

Dr. Whitby chuckled. "No. It is not. Her mother—bless her heart—was a great enthusiast of the Greeks."

"Ah," Adam said, "Hero and Leander. Faith and love."

Miss Whitby immediately picked up on that. "You remember the story, then? Can you recall the circumstances under which you might have heard it?"

He closed his eyes, muttering the names Hero and Leander. He felt the answer was there—just beyond the edge, but he could not grasp it. Finally, he admitted, "Sorry. I just cannot do it."

"Never mind, lad—Adam," the doctor said. "Don't work at it too hard, and one day—soon, I hope—it will come tumbling back. For now, I want to look at that wound on your leg, then Stewart and I will set about giving you a bath."

"A bath?" Adam squeaked, with a glance at Miss Whitby.

"Not to worry. We will chase her away, but she needs to see that wound. The stitchery is her handiwork," the doctor said, removing the sheet carefully from the injured leg. He untied the bandage and Adam felt cold air on the wound. He flinched as the doctor pressed swollen flesh around the cut, which, even to Adam's untrained eye, was beginning to mend.

"Mm...mm," the doctor muttered. "Looks good, eh, Hero? Little danger of infection now."

She merely nodded and handed the doctor a wad of cotton soaked in what Adam assumed from the smell to be an alcohol compound. He felt the cold liquid, then a stinging sensation as the wound was cleansed. Somewhat to Adam's surprise, it was the daughter who put the new bandage in place, tying the end strips with expertise obviously born of practice. *Well, well,* he thought, but he was glad when she picked up the breakfast tray and, saying, "I shall return," started to leave the room.

"Wait!" he called. "You forgot to remove the binding on my ribs last night."

She flashed him a grin. "I did not forget. Perhaps you can discuss it with my father."

"Saucy female," Adam muttered under his breath, but he did discuss it with her father, and the doctor reluctantly agreed to leave that restrictive irritation off after he and Stewart had given their patient a thorough wash and a shave. They then dressed him in what Adam assumed to be one of the doctor's nightshirts. The whole process necessitated a good deal of their rolling him about on the bed, but he readily admitted it felt good to be really clean again. By the time they were finished, both his leg and his head were throbbing and every breath was painful. He welcomed a second dose of laudanum and the healing sleep it offered.

Adam. Hero liked thinking of him as Adam. The primeval man. The name suggested something earthy and fundamental. From the very beginning she had felt some elemental attraction to this man. Now he had a name that justified her wild musings. *You are being decidedly silly*, she chastised herself.

She went to the nursery to spend time with Annabelle—always a great way to escape dealing with any issue in her life that she wanted to avoid facing head-on. The little girl was learning her numbers and letters—still getting them mixed up, but Hero was sure she would have them mastered within a week or so.

During the next three days, her life returned to some semblance of normal. As with any long-term patient of the clinic, she checked on Adam at least twice a day. A clean-shaven Adam was remarkably attractive— and he was personable too. He had a cheerful demeanor and a smile that revealed deep laugh lines in his cheeks and around his eyes. Sapphire-blue eyes that suggested a layer of amusement at the world around him and often at himself. She liked a man who could laugh at himself. She knew he was often in pain, but he tended to ignore it, rarely asking for the pain-relieving laudanum.

"That stuff is dangerous," he said.

"Yes, it can be," she replied, "but I think you are in little danger of becoming addicted—yet!"

"Still…"

Assured that he was on the mend, and eating properly, she accompanied her father on house calls, but Adam was the patient who dominated her thoughts. She fervently wanted to help him recover his memory. To this end, she pored through her brother's up-to-date medical books and her father's more dated tomes, but she found little to help her. She did not ignore the issue—at least not deliberately—but she found herself caught up in other problems: The Wellman twins had contracted chicken pox and spread it to their playmates; old Mrs. Petersen's rheumatism was acting up; a stable boy at the coaching inn sprained his ankle; and so on and on...

One afternoon, she visited Knowlton House on her own. Sally had only two pregnant young women residing there at the moment and neither of them was close to term. Hero examined each of them and gave them her standard pep talk: "Eat your vegetables and exercise."

When she had finished, she and Sally sat in Sally's small office to compare notes. The room was barely large enough for Sally's rolltop desk, two chairs, and a chest-high bookcase that contained more loose papers than books. As midwives, the two women were more or less equal, balancing each other's expertise and readily sharing new insights. A woman in her midfifties, with gray streaks in her raven-black hair, Sally could not remember precisely how many babies she had helped usher into this world.

"Probably enough to populate the whole parish," she often said with a laugh.

Hero, on the other hand, read voraciously and often mentioned some new—or old—technique she had come across, and she and Sally would discuss the practicalities of such. Sally's big news today was that she had received an inquiry about yet another young woman who needed their help.

"I thought you were going to cut back some," Hero said.

"I am." Sally sounded defensive. "I can handle three well enough. You know I once had six girls here."

"Yes, I do know. But you've hardly the room, let alone the resources, for that many. And you work yourself to a frazzle over each and every one of your girls."

"It's just that the need is so great. And I do have help. Weyburn people help when they can. Mostly. You and your 'H' friends have been invaluable to us." Sally referred to Hero and her former school friends, Henrietta and Harriet, who had readily answered Hero's call to help women and girls whom society would gladly assign to a trash heap.

"I've had another letter that you will certainly find interesting," Sally went on.

"Not another one, Sally. Really, three is all you can handle comfortably."

"No. No. Nothing like that. This came from a solicitor in Lancashire." She rifled through a stack of correspondence on her desk. "Ah, here it is. He refuses to name his client, but insists he represents someone who is very interested in whether Barbara Gaylord, who is said to have died of influenza in 1812, was ever a guest of mine."

Hero felt a chill of apprehension. *No. All these years later—No. It cannot be.* "Have you answered him?"

"Not yet. I wanted to consult you first."

"The timing is right," Hero admitted, "but Barbara is a rather common name. I do not remember our Barbara ever using a family name."

"No. She did not. But then they rarely do—at least, not a real one." Sally's tone hardened. "Why would someone suddenly care now? I remember her arrival so clearly. A post chaise drove up the driveway, the coachman got down and rapped on my door. Asked me if this was the Knowlton House. When I said yes, he nodded at the carriage; the door opened from the inside and Barbara climbed down with a small valise. I felt so sorry for her. She was so alone."

"I do not recall her ever talking about her family," Hero said, "but I did not see her every day as you did."

"No. Never mentioned them. Talked of her school days and a few balls she had attended, but not her family. I received compensation for her stay here from a London law office. When she died, that office merely instructed that she be buried locally."

"How cold."

"Yes, well…" Sally spread her hands in a what-can-one-say sort of gesture, then added, "I think she was happy here—content at least. She got on well with me and the other girls. Shared a room with a former governess. She did say once that her babe's father was killed in one of those sea battles leading up to the war with America."

Hero read the solicitor's letter in its rather stilted legalese and passed it back to Sally. "How will you respond to this?"

"With the truth. I never knew of a Barbara Gaylord, but the name Barbara is quite common. Let his unnamed client take it from there—if they care to—which I doubt."

Hero agreed with this plan and the sentiment, but she could not shake a nagging worry. That night after the bedtime story and prayers, she hugged Annabelle ever so tightly. *Oh my God! What if I ever had to give her up?*

* * * *

For his part, Adam welcomed Hero's visits to the clinic. Other members of the Whitby household checked on him from time to time, servants brought him meals three times a day, and both Mr. Stewart and Mrs. Hutchins seemed to take a warm interest in his welfare. Outside visitors were often invited to stop by his bedside briefly. There were a surprising number of these, but the doctor had reasoned that perhaps one of the neighbors would recognize the patient—or trigger a memory response from the man himself. But it was Hero's smile he looked forward to most.

Anxious to learn anything he could of his own identity and his possible reason for being in this area of southern England, he encouraged all his visitors to talk. Most were eager to do so. In this way, he gained a good deal of information about the town and its inhabitants as well as those in the surrounding area. The principal holding in the area was Weyburn Abbey, which controlled several thousand acres of farmland as well as a copper mine.

"All that farmland and a mine? Must require an army of workers to keep it up," Adam commented.

"Used ta do," replied Stewart, the caretaker-visitor of the moment. "Lots of 'em been let go since Sir Benjamin died seven, eight years ago. He was the last owner. Fine man he were too. Took care of his people and his property. Not like now."

"Who owns it now?" Adam asked, shifting his seat in the bed with a sharp intake of breath as he moved the injured leg too abruptly.

"Some nob name o' Sterne. Sir Benjamin's godson. But he ain't seen fit to even visit his holding. Can ye believe that? A duke's son. Got no sense of responsibility if you ask me."

"There must be somebody in charge, though."

"There's a steward named Teague. But he don't seem overly innerested in the Abbey an' its concerns. My brother's a foreman in the mine. He's real worried about safety there. But Teague jus' told 'im to tend to his own business an' carry on."

The next afternoon, Dr. Whitby ushered in two men in fishermen's garb. "Thought you'd like to meet these fellows, since they likely saved your life. The Jacobses—father and son." Whitby gestured at each in turn.

Adam sat up straighter and reached—not without a sharp protest from his chest—to shake their hands. "I am most pleased to meet you. How can I ever repay you?"

"No need o' that," the older Jacobs said. "We was jus' wonderin' how ye was a-doin'—heard you'd finally come to."

At Dr. Whitby's prodding, they reiterated the story of their finding him. "Whoever done it likely got innerrupted," the younger man said. "We looked around. Lots of signs of a scuffle. I think they was two, maybe three of 'em. Ye musta fought 'em real hard. But we didn't find anything else."

"Nevertheless, I appreciate your rescuing me. When this is all sorted out, perhaps I will be able to thank you properly." Still standing at his bedside, they shuffled their feet and looked embarrassed, so Adam changed the subject. "How goes your fishing?"

"Fine—when we ain't chased off the water by either smugglers or the militia takin' *us* to be smugglin'," the older man said.

"Now, Pa..." his son admonished.

"Sorry, Ronnie, but I'm tired o' bein' mealymouthed about it. We're losin' money we can't afford to lose."

At the son's urging, the fishermen expressed their pleasure at finding Adam recovering so nicely, and left.

Dr. Whitby took the bedside chair and asked, "Did their account trigger any memory of the incident?"

"Afraid not, Doc. It's almost as though it happened to someone else. Except when I move!"

"Don't try to rush it, son."

They sat in silence for a few moments; then Adam said, "Smuggling? Has that not decreased appreciably with the end of the French embargo?" He did not bother at the moment to wonder where *that* thought came from.

"Some," Whitby replied. "Government turned a blind eye to it during the war. Token enforcement only. Now, Westminster needs all that tax money. Increased the local militia, but it—the militia—is 'taxed' to its utmost—if you'll pardon the pun."

"Are you suggesting the militia cannot handle the problem?"

"I do not honestly know. I think much of the problem is that militias are often made up, at least partly, of local men who are reluctant to see friends and family members fired upon—or arrested and transported—for trying to put food on the table."

Adam merely nodded his understanding.

"I am sure it will get worse before it gets better." The doctor sighed and changed the subject. "Are you a chess player?"

"Chess? Hmm. Yes, I think I am, though it has probably been a while..."

"Good. I'll bring the board next time."

The next afternoon, Dr. Whitby arrived with the chess set and board under his arm. He was accompanied by the footman named Davey, who was half pushing, half carrying a rather strange piece of furniture.

The doctor announced, "Since you are likely to be here a good while— takes at least six weeks for broken ribs to mend, and even longer for that leg to heal—this should help you get around until you become proficient with crutches."

"What is it?" Adam asked before he had a clear view of the contraption.

"It's called a Bath chair. Lots of invalids in Bath, you know. The wheels give patients mobility. My daughter got this one for me when my gout was at its worst."

Now Adam saw it quite clearly: a wicker armchair with a padded seat and a platform for one's feet. It was set on two large wheels, with a small third wheel in front to steer by.

"Davey here will help push you around until you feel you can handle it on your own. Just ring the bell for him." With that, the doctor pushed the chair near the bed, and he and Davey, a strapping lad in his teens, helped Adam transfer to the chair.

They pushed him out to a terrace just outside the side door of the room. Facing the sea, the terrace, one of three on the northwest side of the building, was paved with granite slabs and had a wooden bench, a table, and three chairs. Adam noted planters displaying colorful spring flowers—daffodils, wild irises, and tulips. He turned his face up to the sun, luxuriating in just being outdoors. Dr. Whitby tossed him a small blanket for his legs, set the chess game on the table, and wheeled Adam closer before taking a seat at the table himself.

"Any progress on the memory?" the doctor asked.

"Not much regarding recent weeks. I am remembering certain scenes of Waterloo—not such as one would discuss in a drawing room, mind you!—and I am getting a better grip on my time in the Peninsula."

"Nothing about family? Schooling? Friends? Somebody somewhere must be concerned about you."

Adam shrugged—and winced as he felt the action in his ribs. "I suppose so."

"As I've said before, it will all come back to you. Something is sure to trigger a memory and everything will come rushing back."

"I hope so. I do hope so. For one thing, I am mindful of my obligations to you and Miss Whitby."

"We shall deal with that in due time," the doctor said. "Meanwhile, concentrate on getting well. And playing well," he added, dumping the box of chessmen on the board.

Chapter 5

He was gaining strength every day, but Adam had not yet built up any endurance. He felt a distinct sense of frustration at not being able to remember even his own name, though he was schooling himself to be this person called Adam. And he deplored the fact that he really needed his afternoon naps.

On a warm spring day he had just awakened from one of these, and was considering ringing for someone to help him out of bed and into the Bath chair when he became aware of voices on the terrace. Both the window and the outside door had been left open to "air the room out," as Mrs. Hutchins had put it when she came for his lunch tray. She did that most days instead of sending a maid for it, and she usually chatted with him for a few minutes. He found her a veritable fountain of information.

But why ring when he could just yell at someone on the terrace who would see that he had help? He hesitated when he failed to recognize the male voice he heard first.

"Ah, Miss Whitby. Your father told me I might find you out here." The voice moved as the speaker was apparently coming from around the corner of the building.

"Mr. Teague." Her voice sounded guarded to Adam. "Is there something particular you wanted of me?"

"No. Just thought I'd drop by and see how your long-term patient was doing. Mind if I sit with you for a while?"

"No. Of course not. Do have a seat." Again Adam perceived hesitancy in her voice—which surprised him, for in Adam's experience she had never been anything but open and friendly with others. He heard the sound of a chair scraping across the slate floor of the terrace.

"Wellman tells me your patient has regained consciousness," the male voice said.

"Yes, he has. Mr. Wainwright awoke four days ago."

"Wainwright? That's his name, eh?"

"Adam Wainwright."

"You sure that's who he is?"

"I am as sure as one can be about anyone one happens to meet."

"Know anything else about him?"

"He has been a soldier and he curses in three languages." Adam heard amusement in her voice.

"Soldier, eh? How can you know that?" The man was skeptical.

"He has battle scars older than this recent beating. Before regaining consciousness, he mumbled incoherently about a military encounter."

"Nothing else?" The man was persistent.

"Not yet. Mr. Teague, the man suffered a thorough beating. The blow to his head could have killed him. We are not pressing him to remember."

"Well, when he *does* remember, I'd like to be kept informed." Now the man sounded pompous to Adam.

"Why?"

"Why what?"

"Why do you wish to be informed? Your interest seems rather unusual. You have never before concerned yourself about any of our patients."

"Ah, but I generally know Weyburn folks, don't I? As the man in charge of Weyburn Abbey and all its concerns, I am quite naturally interested in any stranger to the area." *Definitely pompous*, Adam thought.

"I assure you that as soon as Mr. Wainwright regains his…uh…faculties, my father and I will notify his family, or whomever he tells us needs to be informed."

"Hmpf," the man grunted. There was silence for a moment, then Teague went on in a much warmer tone. "I have given you several days to think over that matter I mentioned to your father—"

"Mr. Teague, I…uh—"

"Willard. Call me Willard, Hero."

"I am not comfortable doing that, Mr. Teague." She sounded distinctly uncomfortable to Adam.

"That is quite all right, my dear." Teague was affable now. "I know many wives who address their husbands only by their surnames."

Wives? Miss Whitby was going to marry this man, Teague? A man about whom Adam had heard little to recommend him, though others tended to be guarded in discussing him with a stranger. Just why the possibility of

Miss Whitby's marrying him was such a shocking idea, Adam could not immediately say, but it seemed wrong somehow. *Come now. You've not even met the man*, he told himself. He knew he should call out, let them know he was an unwilling party to their discussion, but why embarrass them? Miss Whitby's next words cheered him. "Mr. Teague, I am afraid you are jumping to an impossible conclusion. I am mindful of the honor you do me, but—"

Aha! She is refusing him.

"You need not act the coy miss with me," Teague said, his voice harsher now. "We both know that at your age you are not likely to get a better offer. Truth to tell, who's to say I won't be getting damaged goods, eh? What's more, I am not only willing to marry you, but I'll take that bastard child you're so fond of as part of the bargain. What's one more brat anyway, eh?"

"Mr. Teague!" *Indignation*, Adam noted to himself. There was the sound of scraping chairs; Adam assumed they were both standing now. In a tone that sounded as though she were trying for control, she continued, "As I say, Mr. Teague, I am sure others would find your offer most flattering, but it is not one I can consider."

"So. You want to be wooed. Is that it? Well, I can do that, but you have to keep me interested, you know."

"Mr. Teague!" Her voice rose in something like a yelp.

"Ah, come on. One little kiss is not going to kill you."

"Mr. Teague." Controlled anger now.

Adam had had enough. He wished he could charge out and plant a facer on this Teague person. But—hell and damnation!—he needed help just to get into and out of bed. He reached for the ceramic water pitcher on the nightstand and sent it crashing to the floor. "Damn!" he said loud enough for them to hear.

Miss Whitby rushed through the open door. "Mr. Wainwright. Are you all right?"

He tried to sound as though he had just awakened. "T-tried to get a drink of water."

"I will help you with that," she said, either ignoring or not seeing a half-filled glass on the nightstand. She reached for the bellpull above his head.

Teague loomed in the doorway and gave Adam a suspicious look. Adam noted he was tall, blond, and dressed as a country gentleman with a well-fitted dark green coat over a gray silk waistcoat, dark gray trousers, and an intricately tied neckcloth. *Not exactly working attire*, Adam thought. Miss Whitby introduced them and Adam offered his hand, noting that Teague had an intensely firm grip.

"Hero tells me you are having trouble remembering things," Teague said. Adam thought his brazen use of Miss Whitby's given name was deliberate—an attempt to establish possession or to intimidate.

"Yes. I am, but *Miss Whitby* assures me the problem is likely to be temporary, and I have confidence in her expertise." He deliberately emphasized the correct form of her name and noted the other man's lips tighten.

"Well, if you do remember why you came to Weyburn, I stand ready to help you about your business," Teague said.

"Thank you, but as you can see, it will be a while before I am 'about' anything."

Teague turned to Miss Whitby. "We'll continue our discussion another time, Hero."

Again Adam resented the man's making free use of her name, but mentally chastised himself as having absolutely no right to his resentment.

"I do not think that will be necessary, Mr. Teague," she said.

"But *I* do," he said emphatically and left.

She sighed and began to pick up the pieces of the broken pitcher.

"I'm sorry," Adam said, and was about to go on when the maid Dorcas appeared at the inner door.

"Oh! Miss Whitby. I thought Mr. Wainwright needed something." She gave Adam a brilliant smile.

"He does," Miss Whitby said. "Please have Davey bring him a pitcher of fresh water and he can help Mr. Wainwright out of bed."

"Yes, ma'am."

Adam shared a knowing glance of amusement with Miss Whitby, who did not seem fully recovered from her talk with Teague.

"How much of that did you hear?" she demanded, with a gesture at the open side door.

"Most of it," he admitted. "I apologize for eavesdropping."

"You should have let me know you were awake."

"Yes. I should have. I—I did not want to interrupt, to embarrass—er—any of us."

She continued to pick up bits of the broken pitcher and consign them to a wastebasket. Finally she stood and looked at him. "Mr. Teague has four young children for whom he needs a mother."

"I somehow doubt that is his only interest," Adam said.

She did not respond to this, but her blush told him she had understood the implied compliment.

Davey's arrival forestalled further discussion.

* * * *

Embarrassed that Adam had overheard that discussion with Mr. Teague, Hero deliberately avoided her most intriguing patient for the rest of that day. Her father, however, was becoming quite fond of the man, spending time with him just chatting or playing chess. It came as no surprise to her when, after putting Annabelle down for the evening, she entered the library to find that her father had wheeled the man into the library.

Over his own newly mended shirt, Adam wore a dark blue dressing gown that Hero recognized as belonging to her brother Michael. The color enhanced the blue of Adam's eyes. A blanket covered his legs, the good one bent at the knee in a natural, relaxed position, but the other one—held in place by splints and bandaging—thrust rigidly to the side and rested on the foot stand of the Bath chair. The position looked uncomfortable.

"I'm becoming quite proficient with this chair," he announced. "But I still need some help getting into and out of the bed."

"I've noticed," the doctor said. "I'll wager your arms are getting a monstrous workout."

"Oh, yes," the patient responded ruefully. "I did not realize arm muscles were quite such complex mechanisms. Every little part makes itself known."

"We've some liniment that will help," Hero said from her place on a beige leather couch. She rose and rang for the tea tray.

"I'd appreciate that," Adam said. "And I must say, troublesome as it is, I am thankful for this chair. Just being upright for a good portion of the day is a boon."

"That wound on your leg should be healed enough to get you on crutches in a day or two," the older man said, pushing the chair into position near a small table on which the chess board had already been placed.

"Wonderful," Adam said. "A whole new set of muscles to discover."

Stewart entered with the tea tray and Hero welcomed having something to do; she set about preparing each man's tea as he liked it, then handed it to him. At first she had feared that her father or Adam might bring up the subject of Mr. Teague's visit, but when neither of them did so, she relaxed into her book and listened only intermittently as they discussed their game and items they had read in the most recent London newspapers: the Prince Regent's angering his Whig opposition with his newfound interest in the reign of the Stuarts; fear in aristocratic circles of a French-like revolution; popular unrest as the once booming wartime economy stagnated.

"The situation is likely to get worse before it gets better," she heard her father say.

"Why?" Adam asked.

"Why?" her father repeated rhetorically. "As I see it, mainly because people like his noble lordship of Weyburn Abbey are content to ignore people who depend on them for leadership. They leave things in the hands of surrogates like Teague, who cannot—or will not—do right by folks. The owners are content so long as the money keeps coming in. Weyburn people are not desperate yet, but those workers in the Midlands are really hurting. The paper talks of a resurgence of the Luddites."

Hero glanced up from her book to see Adam's brow wrinkle in consternation. "Luddites? Luddites? Ah. Smashing machinery in textile mills."

"You remember that, do you?" the doctor asked eagerly.

"Only vaguely." He pressed the heel of his hand against his forehead, then shook his head sadly. "I have an image of a group of officers in a mess tent sharing mail and news from home."

"Officers," the doctor said. "Do you remember any of their names?"

"Ollie. Fitz. Oliver Windham. Fitzgerald Williamson. Charlton Stirling. There were others…." His voice trailed off.

Seeing that her father would have pursued the discussion and that their patient was either tired or emotionally drained at even that much memory, Hero interrupted. "Don't press him, Papa. Let it come as it will." She stood and added brightly, "How about a bit of cognac to top off our day?"

"Splendid idea, my dear," her father said, accepting her putting an end to the evening.

Hero went to a sideboard and poured three glasses of the amber liquid. She handed one to each of the men, returned to her own seat, and raised her glass in a salute. "To your progress," she said, gazing into Adam's deep blue eyes.

"Hear! Hear!" her father said.

"Thank you." Adam held her gaze for a long moment before taking a swallow of his drink.

The two men finished their game, but Hero thought Adam's heart was not in it now.

"Checkmate," her father said. Adam nodded and laid down his king. Her father drained his glass and stood. "It has been a long day. I am off to bed. Hero, will you ring for Stewart to see Wainwright here to his bed as well?"

"Of course, Papa. Sleep well."

To reach the bellpull, she had to walk around Adam's wheeled chair. As she did so, he reached out to grasp her hand.

"Can we hold off on that for a moment, Miss Whitby?"

"If you wish." His touch elicited an unfamiliar—and very physical, almost breathless—reaction in her. Flustered, she quickly disengaged her hand from his and sat down in the chair her father had vacated.

"I... uh...wanted to apologize again for this afternoon," he said. "I did not intend to embarrass you, Miss Whitby."

"I know. Apology accepted." She held his gaze. "Actually, your interruption was rather timely—but I suspect you know that."

He grinned. "Guilty as charged. Sorry about that pitcher."

"I should thank you, Mr. Wainwright. You helped me avoid—or at least postpone—a confrontation."

His expression sobered and he continued to hold her gaze. "If I can help in any way, Miss Whitby, you must let me know."

She smiled. "Hero. Call me Hero, please."

"And I am Adam—I guess."

"For the time being anyway." She rose to reach for the bellpull. "Tell Mr. Stewart to wait here while I get that liniment for you."

* * * *

Hero lay awake staring at the underside of the canopy of her bed. Three things kept her from the sleep that beckoned just beyond her reach.

The first was what to do about Mr. Teague. She supposed she might simply ask her father to warn the man off, but that went against the grain. Hero Whitby was accustomed to handling her own problems. Marriage had never—in her adult life—held any real attraction for her. Marriage to Teague was a decidedly repugnant idea. She knew he had enjoyed his reputation as something of a ladies' man even while his wife was still alive. Hero had seen Teague's wife through two of her four pregnancies, the last of which had killed her. Women in the throes of childbirth were often less than discreet in their talk. Aside from the fact that she was quite content with her life as it was, Hero was furious at his presuming she would welcome his advances. However, she knew he was not a man to handle well any hint of criticism or rejection.

And he could be vindictive.

Henry Thompson, one of the Abbey's tenant farmers, had been somewhat the worse for drink when he complained at the inn about his barn that needed repair and how the Abbey steward refused to do anything about it. A few days later the barn mysteriously caught fire. Teague accused the farmer of arson. Thompson vehemently protested his innocence—and half the parish believed him. Nevertheless, Teague summarily evicted the whole family. Most Weyburn folks thought it had been done as a warning to others. That farm was still mostly idle.

But it worked, did it not? she thought. *Diana and Malcom are certainly reluctant to say anything about their roof, which leaks profusely with every storm.* Hero gritted her teeth at the thought of her sister's rearing four children—one just an infant—in such an environment. She recalled Teague's smug comment about that being a problem that could be remedied. Was that a threat? A bribe? Aimed at her?

The second cause of her sleeplessness was also a man: Adam Wainwright. However, this issue was more pleasant to contemplate. She recognized a sense of personal power in Adam Wainwright—or whoever he was—that came with the authority granted the most privileged class. He might not be the lord Mrs. Hutchins had dubbed him, but he was close. His accent proclaimed that about him. He'd not merely been in the military, he'd been an officer. It was true that many officers—such as her own brother—came from the gentry class, but it was equally true that most had family ties to the aristocracy. Had not Michael written of them often enough?

Still, she could not deny that Adam was one very attractive man. Not since she was in her teens had she been so physically aware of a man, so alert to his presence whenever they were in the same room, so sensitive to his slightest touch. She had been fully sensible to him as a man even while he was unconscious, just lyng there helpless, exuding masculinity. But her awareness had intensified exponentially with his awakening. Those blue eyes were downright mesmerizing.

Stop! she admonished herself. *You do remember—do you not—what an utter disaster followed that youthful infatuation?* No. She would not relive, yet again, the terror—the pain—the betrayal—the humiliation of that event. She would not! She had managed to get beyond it years ago. Nevertheless, Teague's casual reference to "damaged goods" rankled.

The third matter keeping her from dreamland was perhaps a more universal sort of issue: what the future might hold.

At eighteen, fresh from Miss Penelope Pringle's School for Young Ladies of Quality, Hero had joined her friends Henrietta and Harriet as they made their debuts in London Society. Harriet's older sister, the Countess of Sedwick, had generously offered to sponsor the daughter of a country doctor. Hero was sure Harriet had insisted that Lady Sedwick do so, but she had enjoyed London immensely, agreeing with Samuel Johnson of the previous century that "when a man is tired of London, he is tired of life." None of the three H's had "taken" on the marriage mart, but Hero, at least, had had no illusions that she even wanted to do so.

She had come home to devour her brother's medical books and badger her father into letting her help in his clinic. He had been adamantly opposed in the beginning: This was not a milieu for females; she should find a husband and have children; that was what her mother would have wanted for her. Hero would not have minded having children, but the husband part of that was not exactly enticing. Gradually, she had managed to become her father's apprentice, in fact if not in name. The two of them were an efficient team.

Her brother Michael was the one who had been prepared to be their father's medical partner. But Michael had gone directly from medical school in Edinburgh to working with Dr. James McGrigor, Wellington's chief medical officer, first in the Peninsula and then with the army of occupation in Belgium. Now that so many of that army were being demobilized, Michael was sure to come home to take his rightful place here. And where would that leave Hero? Except for those years at Miss Pringle's school, Hero had, since her mother's death and her sister's marriage, managed her father's household as well as working in his clinic. What would happen when Michael married, as he was sure to do at some point?

What will I do? What about Annabelle?

Oh, do stop borrowing worry from the future...

She pounded her pillow into something offering comfort and willed herself to sleep.

Chapter 6

In the dim light of an oil lamp, the wick turned as low as it could go and still wage a weak fight against darkness, Adam too lay awake after leaving the library. Staring at the whitewashed ceiling and walls of his hospital room, he tried, as he did every night, to bring up something of his past that would prompt a real return of his memory.

Nothing.

He turned to a review of this day.

Though his own taste in women ran to willowy blondes, there was something about Hero Whitby—with her sturdy figure and ready smile—that he found comforting. Her cheerful optimism and generous nature reminded him of his mother. *Whoa! Where did that come from? A mother?* His *mother?* He tried to conjure up a perceivable vision, but the image eluded him. He let his mind drift back to Hero and that conversation he had overheard. As he reflected on it, he wondered if he had detected a note of fear in her attitude toward Teague. Fear and anxiety were not emotions one would immediately associate with Miss Whitby.

To Adam, Teague had seemed an overbearing sort—the type of man who tried to turn a simple handshake into a power struggle—but not an especially frightening fellow. Perhaps women would view him differently; he had the sort of looks that women often found attractive: good-looking well-built, exuding self-confidence. But as Adam considered the matter further, it occurred to him that whenever Teague's name came up, people tended to be rather circumspect in what they said.

Food for thought there.

He turned to lie on his left side as much as his splinted leg would allow, and set about willing himself to sleep. His back was to the window, which he had asked Stewart to leave open a bit when the servant had locked the outside door. Always a light sleeper, Adam could not immediately pinpoint what it was that woke him. He lay very still and listened. He conjectured that it must be two hours or more past midnight.

There it was! A faint scraping of metal against metal and what could be a shoe sliding on the slate outside the door. Someone was trying to pick the door lock. Whoever it was could have nothing good in mind.

Adam reached above his head to tug on the bellpull, hoping that at this hour someone might even hear it. Then he lay still, feigning sleep, but he was intensely alert. He slid his right hand under his pillow to grip the pistol Dr. Whitby had given him a few days earlier. He heard a click as the lock gave way, and watched through slitted eyes as two figures came into his line of vision. As they approached his bed, one behind the other, the one in the rear gestured to the other bed.

"Grab that pillow," he whispered, "in case he wakes up."

Adam raised himself on one elbow, cocked the pistol, and pointed it at the man reaching for the pillow. "He's awake. Whatever you have mind, you'd best forget it," he said calmly.

The man in front gasped. "Blimey, George! He's got a barker!"

George, who was closest to the now open side door, looked as though he would run for it until Adam turned the gun slightly in his direction. "Don't even think about it," Adam ground out in the manner of a military officer issuing an order to a subordinate. "I am accredited to be a good shot and I could hardly miss at this distance."

"Oh, Jesus, Mary, and all the saints! He never told us he'd have a gun!" This came as a near whine from the man standing nearest Adam.

"Shut your mouth," George growled at his companion. He was bigger than the other one; even in the dim light Adam saw that both were unshaven, wore dark clothing and dark knitted caps. George turned his gaze to Adam and said, "What now, fancy boy? You can't shoot both of us at once."

Adam pointed the gun more firmly at George. "There is more than one bullet. You first, then the whiner."

"I ain't no whiner," the whiner said.

"I told you to shut up," George said.

Just then the inner door to the surgery swung open and Stewart entered carrying a bright lamp. "You need something, Mr. Wainwright?"

The man George took advantage of this distraction. He dropped a length of rope he carried and made a dash for the open side door. Adam fired the gun and George yelped, but kept on running. Adam turned the gun on the whiner who now seemed frozen in place.

Stewart held his lamp higher to shed light more fully on the intruder. "Trevor Prentiss? What are you doing here? And at this hour?"

"I…uh…George 'n' me—"

Adam broke in. "Had a little matter of murder in mind, did you not? You and your friend George? Thought to finish what you started several days ago, did you?" Adam did not stop to think about what he had just said, but he barked an order. "Keep your hands up where I can see them."

"Y-yes, sir. Jus' don't shoot me. Please,"

"Stewart," Adam said, never taking his eyes from Trevor Prentiss, "if you would, set that lamp down and tie this miscreant's hands behind his back. Use that rope they intended to use on me. Then make him sit on the floor over there in front of that closet where we can keep an eye on him."

Stewart did as Adam directed and was just finishing when Hero burst into the room, holding a lantern. She was followed closely by her father.

"What happened?" she demanded, sounding anxious and somewhat breathless. "We heard a shot!" Her gaze landed on the prisoner. "Trevor Prentiss?" Her voice rose in surprise. She whipped her attention to Adam. "Adam. Are you all right?"

Adam laid the gun on the nightstand, pulled himself to a sitting position, and turned up the wick of his own lamp. "Yes. Luckily, I am a light sleeper." He explained what had happened, ending with, "I may have winged this fellow's friend George."

"That would be George Kempf," Stewart said from where he stood, keeping watch on Prentiss. "Kempf and Prentiss here are part of Teague's gang."

"Yeah. An' Mr. Teague ain't gonna like this one bit," Prentiss said in a show of adolescent bravado.

Adam looked at him closely and was not surprised to find he was quite young—fourteen or fifteen at most. "Prentiss," Adam said, "you would be wise to take your friend George's advice and be quiet. Attempted murder is a hanging offense."

"Transport to the penal colony in New South Wales at the very least," Dr. Whitby said, sitting on the only chair in the room other than the Bath chair.

The boy's complexion paled visibly. "We wasn't gonna kill anybody. Jus' scare 'im."

Hero set her lamp on a sideboard and went over to kneel beside him. She spoke gently. "Trevor. Why? How did you come to be involved with the likes of George Kempf? And, I suppose, Henry Slater?"

Dr. Whitby explained to Adam, "Kempf and Slater are a couple of young toughs about five or six years older than Prentiss."

"They're my friends," the boy said, refusing to meet her gaze.

"I thought Jonathan was your friend." Adam knew Hero named one of her brothers, the doctor's youngest child.

The boy shrugged. "Jon ain't here, is he? Off to some fancy school, he is. An' me ma and sisters—they hafta eat, don't they? A sergeant's widow don't get much, you know."

Hero looked distraught. "Oh, Trevor, why did you not come to us? We would have helped you and your family."

The boy just stared at her.

"You are Jonathan's friend. We would have helped you," she repeated.

"We ain't takin' handouts," he finally said. "Prentisses take care of our own. Don't need no charity."

"It is not charity when it comes from friends," she said, gently patting his shoulder. He shrugged her away.

Adam surmised that his belligerence kept him from showing tears of weakness. *A sergeant's widow?* Adam felt an inkling of recognition. "Prentiss!" he said sharply. "What was your father's name? His regiment?"

"What's it to you?"

"Just answer the question."

Something in Adam's tone got through, for the lad responded. "Spencer Prentiss. The Ninety-Sixth Rifles."

"Ah, God." Adam sighed heavily.

Hero stood and turned to Adam. "You knew him? You remember?"

Adam shook his head. "Not well. Not my regiment. Stirling's. My friend Stirling."

"You knew Major Stirling? My pa really liked him." The boy's tone was eager surprise at first, but then he clamped his mouth shut, seeming to fear he had said too much.

Adam wiped a hand over his face. "Prentiss saved Stirling's life not once, but twice. Couldn't manage it a third time. They both died at Toulouse."

Everyone was silent for a moment.

"How sad. How very sad," Hero said softly.

"War is a sorry business," her father said. "That battle was particularly so. Napoleon had already abdicated before it was fought."

Again, there was silence as others absorbed this ugly reality.

"Stand up, Prentiss," Adam ordered. "And come over here."

Using the door of the closet as leverage, the young man pushed himself to a standing position and slowly walked over to Adam's bedside.

"Untie his hands," Adam said to Stewart, who seemed none too happy about doing so. Prentiss stood looking at the floor and rubbing his wrists.

Thinking he must be terrified, Adam had to admire the stoicism the boy displayed. "Now look here, Prentiss." When Prentiss looked up, Adam held his gaze. "Your father was a good man. Brave. Loyal. I doubt he would have approved of what you were about this night, no matter what the reason." The boy swallowed hard. "N-no, sir."

"So." Adam paused, then went on with more assurance. "So—out of respect for Sergeant Prentiss, I am letting you go. You might say the sergeant is saving yet another life. Find another way—a more honorable way—to help your family."

"Yes, sir."

"And, Mr. Prentiss?"

"Yes, sir?"

"There is no shame in needing help."

"Y-yes, sir."

"Now go on home."

"Th-thank you, sir."

Trevor looked as though he wanted to say more, but Hero interjected. "Your mother will be worried sick."

"Yes, ma'am." He turned and fled through the open side door.

A cool breeze flowed from the open door and window as the blackness of night was rapidly evolving into the gray beginnings of dawn. Adam and the two Whitbys seemed to release a collectively held breath as Stewart too left the room.

"I hope I was not overstepping there, Doctor," Adam said.

"No. No. I was trying to come up with a solution myself. Let us hope your 'go and sin no more' approach works. He has always been a good lad."

"His father was a good man."

"And you remember that, do you?" Hero had stood quietly in place during his discussion with the boy, but now she moved more firmly into Adam's line of vision. She was somewhat disheveled in a serviceable brown wool robe that she had obviously donned hastily, for the robe, though tied at the waist, was open in the front to show the frilly lace of the neckline of her nightgown. Her hair hung in a single braid over one shoulder and reached to her breast. A firm, rounded breast under that nondescript robe. Her nose and cheeks were shiny, and that sprinkling of freckles went right down to the neckline of her garments—and perhaps beyond. He thought she was beautiful. With effort, he brought his mind to focus on her question.

"Yes, I do. I do remember."

He was surprised at how much he did remember. He realized now that he had not so much recognized Trevor and George individually, but their clothing had brought to mind the men who had beaten him so thoroughly. However, he thought it wise to be somewhat cautious about revealing too much at this point. He trusted the Whitbys implicitly, but theirs was a large household. There might be others like George and Trevor and their friend Henry. And he was hardly in a position to fend for himself much—yet. He would keep his own counsel for the time being.

So, he equivocated. "I do not seem to have difficulty with war memories," he said. "Would that I did."

She gave him a look of sympathy, but said nothing as Stewart returned just then with a flat piece of wood under his arm and a hammer and nails in his hands.

"Thought I'd nail that door shut 'til we can replace the lock," he said. "No sense inviting trouble again."

"Well done, Stewart," the doctor said with a yawn.

"Come, Papa," Hero said. "We can get an hour or two of sleep yet. We shall talk with you later, Adam."

The doctor rose and bade Adam "Good night—er—good morning" as he escorted his daughter from the room. Adam smiled to himself as he overheard the doctor say with a chuckle, "Adam, is it?" He did not hear Hero's response.

* * * *

Alone now with his rejuvenated memory, Adam could no longer sleep. He remembered! He remembered it all: who he was, why he was here, the incident on the road to Weyburn Abbey. Dr. Whitby had been right: Something—even something quite trivial—could trigger the return of memory. In this case, it had been the tension—battlefield tension—as he waited for whoever was trying to unlock that door. His memory had been triggered as soon as he got a clear view of them. He wondered fleetingly if anyone else from his past—a friend or member of his family, say—might have instigated his re-entering his own book of life. It did not matter. He remembered!

This chapter of his life had started in his father's London residence, Thornleigh House, in the Mayfair district of the city. Napoleon finally and firmly banished from the Continent, the Duke of Thornleigh had taken his bride of forty-plus years on a long-promised tour of the Italian provinces, leaving their third son to rattle around in that mausoleum alone with a mere thirty or more servants to see to his needs. But not for long would he be "alone." Thornleigh House was on the verge of being invaded by three other of the duke's children—along with their spouses and assorted children of their own—for the London Season.

Thus it was that the duke's third son, Lord Alexander Benjamin Sterne—until some months ago, *Major* Lord Alexander Sterne of His Majesty's Army—welcomed the escape suggested by a visit from his solicitor, who had handled his lordship's affairs during the major's army years.

The solicitor had arrived late one morning as his client was suffering a monumental hangover—one of many following monumental drinking bouts pursued in part to postpone sleep, which inevitably brought dreams of death and destruction and mayhem. Hamlet was right to suspect that supposed balm to the human soul, Alex told himself repeatedly. Sleep was vastly overrated as offering comfort. And no amount of drinking, gambling, and whoring had yet managed to fend off the major's "slings and arrows of outrageous fortune."

When the visitor entered, Alex had roused himself from a reclining position on a couch in the duke's elegant library to stand and greet the lawyer properly.

"Mr. Montague, your note sounded rather urgent." He motioned the visitor to a winged chair opposite the couch.

Mr. Cedric Montague, middle-aged and prosperous looking, sat and placed an attaché case at his feet. He said, "Perhaps not urgent, my lord, but certainly serious. I shall get right to the point. Revenues from your properties have declined rather precipitously of late."

"Is that not quite normal for a post-war economy?"

"Not, I think, to this degree, my lord. Actually, there have been some serious losses dating back some years now. I have tried to keep you informed in my quarterly reports, but…" Montague's voice trailed off.

"But—occupied elsewhere—I tended to pay them little attention," Alex filled in for him. "I seemed always to have enough of the wherewithal to suit my needs."

"Yes, my lord. We saw little problem in the first years after you inherited from Sir Benjamin Harwood. There were few expenditures that one might consider extraordinary. All seemed in order. But last summer I took it upon myself to visit the properties. And I must tell you—something is not quite right there. You have laid out monies for repairs and maintenance that seem not to have been done. I did write up my findings in a report then, but as the Battle of Waterloo had so recently occurred, I quite understand how you may have overlooked it."

"I think you mean to say I ignored it," Alex said.

The lawyer reached for his case and extracted some papers. "I would hesitate to put it in exactly those terms, my lord." He reached across a low table to hand over the documents. "When you have examined these, I think you may want to hire an investigator to determine the true state of affairs at Weyburn Abbey."

"Or go myself," Alex muttered.

The next day he had sent a letter to the Abbey's steward, one Willard Teague, informing him that he would be journeying to Weyburn on thus-and-such a date and he would welcome a full accounting from the man when he arrived.

Alex studied carefully the documents Montague had given him, and over the next several days he afforded the situation a good deal of thought. The lawyer was right: Things were not exactly as they should be at Weyburn Abbey. Ordinarily, Major Sterne's inclination would have been to charge in, take command, and put everything to rights again. His gut told him that approach did not seem advisable in the civilian world. So he decided to reconnoiter matters first. To this end, he would forego the usual trappings of travel for a member of a duke's family.

He would journey to Cornwall incognito, leaving Jeremy MacIntosh, his sometime batman, now his valet, in London; employ a post chaise for the first part of the journey; then switch to a rented saddle horse on the last day. Spring rains had slowed the carriage travel, but Alex welcomed fairer weather on that final day. All had gone as planned. He stopped in the town for lunch and, as a ruse to reinforce his traveling incognito, he asked directions to the Abbey. He then rode on, enjoying the fine day and pleasant scenery: a lane lined with trees showing that first green-gold of new foliage and allowing occasional glimpses of a sparkling sea.

Suddenly, his hired hack was startled by something; the horse reared, nearly unseating its rider. Before he could control the animal, three men darted from a copse of willows, shouting and waving their arms, startling the horse further. As they tried to drag Alex from the saddle, he reached for his pistol in a holster attached to the saddle. He managed to get off a wild shot before they succeeded in dragging him from his mount. He recalled hearing a loud crack and landing with his right leg at a horrible angle. He also remembered the mismatched scuffle that followed—with grunts and yelps of pain all around. He was sure he had managed to land a punch or two of his own before a blow to his head—with a rock?—had sent him reeling. He remembered the gritty gravel against his cheek and hands and he felt a couple of kicks to his torso before he lost consciousness.

Now, days later, and after a second attempt on his life, he cursed himself for a fool. He should never have announced his intended visit. Alex had inherited the Abbey from his Uncle Benjamin. His mother's childless brother had also been Alex's godfather. Willard Teague had served his uncle as both the Abbey's land steward and as general manager of the copper mine. Sir Benjamin had trusted the man, so Alex, occupied at the time with one battle after another on the Iberian Peninsula, had readily agreed to the solicitor's suggestion that the new owner retain the steward so long as said owner was out of the country. In view of this recent visit from Kempf and Prentiss, it was quite clear that the attack on the road to the Abbey had not been a random encounter. *Did not think this visit to Cornwall quite through, did you?* he grumbled to himself. He also readily admitted—so long as he was chastising himself—that he had simply ignored the Cornwall-Devon property as he wrestled unsuccessfully with the demons plaguing him since his return to England.

That assault on the road to the Abbey might have been passed off as the work of ordinary highwaymen; this most recent one could not. It was clearly directed at a specific target: the owner of Weyburn Abbey. Had Teague—perhaps innocently—informed others of the intended visit? Surely a visit from a long-absent owner of such a huge holding would have been cause for gossip in the area. Stewart had said the Prentiss boy and Kempf were "part of Teague's gang." What did that mean? Why did folks become guarded when Teague's name was mentioned?

Teague clearly suspected that "Adam Wainwright" was not who he said he was, but Alex knew that, other than timing, there was no way the man could be absolutely sure. Major Lord Alexander Sterne had operated as one of Wellington's spies often enough that he knew one operated in enemy territory without carrying identity papers. And this certainly *seemed* to be enemy territory.

But why?

Perhaps Adam Wainwright should continue to reconnoiter for that other fellow, Alexander Sterne.

Chapter 7

When she left the clinic with her father early that morning, Hero fully intended to first, sleep for a while, and then, after breakfast and time with Annabelle, confront Adam about how much of his memory he had regained. Her plan for the day was sabotaged almost immediately. She had scarcely settled into her bed when Stewart was again knocking on her door.

"Sorry, Miss Hero, but there's some folks needing help down below. Gunshot wounds."

"Gunshots? Oh, good heavens. How many injured?"

"Three, I think."

"Wake my father, please, Stewart. Then go and get the most serious case on the surgery table. We will be right there."

"Yes, ma'am. Mrs. Hutchins is already seeing to hot water."

"Good."

She dressed hastily in a worn, loose-fitting day dress, grateful that she need not ring for a maid merely to help her dress. She might not be fashionable, but she could usually dress herself in something presentable. Still, it took her longer than it did her father; he would already be dealing with the first patient by the time she arrived. She dismissed any further musing about her dress; she would be enveloped in a covering apron once she went downstairs. *Why do these emergencies always come so early in the morning? Not even six o'clock yet.*

In the wide hallway outside the surgery, she found two red-coated militiamen standing over two wounded men. She lifted her lantern for a better look at these two. They were both conscious and both were young—barely in their twenties, she guessed. One, sitting against the wall, wore the militia uniform. He had a blood-soaked rag wrapped about his head and he held his arm carefully in a makeshift sling. The other, dressed in the garb of a local seaman, lay supine on what she took to be a piece of canvas sail. Blood pooled under his right shoulder, and the left leg of his trousers was ripped and bloody. She recognized this one and knelt beside him.

"Billy Jenkins. What happened to you?"

"Caught a bullet in my shoulder and a knife in my leg." He sucked in a painful breath. "Shoulder hurts. Hurts like fire!"

"I am sure it does. We shall see to both of you just as soon as we can," she said as she stood up.

The youngest standing militiaman used his boot to nudge Billy Jenkins's foot. "Yeah. Fix you up good for the hangman's noose, maybe."

Jenkins howled, but Hero thought he did so for show—or out of fear—for the militiaman had merely touched what she took to be his uninjured limb.

"Enough, Taylor!" The older militiaman, who wore an officer's insignia, barked at his subordinate, then bowed to Hero. "Captain Howell. At your service, ma'am. Patrolling the coast, we ran into this gang of smugglers. They were armed and chose to fight. These two"—he pointed at Billy and at the open door to the surgery—"have lived to pay for their deeds."

"Let us hope the payment does not exceed the magnitude of the deeds," she said and hurried past him through the door.

"They are smugglers!" he called after her.

She found her father already dealing with the man on the table, assisted by Stewart and a middle-aged maid named Nellie Matson. Nellie, who had worked for the Whitbys for years, had returned only yesterday, having been attending to her dying father for the last month. She was an accomplished nurse—and she was not squeamish.

"Ah, Hero," her father greeted her. "This one's serious. Caught a knife across his face and a sword slashed his belly. There is a bullet in his upper thigh—nicked the bone, I think. We need to get that bullet out, and your hand is steadier than mine."

She accepted the large encompassing apron Stewart held out for her and wrapped the sashes about her to tie it tightly in the front. She noted that Nellie, similarly garbed—as was her father—was gently cleaning the man's face. Their patient, lying under a sheet already spotted with blood, was Jake Harrison. Hero had attended Sunday school lessons with the Harrisons. She tried not to think about how worried Jake's wife would be.

He was conscious, obviously apprehensive, and obviously in pain, but his amiable personality was sustaining him. "You be careful of the family jewels there, Doc." He managed this remark despite the cut on his face that ran from his nose to his jawline.

"Just lie still. My daughter will do her best to see that you are able to add to that long line of Harrisons."

"I don't want no woman cuttin' on me in tender places. 'Tain't decent."

"Fine," Dr. Whitby said. "We shall leave that lead in you, and you will likely die of gangrene. You might anyway. That would deal effectively with the Harrison dynasty."

"Ah, Doc—"

The patient's words ended on a high note of pain as the doctor lifted the sheet and moved the injured leg to reveal the wound to Hero. Jake subsided into silence. Hero thought he was gritting his teeth against pain. She saw Nellie give him a folded cloth to bite down on.

She knew her father's blunt impatience came from his own pain and fatigue. Trying to stay out of Jake's line of vision, she gently elbowed her father out of the way and began to probe for the bullet. Her father moved to deal with the cut across his midriff.

Finding the intrusive lead proved easier than she had feared, but extracting it required delicate work. No matter how careful she was, the wound was bleeding anew and she was aware of causing Jake excruciating pain. She was glad when he fainted. Once she removed the foreign object, she cleaned the outside of the wound and stitched it shut. She joined her father who, with Nellie's help, was dealing with a deep diagonal slash across Jake's belly.

The doctor stood up to ease his own back muscles and said to the now unconscious patient, "Well, son, you are lucky. That saber—or whatever it was—missed any vital organs so far as I can tell." He turned to Hero. "It nicked the liver. I've managed to control the internal bleeding for the moment. Have to just hope he doesn't manage to get it started again. He's going to have a sore belly and little appetite for a while."

"You sit for a few minutes, Papa. I will finish with Jake, then we'll bring in the other two."

She steeled herself for more stitchery, telling herself yet again how she hated sewing pieces of human flesh together. She was glad to see that the facial wound, once Nellie had cleaned it, required only three stitches in the fleshiest part of his cheek. But he had wakened from the faint, and winced with each poke of the needle.

"Sorry, Jake," she murmured. "Stay with me now. Just a little bit more. Then I will give you some laudanum for the pain, and you'll sleep."

He said nothing, but his deep brown eyes reflected trust, gratitude, and resignation. She finished and instructed Stewart and Nellie to bring in the second bed from what she now thought of as "Adam's room." The two helpers had been busy throughout, exchanging basins of bloody water for clean warm water. They transferred Jake to the bed and Hero and Stewart wheeled it into the other room as Nellie and Dr. Whitby prepared for the next patient.

Hero was not at all surprised to see that Adam was wide awake.

"Busy morning, eh?" Adam watched as Hero and Stewart pushed the second bed into position and set the blocks to stabilize it. The new patient was already drifting into sleep from the laudanum she had given him.

"Yes, and it is far from over," she replied. "We need your bed."

"That should not be a problem. I shall just jump right down and give it up. Would you like me to do a jig as well?"

She smiled. "Try not to be such a wiseacre. Stewart will help you into the Bath chair and wheel you into another room. I think you will like it—it is directly across from the library."

She rang the bellpull for another maid to come and change the bed Adam had been using, then left as Mr. Stewart was helping him out of the bed.

Back in the surgery, she found Billy Jenkins lying on the table and the wounded militiaman sitting on a straight-backed wooden chair. The other two militiamen stood leaning against the wall. The hole in Billy's shoulder turned out to be merely a flesh wound, but she still had to probe for the bullet and stitch the laceration. Billy was not nearly so stoic about pain as his friend Jake Harrison had been. He loudly sucked in his breath or yelped with each stitch. She dealt with the leg wound, which also required stitches, then left her father and Nellie to deal with Billy's bandages.

While Hero and her father had dealt with Billy, Nellie had cleaned the militiaman's face and his wounded arm. She had also correctly deduced that the arm was broken midway between the elbow and wrist and retrieved the necessary splints from a cupboard. Stewart helped Hero set the bone and splint it. She was glad to see that the actual tear in the skin on his arm was superficial and would require no needlework. The man was young and was distinctly embarrassed as he howled in pain when the bone was put back in place and the splints were set to keep it there.

"I'm sorry. I'm sorry," he said in near sobs.

"Never mind," she assured him. "The worst is over now. Let's see what you are hiding under that bloody cloth on your head."

As she removed the rag, hard with dried blood, she was dismayed to see the wound begin to bleed again. He looked panicky as blood streamed down his face.

"Not to worry," she said softly, touching his jaw to turn his head so she could get a better look. "Head wounds always bleed like this. And—it looks as though you are luckier than some. You must have turned your head at just the right moment. It was a bullet, was it not?"

"Y-yes, ma'am."

She mopped up the fresh blood and cleaned away the old. "The bullet plowed a crease just above your ear. Another quarter of an inch and…" She let her voice trail off and just shook her head. She gave him a small cloth folded several times. "Here. Bite down on this as I stitch that crease together."

Stewart had helped transfer Billy to the bed Adam had vacated. In a matter of minutes, it was all over but for the mopping up and restoring order to the surgery. Nellie and Stewart would, with whatever help they needed, tend to that.

The senior militiaman took charge and assigned his uninjured subordinate to stand guard over the two injured prisoners. The injured militiaman was to stay there as well until Captain Harrison was ready to leave. Hero saw to it that chairs were available for both of them.

Dr. Whitby said, "Captain Howell, my daughter and I invite you to join us for breakfast. We shall have a tray sent out for your guards and their charges, though I doubt Harrison will wake up to partake—or even feel like doing so."

The captain bowed slightly. "Thank you, sir. That is most generous."

Hero returned to her room and rang for a maid to help her change into a more presentable day dress of yellow cotton embroidered with white daisies. She had had the dress made by a London dressmaker over a year ago and thought then that the neckline was scandalously low for day wear. Her friends assured her it was quite fashionable, and privately she thought she looked very well in it. She refused to acknowledge that she had chosen it today with her planned meeting with Adam in mind.

When she entered the dining room, she found not only her father and the militiaman, but Adam Wainwright as well.

"I thought it was time Adam joined us," her father explained. "Good food should be enjoyed in the company of others."

"Of course," she murmured with a smile at Adam. He raised his eyebrows and nodded slightly with what she thought might be approval of her appearance. She was glad she had worn the yellow cotton. She quickly took her seat, and the other two men, having risen when she came in, resumed theirs.

"Every day brings a mite of normality back to my life," Adam said. "I am remembering more too. I am not fully there yet, but it is coming. Slowly, mind you, but coming."

He gave Hero a direct look and held her gaze for a moment. She took this to mean he was warning her off talking of his memory return. *Well, if that is what he wishes...*

The Bath chair was positioned so that, by turning his upper body slightly, Adam could join in the meal almost naturally. Hero sat across from him; the captain was on the same side as Adam in the place of honor at his host's right. Two footmen entered with trays, and as one removed the covers and served generous plates of sausages, bacon, and scrambled eggs, the other placed a basket of muffins on the table and poured coffee, finally setting the pot near Hero.

"Thank you, Ross. Carter." The doctor dismissed them, then turned to the militiaman. "Captain Howell, do tell us as much as you can about last night's adventure."

Captain Howell drank some coffee and set the cup down. He was a husky man of perhaps forty, with thick sandy hair that showed strands of gray at the temples. He had brown eyes and thick brows darker than his hair. His uniform showed little of the muss and soil Hero had seen in those of his younger companions. He gave her an apologetic look as he began.

"It is not a tale one would ordinarily share with ladies, but Miss Whitby has shown herself to be of sterner stuff, you might say, than most females of her class. Very unusual to find a woman of any class performing as you did this morning, Miss Whitby."

Hero gave him a smile of encouragement, though she thought he had not quite decided whether he approved of her unwomanly performance.

"Hero does fine work," her father said, "but we are all keen to hear your story."

"Yes, sir." Howell shifted position in his chair, leaning back more casually. "An informant alerted my superior—Colonel Phillips at headquarters in Appledore—that we could expect some illegal activity last night on the beach near Weyburn. As you probably know, we have increased patrolling in coastal areas since the war. We lacked the manpower before, what with so many of our fighting men on the Peninsula or off to America. But, frankly, even with more force now, we cannot be everywhere. England simply has too much coastline. Too many tidal streams. Too many coves that protect nefarious endeavors."

"So you had an informant," Dr. Whitby prompted.

"Yes. A French ship would anchor off the coast here; two fishing boats would sail out for the contraband goods and deliver them to that cove below Weyburn Abbey."

"Did it go as planned?" Hero asked, spreading strawberry jam on a muffin.

Captain Howell nodded. "At first it did. But then one of our new recruits must have lost his nerve. The plan was to wait until both the small boats were beached and being unloaded and then move in for the arrests. This fellow's weapon went off just as the first boat touched the beach. Two men in the boat returned fire, and the fight was on. Hand-to-hand when my lads rushed the boat. One killed. Two injured. Three escaped. The second boat immediately set sail and ran. They probably have another of these coves they use for such contingencies."

"Your men actually fired on those in the fishing boat?" Dr. Whitby asked.

"No. I don't think so. Or, if he did, he missed by a mile."

"Is there any chance this shot, which obviously warned at least some of the smugglers away, was intended for just that purpose?" Adam asked.

"That possibility has occurred to me. Local militias are often that—local to a greater or lesser degree, depending on the area. As you must know, Dr. Whitby, I am fairly new here. I simply do not know my people well yet."

"That's unfortunate," Adam said. "Makes command difficult, I'm sure."

"That it does." Howell gave Adam an assessing look.

Motioning her father and the captain, both of whom could stand, to stay seated, Hero rose to refill coffee cups. As she reached awkwardly across the Bath chair to refill his cup, Adam winked at her. She tried to ignore a slight thrill at the intimacy of this exchange. She returned to her seat and busied herself with refilling her own cup.

Adam seemed to shift the topic of discussion—subtly, but deliberately, Hero thought.

"What do you know of these particular smugglers?" he asked the captain.

"Mostly only what I've been told. Last night was my first encounter personally. The general word is that this lot are fast, clever, and hard to catch. The gang is said to number anywhere from eight to twenty, depending upon which incident report one reads."

"How many incidents?" Adam asked.

"Dozens. The reports on this bunch go back about six years." Howell was beginning to look uncomfortable.

"And neither the local authorities nor the militia has caught any of them?" Adam shook his head in disbelief.

"Locals on all England's coasts tend to turn a blind eye," the doctor interjected. "Too many people depend on—or profit immensely from—that income. They pay attention only when someone is hurt—as happened last night."

"There *have* been arrests," Howell asserted, "especially since Parliament and Whitehall stepped up efforts to collect those taxes."

"But there have been no arrests here—in Weyburn—in many months," Hero said. "And few deaths—ever." She turned toward her father. "The man killed last night was Bertram Larson. Billy Jenkins whispered that to me when we took him into the other room."

"Oh, good Lord," her father said. "The man has—had—a sick wife and seven children," he explained to Adam and Howell. "One of the Abbey's tenant farmers. Let's hope the family is not evicted." He exchanged a bleak look with his daughter.

"The oldest son is sixteen," Hero noted.

Howell sat up straighter in his chair and pulled at the neck of his uniform. "I am sincerely sorry about the loss of life, but you do understand that the militia is charged with a certain mission—"

"Yes, of course. We do not blame *you* personally at all." The doctor sighed. "And we understand the government's need to stop this drain on the nation's economy. We understand—in the abstract. It is just hard to watch one's flesh-and-blood neighbors suffer from abstractions."

"Our local situation could be alleviated a great deal—a very great deal—if the owner of Weyburn Abbey—"

"Now, Hero," her father cautioned amiably, "we deal with what we can."

"Yes, Papa."

Adam gave her a questioning look, but after a moment he turned again to the captain to say, "I assume you investigate and interrogate on a regular basis."

"Interminably. But folks are pretty tight-lipped. And, to be frank, these rascals are good at what they do. Incredibly fast moving—with huge amounts of contraband goods. They often seem to just disappear into thin air. Locals fear and hate the militia. But they fear the leaders of the smugglers even more."

"Do you know who they are?"

"We have a few names, but no solid proof. Those who supply names have a habit of vanishing—or declaring later that they must have been mistaken."

Adam reached for his coffee cup and seemed ready to drop the subject. "Yours is a hard job, Captain."

"'Tis that. And I'd best be about it." Howell stood. "Thank you, Dr. Whitby, Miss Whitby. For breakfast, and for taking care of my men. With your permission, I will leave Taylor here to guard the prisoners until they can be moved. I shall take Roberts with me—I doubt his broken arm will preclude his riding once we get him mounted."

The doctor, standing now, nodded his agreement, but Hero cautioned, "Do keep an eye on Mr. Roberts. His head wound *could* cause dizziness."

"I shall do that. Thank you, miss."

When he had gone, the doctor sat back down and passed his cup to Hero for a refill. She lifted the pot in Adam's direction, but he shook his head. She pushed her plate aside and said, "What a day! And it is not even noon yet!" She looked at Adam across the white expanse of the cloth-covered table. "How do you like your new quarters?"

"That chamber is quite splendid. I cannot believe it was intended as part of your medical facilities."

She exchanged an amused glance with her father, who chuckled and said, "It was designed for me—when I reach my dotage and can no longer climb the stairs to a bedchamber. Used it when the gout hit me hard last winter, but so long as I can climb the stairs..."

"Planned ahead, did you?"

"Seemed prudent so long as we were adding to the house anyway," the doctor said.

Hero added, "The main part of this building was once the manor house of a large estate. It is not as old or as grand as the Abbey by any means, but it dates back about a century and a half. My great-grandfather sold some of the land, but we still have the main farm and two others as well."

* * * *

Knowing that the doctor and his daughter had had little sleep last night, Alex excused himself and managed to wheel himself back to his chamber with only minimal help from the footman Ross, whom he found hovering in the hall, waiting to clear the dining table. Alex was glad to have avoided a discussion of the return of his memory, but he was certain that it had not been *avoided*—merely postponed.

He marveled anew at the change in his quarters. Whereas the hospital room had been all whitewashed sterility, this room displayed such tasteful grandeur as befitted a man of some wealth and education. It was not merely a bedchamber, but a bed-sitting room. A sliding French door led to a terrace like the one outside the hospital room, and, like that one, this one sported a profusion of potted plants, many abloom with yellow, white, blue, and red spring flowers. This terrace too had furniture that simply invited one to enjoy being outdoors.

The room itself was equally inviting. Drapes and bedcoverings had a pattern of muted blues and grays, with splotches of white. A couch and overstuffed chair were dark gray. Brightly colored pillows and the cushions on the chairs at a small dining table delighted one's eyes. A screened alcove offered ample room for taking care of personal cleanliness, and there was a large armoire for clothing. *Quite as comfortable as any chamber in the duke's London house*, Alex thought.

But for him, the most enticing aspect of the room—apart from that comfortable bed, which he could get into and out of without help, and which cried out to be shared—was a well-stocked bookcase. Alex grunted with pleasure at finding within his reach a copy of one of his favorite works, *The Iliad*. His pleasure at this find doubled when he discovered it was a translation he had not encountered before. *Well, Doc*, he mused silently, *you will surely be comfortable in what you referred to as your "dotage."* Alex settled back into the Bath chair and opened the book.

Later, after a lunch Davey brought to him on a tray and served at the small table, Alex managed to open the drapes and the French door and wheel himself out onto the terrace. Feeling no small degree of success at that achievement, he reveled in the sun, which had made its way to this side of the house. He immersed himself in the familiar quarrel between Achilles and Agamemnon outside the walls of Troy, though he looked out from time to time at the sparkling sea in the distance. *Not exactly Homer's idea of a "wine dark sea," but it will do. Indeed, it will do very well.*

Allowing himself to be distracted from Homer's tale, he turned his thoughts to that discussion of smugglers earlier. He had little doubt that the attacks on him were somehow connected to the smuggling operations. He suspected—given the caution exercised about talk of Teague—that Teague might well be leading them. Hadn't he heard Stewart refer to "Teague's gang"? Suspicions were not proof, however, and any search for evidence would have to wait until he gained more mobility.

Besides the issue of smugglers, for Alex there was the added problem of how the local people regarded the heretofore absent owner of the Abbey. *What did you expect?* he asked himself. *After all, you do remember reading that famous essay written by the Irishman Jonathan Swift, do you not? Are you really so stupid that you think people of modern times would be any more tolerant of landlords who abrogate their responsibilities than Swift was, nearly a hundred years ago?*

But I did not know.

You chose not to know.

Even now that I am more aware, I haven't a clue as to the extent of the neglect.

Then get one. Find out what is going on.

These thoughts were interrupted as he heard voices coming from around the far corner of the house. He recognized Hero's voice. He did not recognize that of what could only be a small girl child.

Chapter 8

Having treated herself to a short nap, Hero, again wearing the yellow day dress, had lunch with Annabelle in the nursery, thus giving Clara Henson an unexpected break. Afterwards, she watched from the paddock fence as the man in charge of the Whitby stable gave Annabelle a riding lesson. Daniel Perkins, Hero noted yet again, was as gentle and patient in teaching Annabelle as he had once been with a very young Hero and her siblings. Annabelle delighted in showing off her skill to her audience of one.

Although she would have expected nothing less in her father's household, Hero was grateful that the Whitby staff members had all readily accepted Annabelle as a member of the family. She knew that what society might view as a "baseborn brat" would not have been so accepted in many a household. She feared that sooner or later Annabelle would be forced by some cruel idiot to recognize her origins. But for now, her "Auntie H'ro" was determined that that day would come later—much later—in the little girl's life. Moreover, Annabelle would already have learned the truth from those who loved her. Meanwhile, Hero sometimes thought she was overprotective of the child, but so be it.

She and Annabelle—along with Tootie and Bitsy—were returning to the house from the stable with a brief side trip to the clinic so Hero could check on the patients there. Nellie had reported after lunch that all was well; the militia guard was on the job and, to relieve his boredom, he was helping care for the two wounded smugglers. As she and Annabelle strolled along, it occurred to Hero that Annabelle would have to have a proper riding habit, but today the child wore a blue print dress and a white pinafore apron and was, as usual, full of questions and commentary.

Having dealt with continued praise of the pony, Sandy, and why daffodils had yellow flowers but green leaves, Annabelle pulled yet another topic from her fertile, eclectic view of the world.

"Why do I have to wear a dress all the time an' Freddie gets to wear trousers? If I wore trousers, I wouldn't have to use that silly sidesaddle, would I?" Freddie, the third child of Hero's sister, Diana, was a year older than Anabelle and one of her occasional playmates.

"Ladies ride sidesaddle," Hero answered.

"But why?"

"Just because." Hero remembered wondering the same thing herself on many occasions.

"I'd rather be a boy."

"I quite like you as a little girl."

"It's easier for boys to climb trees."

"You seemed to do all right climbing up that apple tree last week. Davey said he rescued you from a *very* high limb."

"But I couldn't get down 'cause of my dress—it kept getting caught—an' 'cause I had to hold onto Bitsy. She was real scared."

"I'm sure she was." Hero squeezed the little hand Annabelle had tucked into hers while the other arm held the errant Bitsy. "But next time you must get someone to help you. What if you had fallen and broken an arm or a leg?"

"You could fix me. I know you could."

Hero smiled at this expression of blind faith, but she gave the hand a shake. "Next time, you call for help. All right?"

"Uh-huh. I will."

They rounded the corner of the house to see Adam in the Bath chair on the terrace outside his new chamber. He had a book in his lap.

"Hello there," he called.

As they came closer, Annabelle said, "Oh, look, Auntie H'ro. It's the sleeping prince."

"Would you ladies care to join me?" he asked with a gesture at a pitcher of lemonade on a small tray with glasses and a plate of Cook's ginger biscuits.

Annabelle giggled at being so included, but she looked up at Hero to ask, "Can we, Auntie H'ro? Please?"

"May we," Hero corrected automatically. "If we are not disturbing you," she said to Adam. "Allow me to introduce one of my favorite people. This young lady is Annabelle. Annabelle, this gentleman is Mr. Wainwright."

Hero felt a touch of what could only be described as motherly pride when Annabelle gave him a very proper "How do you do?" and executed an equally proper curtsy.

"I am pleased to make the acquaintance of such a pretty girl," he said, gesturing to padded wicker chairs at the glass-topped wicker table.

Annabelle handed Bitsy to Hero and clambered onto the chair nearest Adam, then reached for the kitten again, and settled it in her lap. "You and Tootie can sit across from us," she announced officiously to Hero.

"Why, thank you," Hero said, exchanging a smile with Adam.

Hero poured glasses of lemonade for herself and Annabelle and topped off Adam's glass while Annabelle continued to chatter.

"You're not asleep today. You was asleep afore."

"No. I am quite awake now."

Annabelle turned to Hero. "Did you kiss him?"

Hero nearly dropped the glass she was handing to Annabelle and felt warmth suffuse her face. "Annabelle!" she said aloud and muttered under her breath, "Oh, my heavens." She looked at Adam to see him struggling not to laugh aloud.

Annabelle drank from her glass and set it down very precisely. "Well— did you? That's how it happened in the story. Only it was a princess," she explained seriously to Adam.

Hero could barely bring herself to look at Adam, but she had to say something to Annabelle. "Sweetheart, I told you that what happens in our stories is not necessarily the way things happen in real life."

"Oh." Annabelle was quiet for a moment. "I guess I forgotted. Tootie forgot too. Can I—may I have a biscuit, please?"

Glad for the diversion, Hero handed Annabelle a ginger biscuit and said to Adam, "'Sleeping Beauty' is one of her favorite stories."

"Ah, I see," he said.

Adam was very quiet and seemed lost in thought. Hero felt a moment of panic. *Oh, good Lord. Did he remember that kiss? After all, his eyes did open briefly. No. Don't be silly. He was unconscious!*

"It's a really good story," Annabelle assured him.

"Yes, it is," he agreed.

Hero was sure Annabelle would have launched into a detailed retelling of the story, but at that moment Clara Henson approached from the rear of the house.

"There you are," she said. "Miss Hero, it is time for someone's N-A-P. Shall I take her?"

"I know what that means," Annabelle declared. "An' I don't want a nap. I want to talk with Mr. Ainrye."

"Annabelle," Hero said sternly. "You must have your nap. See there— Bitsy is already asleep."

Annabelle's expression turned mutinous for a moment, but then she heaved a dramatic sigh and said, "All right. But I want a new story later. And another biscuit now." She hopped off her chair and curtsied to Adam again. "Mr. Ainrye, we shall talk again."

"Oh, I do hope so, Miss Annabelle."

Annabelle went around the table to kiss Hero's cheek, grabbed the biscuit she had demanded, and skipped off beside Nurse Henson, uttering an admonishing "Come along, Tootie."

Alex simply gazed at Hero for a moment. He moved his chair to close the distance between them and said, "Tootie? Did I miss something?"

"Annabelle's imaginary friend. A fairly new addition to the family."

"I assume Annabelle is the child Mr. Teague referred to yesterday."

Hero's guard arose instantly. "Yes, she is."

"She is a charmer. But she is not your daughter."

She noted that it was a statement, not a question. "Not by blood. Not legally. But I am the closest thing she has to a mother." She began to twist the corner of a serviette that had accompanied the lemonade to the terrace. She knew she probably appeared both nervous and slightly defensive as she explained briefly the circumstances of Annabelle's birth, ending with, "So you see, she is, as far as the world is concerned, mine. Ours. Annabelle is a Whitby in all but name. Certain elements of English society find it easy to ignore abandoned children."

* * * *

Alex had listened with interest to this account of Annabelle's history with the Whitbys. He had known of such places as Sally Knowlton's establishment, but never before had he come face-to-face, even indirectly, with the plight of society's discarded children.

Not in England.

"Orphans are not merely an English phenomenon," he said. The image of a small boy of perhaps three years flashed into his mind. It had been after the Third Siege of Badajoz, where there had been hundreds of civilian deaths. Alex was charged with the task of gathering the remnants of the drunken, marauding English soldiers who had finally taken the city. The army was moving out the next morning. He remembered many hungry children of all ages on the streets of the city that had been under siege by the allies three times in two years. He could not say why, but the image of that one child had seared itself on his soul: a small boy in rags, dirty blond hair, dirty bare legs and feet, tears cutting light streaks down his cheeks. Other children ignored him as he toddled from group to group with his little hands out. Alex was sure he was hungry—that they were all hungry. Even then he had wished he could just sweep them up and carry them off, but caught in the tide of war, he had simply pressed on. Nevertheless, that image of one child on a dirty, war-torn street, had haunted him ever since.

"I know it is not confined to England," Hero said softly, apparently responding to something she saw in his eyes. "But, as my father tells me repeatedly, we do what we can. We can do no more."

They were both lost in their own thoughts for a few moments, but it was a shared silence of mutual empathy.

Hero perked up. "Now—tell me about this return of your memory."

"Ah, I thought you would get around to that."

"So. Who are you? Why are you here in Weyburn?" She leaned forward eagerly.

"*Who* I am is of little significance at the moment. I would prefer to remain Adam Wainwright for the nonce." He smiled. "Or, in certain quarters, 'Mr. Ainrye.' I hope you will accept that." He held his breath for her response. Yes, it would serve his purpose as owner of the Abbey to hide his identity, but he also wanted to prove himself to her, to show her he was not the heartless scoundrel she thought him to be. Just why, he could not have articulated at the moment. Lord Alexander Sterne had rarely before felt a need to prove himself to anyone. And certainly not to a woman in whom he had developed a passing interest.

"Perhaps," she said slowly. "Perhaps I can deal with Adam Wainwright for a while yet. But why?"

"Because I am here—in Weyburn—on a mission of sorts, but now, with this infernal leg, I need more time to complete it." *Well, it is not exactly a lie, is it?*

She held his gaze, then looked away. She seemed to be struggling with this idea. She jerked her gaze back to his. "Oh! I think I understand. Lord Alexander Sterne cannot tear himself away from the pleasures of London to answer the pleas of folks dependent on him, so he sent you instead to investigate. Years later—years!—he sees fit to take an interest. Better late than never, I suppose."

"Yes, you might say that," he agreed. *Good job, Sterne. At this rate her opinion will be going ever lower instead of in the direction you'd like.*

"I am sorry that you too have had to suffer for his negligence." Her lips—those kissable lips—tightened into a grimace. "I do believe your being in that wheeled chair may be laid at his doorstep."

Ignoring her sympathy—and how kissable her lips were—he honed in on something she had said. "What did you mean by 'answer the pleas of folks'?"

"Just that. For the last five years or so, Mr. Teague has requested that his lordship concern himself—or assign a surrogate to deal with certain major problems. Some people—my sister, for one—have written him directly, but got no response."

"Let us hope there is some explanation for that," he said, thinking he sounded rather pompous. But he knew for a certainty that neither he nor the solicitor, Montague, had received direct communication from the steward or anyone else regarding the estate in Cornwall. He shifted the subject slightly. "You do not think much of one Alexander Sterne, do you?"

"No, I do not." She emphasized the last word. "Men of his ilk take advantage of their positions with little regard for others. They take whatever they want at the moment and—and leave devastation in their wake."

"I…uh…see," he said, confused by the vehemence of her response. "Um—have you ever met him?"

"No," she admitted. "I was away at school when he last visited the Abbey some years before Sir Benjamin died. Later we heard he had joined the army and was fighting the French." Her expression brightened. "Perhaps you knew him in the army."

"Uh—the army is a huge entity. I believe he was a staff officer for General Beresford." He hoped that sounded vague enough.

"Then how *did* you come to be involved with him?"

He had been expecting this question, so he was ready. "One of my friends is a Bow Street Runner. We were corresponding officers—spies, if you will—for Wellington. Sterne knew Bow Street to have capable investigators." At least all of this was true.

"And this friend asked you to help with Lord Alexander's Cornwall problem. Was that it?" She leaned forward, her breasts resting against one arm folded on the table in front of her; the other hand lay near her glass of lemonade. Alex found himself treated to a disconcerting view of delectable cleavage, but he doubted she was aware of that.

"You might say that."

He shifted uncomfortably in the Bath chair, causing the wicker to produce an audible squeak.

Again, they sat quietly for a while, both staring out to the distant sea.

Finally, Alex broke the silence. "Will you keep my secret—allow me to remain Adam Wainwright for a while?"

She nodded. "I think so. For a while."

"There's more." She merely held his gaze, waiting, so he went on. "According to the good Dr. Whitby, it will be a few weeks until I am truly able to get around with ease on my own. I promise not to impose on you inordinately, but I wonder if I might persuade you to help me in my investigation?"

"Go around with you in a carriage, you mean?"

"Yes. And—well—show me things I need to see in order to have a complete picture for my—uh—report. You know the area and the people far better than I..." He let this observation hang between them as he tried to assuage his nitpicking conscience. *It is all true*, he told himself. *Just not the whole truth.*

"Yes, I will help you, but..." She paused and looked out to the sea again, then back at him. She seemed embarrassed. "Adam, these are country people. If—if we are seen often in each other's company, they will assume—"

"That I am courting you!" he interjected. "But that is perfect! An excellent cover for what I am really about."

"And when you leave?"

"I am sure you will be able to explain that you simply found me totally unsuitable." He reached across the table to grasp her free hand. "I promise you this: I will not compromise you in front of your friends and neighbors."

She briefly returned the pressure of his grip. "As to that, Weyburn folks have long since accepted me as an oddity. But I am reluctant to fan that flame overmuch." She reached for the pitcher to refill their glasses.

He lifted his glass in a salute. "To our working together."

She touched her glass to his, nodded, and held his gaze. "To success."

* * * *

Hero watched as Adam drank deeply and set his glass aside, his large, capable-looking hands a distinct contrast to the delicate crystal. She was feeling a little overwhelmed by all that had passed between them: She was grateful for his trust, but somewhat mystified by what he had not revealed.

He cast a sly glance at her and grinned. "Now—about this other matter..."

"What other matter?"

"Did you or did you not kiss me as I lay unconscious, helpless, and at your mercy?"

Hero fidgeted with the serviette again. She did not want to lie to him, but she certainly did not want to admit the truth!

So, she equivocated.

"Why on earth would you think that?" She tried to summon up genuine outrage, but her innate sense of humor caused her to smile. "Surely you do not take seriously a child's chattering about a fairy tale."

His eyes—his oh-so-blue eyes—twinkled at her. "You are not answering my question, Miss Whitby. And I noticed earlier that you did not give Annabelle a direct answer either."

She looked away, then back at him. She sat straight and squared her shoulders. "The topic you mention is not one that a gentleman would pursue." She knew she sounded insufferably prim.

He laughed outright, then winced and put his hand to his chest and emitted a controlled cough. "Still not a direct answer. But allow me to tell you a tale." His voice became very serious. "As I lay on that bed, I was vaguely aware of things going on around me. I was in a very dark place. Dark, but somehow the darkness was familiar. Acceptable. If I just welcomed it, there would be no more pain—of any kind. No more physical pain. No more guilt. No more sorrow. No more loss. It would just be gone. All of it. I was very tempted. I thought if I could only grasp the comfort, the beckoning warmth of that darkness—It was so real, almost tangible..."

Hero sucked in her breath. "No. Please—no," she whispered.

He seemed unaware of her interjection and continued in the same solemn tone. "I *wanted* that darkness. Oh, how I longed for it! But suddenly an angel kissed me. Perhaps I was hallucinating. I don't know. But there she was—an angel surrounded by light with hundreds of bright stars all about her—and she kissed me! Immediately, I wanted that light, that brightness."

"Oh, my heavens." Hero again whispered.

He went on, his tone now only slightly lighter. "I am not one for taking stock in hallucinations. I think you kissed me. I think you brought me back from the brink—and for that I can only be grateful."

"I—I did kiss you," she confessed, looking at him directly but apologetically.

"Aha!" He smiled his satisfaction, his eyes twinkling again.

"However," she hurried on, "I have no doubt it was your own strong will that brought you back."

"You have your truth, I have mine," he said. "But I assure you, Miss Hero Whitby, next time there will be no question as to its being a hallucination."

She felt herself blushing, but she liked the implied promise in that comment. Embarrassed, she mumbled something about seeing to her other patients and beat a hasty retreat.

A soft chuckle followed her.

Chapter 9

Over the next weeks, Alex found himself gaining strength. Laughing and just breathing deeply were less painful. Hero removed the stitches from his leg and his head, and her father not only saw to a simpler splint and bandage, but he also presented "Adam" with a set of crutches. Essentially shaped like an elongated T, the upper part that fit under the arm was padded with an old towel, as was a handle set perpendicular to the main shaft. There had been much discussion among the doctor, Stewart, and Mrs. Hutchins as the details of this new device were worked out and proper measurements ensured. Nor had Hero and Nellie Matson hesitated to offer their observations. At first, using the crutches was tiring and Alex resorted to the Bath chair to relieve his shoulders and tender underarms. Gradually, his hands and arms toughened and he delighted in the freedom the crutches gave him.

Hero had asked for and received his permission to share with her father much about the return of his memory and his "mission" to investigate the goings-on at the Abbey. By tacit agreement, neither of them mentioned the "courtship." The doctor readily accepted the idea that their guest would continue to be addressed as Adam Wainwright. All was going as well as might be expected, given that a key actor in this drama could not move about with total ease—even with the help of the crutches.

Aware now of Adam's purpose in coming to Weyburn, the doctor actually aided him by continuing to invite Adam to share discussions when callers visited Whitby Manor. Soon enough Adam had met a number of the area's most prominent citizens. He discussed crops and breeding farm animals with the farmers, religion and providing for the poor with the vicar, and local legal issues with the magistrate. The smugglers, Harrison and Jenkins, had been removed to the town jail, awaiting the next session of the assize court. Alex was aware of Hero's worry about the fate of these two, but, as Adam Wainwright, there was little he could do about the situation. He had, however, made a point of visiting them before their removal to the jail. He thought it decidedly unfortunate that Willard Teague had visited them first, for that probably explained their reluctance to discuss anything but the weather with Adam.

One day a cold rain kept Alex off the terrace. With Hero and her father away all afternoon making house calls, Alex retreated to the library. He had stirred the fire and settled in a comfortable wing chair with a book on the Peloponnesian War when he heard the loud thwacks of the outside door knocker and then muffled voices as a footman answered the door and presumably informed the caller that the doctor and his daughter were not at home. Then the footman—it was Ross this time—rapped softly on the library door and entered at Adam's bidding.

"I am sorry to disturb you, Mr. Wainwright, but Mr. Teague is asking if he might speak with you."

Alex was surprised, but said, "Show him in." Using only one crutch, he rose awkwardly to a standing position as Teague strolled into the room.

"Do stay seated, Wainwright. I would not put you to any trouble," Teague said, plopping himself down on a couch without waiting for an invitation to be seated.

"Thank you." As he waited for Teague to state his business, Alex noted that the steward was again dressed as a prosperous country gentleman, this time in a maroon coat and buff colored trousers. *And why shouldn't the Abbey's steward dress to fit his position in the community?* Alex asked himself. He forcibly quelled his resentment at having to appear in a hand-me-down coat and a pair of trousers that had been altered drastically to accommodate the splinted leg. Teague merely stared at him for several seconds. Alex thought the stare was meant to intimidate, but he refused to rise to the bait.

Finally, Teague said, "I see you are recovering quite nicely."

"Yes, I am. I have had excellent care."

"I hear you're from London."

"Most recently, yes."

"And that you are acquainted with the owner of the Abbey."

"I have met him."

"I'll just bet you have," Teague said, almost under his breath. In a louder voice, he continued, "Are you planning to return to London?"

"Eventually."

Alex saw Teague's lips tighten at this. "I should think you'd want to return as soon as possible. You've not had what one would consider a warm welcome to Cornwall."

"Dr. Whitby and his daughter have been most hospitable. I find others friendly enough, as well."

Teague made a show of looking around the doctor's comfortable library. "You seem to have settled in here well enough. And I don't suppose it hurts to have such a delicious piece as Hero around to take care of one's needs."

"Miss Whitby has been all that is polite and proper, and any innuendo to the contrary is merely a slur on a good woman's name," Adam said tightly. He wanted to add that any man who would talk so disparagingly of a woman he hoped to marry was a bounder of the worst sort, but he held his tongue.

"Hey! Hey!" Teague made a show of putting up his hands in a mock defensive gesture. "I meant no slur on anybody. Merely remarking that she is a good-looking woman." He paused. "But I don't suppose it matters much as you are here for such a short time anyway."

"Actually, I am considering buying property here." Alex and Hero had lit on this ruse to explain some of Adam's questions as he toured the countryside.

"I am not aware of any property for sale in the immediate area," Teague said discouragingly.

"Are you not?" Alex feigned surprise. "Surely as the steward of Weyburn Abbey, you know that Sterne is considering selling all or part of his holdings here."

"I am aware of no such thing." Teague sounded indignant. "And I feel I should tell you that folks around here do not take kindly to ill-founded rumors. Nor do they take kindly to strangers asking a lot of intrusive questions. That sort of thing can get one hurt."

"Hmm. People with whom I have conversed have been most receptive and tolerant. Not at all suspicious and standoffish. Of course, when I am able to get about more, I may arrive at a different conclusion."

"Yes. I'm sure you will. And you will surely decide then to look elsewhere for property to buy—if, indeed, that is your purpose in coming here."

"Why, what else could it be?" Alex ask in a show of innocent wonder.

"That *is* the question, isn't it?" Teague gave Alex a pointed look. Then he rose and added, "I have enjoyed our little chat, but I fear I must be off. Things to do, you know."

"Enlightening," Alex said. "But don't let me keep you."

* * * *

June had brought an occasional cloudy day and an even less occasional rainstorm. These were usually "one day wonders," as Hero thought of them, but farmers welcomed them—unless they happened to have hay drying in a field. Dreary days were balanced nicely by warm, sunny days during which it seemed Mother Nature was beckoning everyone out of doors.

Hero and her father continued to deal with routine medical issues: a broken arm; two babies born—one in town, one on a farm; more cases of chickenpox, though these seemed on the decrease; a bad burn when a maid's skirt caught fire as she cleaned a hearth; and death claimed not only the smuggler, Bertram Larson, but also old Mrs. Porter, the blacksmith-mayor's long-ailing mother, and Mary Beth Lynch a young farm wife who succumbed finally to consumption. *But not without a good fight*, Hero noted of this last one. The doctor and his daughter rejoiced at the births, encouraged those recovering, and shared the grief of the families suffering losses. After all, these were people they had known for years, their neighbors and often their friends as well.

There was one outstandingly bright spot in these days for Hero: her younger brother, Jonathan, returned from school for the summer holiday. Except for those years when she was herself away at school, Jonathan had always been a shining light in Hero's life. She was eleven when he was born; she had immediately taken over as an "assistant" to the nursery maid, doting on her new little brother. Michael, who was thirteen then, had little interest in babies, though he and Hero, being nearest in age of the Whitby siblings, were also very close, period. Four years later their mother had died of the same disease that had so recently taken Mary Beth Lynch. Hero had missed Jonathan fiercely when she was herself at school, but when she settled in at home again, he was eight and she became a sort of surrogate mother and mentor to the child. Michael was still in medical school at the time, so the relationship between her and Jonathan strengthened.

At sixteen, Jonathan Whitby was a picture of what would be. He towered over his sister now, but she thought he had yet to feel comfortable in a body that was developing a man's physique. His hair was lighter than hers, but his freckles just as prominent, and his grin was as engaging as ever—though it seemed to flash more rarely now. Hero thought he might be struggling to find his "persona" as much as getting used to his gangly, changing body.

"I swear this boy has grown a foot since he was here for Christmas," Mrs. Hutchins said, looking up into Jonathan's laughing eyes when Hero ushered him into the kitchen to say hello.

"Certainly another inch or two," Hero agreed with a mock sigh as she and Jonathan sat on a bench on one side of the long worktable that dominated the kitchen. "And he just had new clothes in December!"

"Can't I go to London for some new ones? I want things more in style. Old Mendel's stuff is so out of date."

"You will have to ask Papa," Hero said. "But you know how he hates traveling. And Mendel has always suited Papa and Michael."

Jonathan grimaced. "Only because he is the only tailor to be found in hundreds of miles."

"I think that is a bit of an exaggeration," Hero said, "but you will have to take up your sartorial problems with Papa."

"But I know he would let me go to London if you'd only put in a good word for me. Isn't that right, Mrs. Hutchins?"

"Umm. Possibly, Mr. Jonathan." Mrs. Hutchins placed a plate of biscuits and glasses of cider in front of them and returned to kneading her bread dough at the other end of the table.

"Jonathan, Papa is unlikely to want to go to London," Hero said. "And you mustn't plague him with doing so."

"Ah, I missed these!" Jonathan crammed a biscuit into his mouth and took a swallow of cider, then mumbled, "I don't need a keeper. I could go alone. Take the stage."

Hero laughed softly. "You know very well Papa would not send a sixteen-year-old to the city alone."

"You could come with me," he wheedled. "You have friends in London."

"Jonathan, I have obligations here in Weyburn. I cannot just ignore them and go traipsing off to London."

"Well, I don't want to spend my entire school holiday stuck in boring old Weyburn. There's nothing to do here."

Hero rose. "I'm sure you will find something."

At supper that evening, she introduced him to Adam, and the boy was duly impressed at meeting a man who had fought at Waterloo, but he seemed determined to pursue his London scheme with his father, who was obviously less than enthusiastic about it. Hero sighed inwardly and hoped the summer would not be marked by contention.

Besides being pleased to have Jonathan home, Hero welcomed these weeks in June as they afforded her opportunities to get to know the man calling himself Adam Wainwright. He now took most of his meals with them in the dining room, though after Jonathan's return, she noted that Adam was careful not to intrude on what he might have viewed as family business. Weather permitting, she often joined him on his terrace in the afternoons. Occasionally her father joined them, or Annabelle insisted she needed to talk with "Mr. Ainrye," but more often than not, it was just the two of them. She was surprised at how comfortable she was with him. Except for her father and her brother Michael, Hero rarely felt at ease with men. Since her disastrous early teen years, she simply had not trusted her feelings and her judgments about men—especially men of the class in which she suspected Adam Wainwright moved freely.

He readily shared stories of his childhood, his family, and his years at school and university. However, she felt that these accounts were missing important details of names and titles and locations. While this made her a bit uneasy, she did not press him—or examine her own feelings too closely. After all, everyone had secrets, did they not? Adam too was entitled to his privacy.

So she dismissed her reservations because she enjoyed listening to his stories of his past and his years abroad, even when she was not directly involved in the conversation—as often happened of an evening when Adam and her father battled it out over the chessboard and she sat curled up with a book, sometimes only pretending to read. She loved his voice and his laugh. She became intensely aware when he entered a room and conscious of his presence afterwards.

* * * *

Both residual pain and the sheer frustration of an active man forced into inaction plagued Alex, but he was finding ways to ignore the pain, usually without resorting to laudanum. As for action versus inaction, he was working on that too. Action, he told himself, was a matter of mind as well as muscle. Early on, he had discovered that the Whitbys' library far exceeded what one might expect of a country squire. Its rather marvelous collection held a number of volumes on local history. He began to systematically examine these—and maps of the area.

In doing so, he recognized that his lack of mobility was forcing him, at long last, to face a glaring need in his life: to gain control of it. As the third son of a very rich man, he had always known he could muddle through—neither his father now nor his brother later would turn his back on him. Pride, along with a sense of societal obligation, would dictate their "taking care" of him—even if ties of family love had not existed.

But of course they did.

Alex realized now that in the first two decades of his life he had just sort of drifted. Second and third sons were not reared to take on the responsibilities of the title and all that went with it. With little sense of direction, Alex had enjoyed his days at Winchester, one of England's most prestigious public schools. University had offered more independence, but he had been diligent in his studies. Because these came to him so easily, he had been equally diligent in raising hell both in Oxford and in London. His father, tired of trying to talk a sense of duty and honor into him, had purchased a commission for his recalcitrant son. At the time Alex had seen this as his father's merely washing his hands of the problem.

Now, he was not so sure.

The army had provided purpose and direction. He had surprised himself—let alone a few senior officers who knew him only by reputation—when gradually he had evolved into what one general had termed "a damned fine officer" as he awarded Alex yet another medal and a promotion.

Praise, promotions, and other accolades had not been enough to drive away the ghosts and demons that began to haunt him almost as soon as he left army life behind. Though he had not articulated it before, he thought now he might have seen Weyburn Abbey as a chance to regain that sense of purpose and direction—not to mention that hard work might placate some of those ghosts and demons.

But not for a while, damn it. Not for a while.

Impatience, he discovered, could be a powerful motivator. He felt driven to doing all he could to further his physical recovery, to exercise and massage the muscles of his injured leg. His ribs were more or less healed now, and he very rarely resorted to the Bath chair. He found himself devouring information about Weyburn and Weyburn Abbey with a view to living here permanently. Careful to guard against revealing too much, he shared information about himself with the Whitbys and encouraged them to talk about their little corner of Cornwall. But keeping up the pretense was not easy.

At supper one evening when Jonathan was out with his friends, Dr. Whitby brought up a subject he had broached before. "Are you sure there is not someone in your family we should notify of your injury and forced stay here?"

Having anticipated that, sooner or later, this question would come up again, Alex stuck to the truth insofar as possible. "My parents are traveling on the Continent now that it is safe to do so. I am clearly going to recover. I would not want them to cut their journey short. My mother has looked forward to this trip for years."

"Brothers? Sisters?" the doctor asked, passing a dish of vegetables to his daughter.

"Two of each," Alex said. "One or another of them would be sure to write my parents and worry them."

"Surely *someone* is worrying about you," Hero said.

"The family is used to not hearing from me for weeks at a time. It has always been the nature of my work."

This, of course, had been true when he was soldiering, but he would have to get word to them soon or his brother, the Marquis of Finneston and heir to the duke's title, would have an army of searchers out looking for him. The mail in England was known to be extraordinarily reliable, but given what Hero had told him earlier of people writing to the owner of the Abbey and getting no response, Alex was reluctant to simply write a letter announcing his presence in Cornwall.

As if she had read his mind, Hero said, "Write a letter. I will see to its being mailed when I go into town tomorrow."

"Into Weyburn?"

"Yes, Weyburn. Really, Adam! Our town is not so remote as to not have mail service. Twice a week we have actual contact with the outside world via the mail coach. Is that not absolutely grand?"

Alex lifted an eyebrow and grinned at her response. "I meant no offense to your sense of civic pride."

"Wellman, at the mercantile store, handles the mail," the doctor explained. "Collects our letters at the store and hauls a bag over to the inn when the mail coach arrives. Wellman sorts incoming mail and sends his boy out to deliver it."

"So Wellman handles all the mail, coming and going?" Alex asked.

"Yes," Hero said. "Surely you know that is a common practice in country towns and villages."

Alex drank from his wineglass and set it down. "I am just wondering why neither Sterne nor his solicitor received those missives you told me Teague and your sister and others have sent."

"I am sure there is a reasonable explanation," Hero said.

The three of them were quiet as a footman removed the dinner plates and served a strawberry trifle for dessert, which elicited appreciative murmurs.

At last Alex laid down his spoon and said, "Do you think it might be possible to send a letter without anyone in Weyburn having an opportunity to intercept it?"

Hero wore a quizzical frown. "Mr. Wellman is a terrible gossip, but I cannot see him doing what you are suggesting. And, in any case, why would he do such a thing?"

"I have no idea," Alex said, "but someone did something with those letters—either here or in London. I think we might start here to find out who and what and why. But meanwhile, I should like to keep my correspondence private."

"He has a point, my dear," Dr. Whitby said. "We could perhaps send Stewart or Perkins to Bentley to mail something."

"That is nearly half a day's ride," she said.

Her father shrugged. "Well…"

"Hmm." She sat in thought for a moment. "I could perhaps time my trip to town to arrive just as the post arrives and give a letter directly to the driver with a plea that I was afraid I might have missed him."

"I am reluctant to impose on you or your staff," Alex said.

"It would not be an imposition," she said. "I can go the next day as easily as tomorrow. As I said, the mail coach comes only twice a week, but it is quite prompt. It arrives at two, changes horses, and leaves ten minutes later. It would be just a matter of timing—and discretion, I suppose."

"You make it sound easy," he said.

"It will be. You have all day tomorrow to get your missive written. I will be happy to help you get it on its way."

She excused herself to go and see to Annabelle's bedtime routine. Alex and the doctor repaired to the library, where a decanter of cognac and the chessboard awaited them.

Chapter 10

The next day Alex settled into the task of writing a letter to his solicitor, Montague, into which he inserted a letter to his brother and another to his erstwhile batman, now his valet. The letter to his brother was rather terse: The family should not worry; he would contact them again in a month. Mr. Montague was to see immediately to getting necessary funds into the hands of one Jeremy MacIntosh, Alex's batman throughout the Peninsula campaign, his valet in civilian life. His letter to Mac instructed him to proceed forthwith to the town of Weyburn in Cornwall, where he would find Adam Wainwright, a guest of the local doctor.

Ten days later, Mac, in the guise of a tourist whose London doctor had advised him that a sojourn near the sea would be just the thing to improve his health, arrived in Weyburn with enough luggage for two men and booked a room at the Weyburn Inn. The next morning he set out on a rented horse ostensibly to make the acquaintance of the local doctor.

"Adam, this fellow says he is a friend of yours." Dr. Whitby, having been forewarned of such a visitor, ushered into the library a man in his midthirties, dressed as gentleman in a black coat and gray trousers. He was short, only a little over five feet, but with a strong physique; his eyes were brown, his head prematurely bald. He carried a small valise.

Alex looked up from a map he had been studying at the long library table. "Mac!" Making no effort to temper his welcome, he stood too abruptly and winced in pain as he put too much pressure on his injured leg. He cursed and plopped back into his chair. "Well," he said ruefully, "I really am glad to see you. Come and sit with me." The two shook hands across the table.

"If you gentlemen will excuse me, I have a patient waiting," the doctor said.

The door closed behind Whitby, and Mac, setting the valise on the floor, took a chair opposite Alex. For a moment he simply stared at his employer, then shook his head.

"I might have known you'd got up to something. You had us worried, my lord, when there was no word from you. Your brother was about to send Bow Street Runners looking for you."

Alex glanced at the door to be sure it was closed. "'Adam'—not 'my lord.' You know me as Adam. It is important that you not make that mistake again."

"Yes, sir." Mac reached into an inner pocket of his coat and handed Alex a heavy purse. "Glad to get this off my mind. I never had so much money in hand at one time before in my life!"

"Thanks for doing this, Mac."

"Got you some of your clothes here too." Mac pointed at the valise. "If I may be so bold as to ask, what's happened to you? And why are we here?"

Alex filled him in on his history with Weyburn Abbey—much of which Mac already knew, for he had served Alex from the time he was a lowly ensign through to the more exalted rank of major and on into civilian life. Alex also gave him a detailed account of the attacks on his person and his current status in the Whitby household.

"So—what do you want me to do?" Mac asked, leaning forward across the table.

"For now, continue as you have started—you are here on an extended stay near the sea for your health. Do what I can't do—yet. Get to know the area. Take long walks about the town and on the beach. Talk to people. Have coffee at the bakery. Buy men drinks at the inn—I'll stand the ready." Alex gave him several gold coins. "Don't act too nosy, but listen for information on matters at the Abbey and about the local smuggling operation."

"Recon work, eh? Kind of like old times."

"And just as dangerous. You watch yourself, Mac. You hear?"

He nodded. "In case we should meet, do I know you?"

"We met today. Both patients of Dr. Whitby. We discovered that we had both served in the Peninsula, but not together."

"But I ask the doc for you by the name you gave me."

"I will clarify things with the doctor."

"Got it."

Alex asked about his family and Mac gave him such news as he was privy to—which was not much, as most of the family members had returned to their country houses. Mac took his leave, promising regular reports as he "visited his new doctor."

* * * *

By the first week of July, Alex had mastered the use of the crutches to the point that one afternoon he accompanied Hero and Annabelle down to the beach. This journey was about a quarter of a mile through a long, low field of grass between the Whitby Manor and the beach beyond. Besides the ubiquitous Bitsy, their companions included the fantasy child Tootie and a black-and-white border collie named Sparks.

The early summer day offered sun and fluffy white clouds dancing above. The air smelled of the sea and the richness of vegetation beneath their feet. A soft breeze carried the sounds of gulls calling to each other, the child's delighted laughter, and yips from the excited dog. Trying to maneuver crutches on a sandy path was no easy task for Alex, as the crutches tended to sink into the soil. Hero, with a blanket over one arm, carried in the other hand a basket shaped like a small valise. She matched his slow pace, laughing with him at the antics of the child scampering ahead and, when it was not barking at a gull, the collie's attempts to herd the child and the kitten.

As they approached the shoreline, Alex was pleased to see several very large pieces of driftwood lying about, including a log half-submerged in the sand.

"Did you know this log was here?" he asked Hero as he sank gratefully onto it and shrugged out of his coat. His still-splinted leg jutted out awkwardly before him.

"Yes, I knew. Had it not been here I would not have allowed you to come with us."

"Right. Were I sitting directly on the sand, there is no way you and Annabelle could help me to an upright position—even with Tootie's help."

They laughed together at this bit of silliness as Hero spread the blanket at his feet and planted her basket and herself on it. She sat with her back against the log, her head near the knee of his uninjured leg. He gazed at her hair, fascinated by the coils of braid and the glints of red caught by the sun. His fingers itched to loosen her hair, run his hand through those richly colored strands, and caress the nape of her neck, which was exposed as she removed her not very stylish straw hat and tossed it aside.

These wanton thoughts were abruptly diverted when she called out, "Annabelle! Do not stray so far away from us. Stay on this side of that great rock."

Annabelle had picked up a small piece of driftwood, which she tossed and the dog dutifully chased to bring it back to her. "All right," the little girl called, taking the proffered stick and tossing it more in the direction of where Hero and Alex sat. It landed in the edge of the surf and a wave caught it, but the collie retrieved it and brought it back to its playmate, who had come to sit next to Hero on the edge of the blanket. Annabelle took the stick, but instead of tossing it again, set it down beside her. Seeing the state of affairs, the dog gave itself a vigorous shake—thus treating the three of them to a shower—and plopped itself down next to the child.

"Sparks!" Hero protested.

"Eeek!" Annabelle squealed.

Alex laughed aloud, for he had seen this coming.

"You laugh," Hero protested in mock umbrage. "Annabelle and I took the brunt of that."

"Indeed, you did," he said, still laughing. "Not very gentlemanly of me, was it?"

"I should think not," Hero said. "What do you say, Annabelle? Should we share our picnic lunch with him or not?" She reached to pull the basket closer.

"Oh, Miss Annabelle, you would not leave me to starve, would you?" he asked plaintively, his hand on his heart.

"'Course not. Auntie H'ro was jus' joking."

He heaved an exaggerated sigh. "That's a relief."

"You little traitor," Hero muttered, but she gave Annabelle a quick hug before delving into the basket.

"This is not much of a lunch," Hero said, "but it will do us until supper." She handed Alex a small knife and two apples wrapped in a small cloth. "You, sir, may make yourself useful by coring and cutting these for us."

She also produced chicken sandwiches, some wedges of cheese, three lemon tarts, a small oiled canvas bag filled with lemonade, and three tin "glasses" of graduated size so they fit together. She laid all this out on a floral printed cloth, filled the glasses, and put the stopper back on the bag.

"I cannot believe you carried all this feast in that small basket," Alex marveled as he handed her the apple pieces and tossed the scraps to the gulls.

"Well, it was either this or force Davey or Ross or someone else to carry a larger basket for us."

"Now you are making me feel truly useless," he said. She started to protest, but he went on. "Tell me about that bag of lemonade. I saw something like it in Spain, but of leather and for wine."

She handed him the bag. "It came to us from the men in the Abbey's copper mine. They carry water in it. It gets beastly warm down those mine shafts, I'm told."

"I've heard that of mining in general," he said.

"Annabelle," Hero admonished, "do not give all of your sandwich to Sparks and Bitsy."

"But they're hungry too."

"Nevertheless, you eat the rest of that yourself."

They all munched quietly for a while, murmuring appreciatively over cook's lemon tarts. Then Annabelle scooted around to swing her gaze from Hero to Alex, and back to Hero. "Can we—I mean, may we go wading today, Auntie H'ro?"

"You and Sparks may do so, but only in the very edge of the water and right here." Hero pointed to an area directly in front of where they sat.

"But you must come too, Auntie H'ro. What if I fall? I could get drownded."

It was apparent to Alex that this was something they had done before and it was his presence that was inhibiting Hero now. "Do go along with her, if you wish to," he said.

"I—it just seems selfish, since you can only sit and watch. Really, I hadn't intended—"

"Never mind me. I anticipated something like this. See?" He pulled a small book from a coat pocket.

She held his gaze for a moment. "A man with foresight, I see."

"C'mon, Auntie H'ro." Annabelle was already divesting herself of shoes and stockings. Then, with Bitsy in her arms, she stepped nearer Alex. "Mr. Ainrye, is it all right if I leave Bitsy with you? She don't like the water."

"Of course. Bitsy and I will keep each other company." He took the small animal in his large hands and shared an amused glance with Hero.

"Don't look," Hero said to Alex as she began to remove her own footgear.

Alex found her shyness charming—and he had not actually *promised* not to look, had he? Thus he treated himself to a glimpse of a shapely ankle and calf before the two females dashed hand-in-hand for the surf. He watched, entranced, as the woman and the little girl lifted their skirts to their knees and both squealed in delight as the waves washed over their bare feet. The dog yipped at both of them. When they eventually returned to the blanket and him, he pretended to have been reading all the while.

"That was such fun," Annabelle said, lifting the sleeping kitten from Alex's lap.

"Yes it was," Hero said, turning her gaze to Alex. "What are you reading?"

"Your father's collection of Mr. Wordsworth's poetry."

"One of his favorites. Mine too. Read me the one about Tinturn Abbey. Please?" she said as she again sat at his knee and Annabelle stretched out, her head in Hero's lap.

He had read only a few lines when Hero touched his knee and pointed to Annabelle, sound asleep.

"Shall I stop?" he asked softly.

"No. Oh, no. I love that poem."

When he had finished, she said, "That is so beautiful. It is such a tribute to the comforting power of memory."

"It is that," he said. "His images of English countryside are often very like things I remembered on those hot, dusty plains in Spain. But not all memories are comforting."

She twisted her head to look up at him directly. "You fought a terrible battle when you were unconscious. Are you still having those—uh—*visions*, for want of a better word? Stewart said he heard you call out one night recently as he was locking up."

"Yes." He tore his gaze from hers and stared out to sea. His tone was closed. "I am sorry to have disturbed the household."

She touched his hand that had been resting on his knee. "You did not disturb anyone. Not at all. Do you want to talk about it?"

"No."

"It might help."

He took her hand in his, lacing their fingers together. "No. Nothing will help. It is just something I must live with—for now. Eventually it will go away. I hope."

"But sometimes—"

He gave her hand a little shake. "Let's not spoil this beautiful day."

"All right." She withdrew her hand. "Read me the sonnet that begins 'The world is too much with us...'"

He found it and read it, then said, "Somehow I am not surprised that a girl named Hero likes this one with its references to gods of old."

They spent another lazy half hour with a couple more poems and just talked about whatever came to mind, sometimes inspired by the reading, sometimes not. Then Annabelle awoke and Hero declared it was time to return to the house.

Back in his own chamber that night, it occurred to Alex that he could not remember a more satisfying day. Never had he felt so utterly content as he had out there on the beach with Hero and Annabelle and the sea and the sun.

The next morning he noted that the ghosts and demons had left him alone for one night at least.

* * * *

Hero lay awake long into the night, reveling in this day's main event. She had felt more comfortable with Adam than she ever remembered being with another man, other than her father and her brother Michael. She had enjoyed such complete rapport with Harriet and Retta, but not with a man. She kept discovering depths to this man called Adam that surprised and delighted her. She would miss him sorely when he returned to his own life.

Two days later her sense of comfort and general satisfaction with the world was shattered by a visit from her sister. Diana arrived in a high state of agitation. Alone and on horseback, she had left her mount in the stable before letting herself in through the back entrance of her childhood home. Hero was working in the stillroom when she was startled by Diana's unexpected visit.

"Is Papa at home?" Diana asked abruptly, somewhat distractedly.

"No, he is not. And hello to you too." Hero laughed, then perceived something wrong with Diana.

Diana said, "Good. I actually came to see you, Hero."

Hero finished tightening the lid on a jar of peppermint oil. "What is it, Diana? You look distraught."

"I am. Let us go into the library so we can talk."

"Umm. The drawing room would be better. Adam may be in the library." Diana had met the Whitbys' long-term patient on an earlier, less stressful visit.

The two sisters made their way upstairs to the drawing room on the first floor. Diana sat on a horsehair couch with an elaborately carved back. She removed her riding gloves and her hat, setting them on the seat beside her. Strands of her almost black hair were escaping her usual tight bun; her deep brown eyes were clouded with worry. She was wearing a rather faded cotton day dress, though Hero knew Diana had a riding habit—old, but a proper, if less than stylish, habit. This fact testified to the urgency of whatever was on her mind.

"What is it, Diana?" Hero took a seat opposite her sister in one of two deep red brocade wing chairs.

"It's—it's Milton. And Anthony. And Jonathan." Her voice caught on a sob. Anthony, Diana's oldest child, was only a few months younger than his Uncle Jonathan. He too had been away at school until the summer holiday. The two boys, so near in age, had been inseparable as childhood playmates and then had gone away to school together.

"Milton and Anthony and Jonathan?" Hero repeated dumbly.

"My husband, my son, and our little brother. Oh, Hero—"

"Oh, dear God." Hero felt her heart tighten in fear. "Has something happened to them?"

"No. Yes. I mean, I hope not." Diana seemed on the edge of hysteria.

Hero quickly moved from her chair to shove Diana's gloves and hat aside and sit beside her sister. She put an arm around Diana. "Now. Take a deep breath and just tell me."

"S-smugglers." Diana choked on a sob. "Oh, Hero—Milton and the boys—they—they've joined with the smugglers!"

"But why? How? Jonathan too?"

Diana seemed to gain some semblance of control. "Mr. Teague came to visit our farm last month right after Billy Jenkins and Jake Harrison were jailed. He wanted to speak to Milton alone."

"About that roof, I hope."

"Sort of. Milton told me later. Teague said he would see to the roof, but only if Milton would help him and his gang transport smuggled goods from the beach to that cave below the Abbey. Said they were short men without Larson and the other two."

"And Milton agreed?" Hero asked, disbelieving.

"Y-yes. He felt he had to. You know how sick Freddie was last winter. Meredith was too, but not so severely."

"Papa said then that he should just pay for that roof himself," Hero said.

"Milton would never have permitted that," Diana said. "He hates that Papa is paying for Anthony's schooling."

"So—tell me the rest," Hero demanded.

"There's not much else. Jonathan was visiting when Teague came, and as he was leaving, he said, 'Bring those two along as well—they can heft a few bundles.'"

"Jonathan has not said a word of this," Hero noted.

"He wouldn't, would he?" Diana sounded bitter. "Milton hates that the boys are involved at all, but Jonathan and Anthony are just children caught up in a kind of game. Robin Hood and his merry men. It's a thrill for them."

"And Milton? A roof? That is his reason for risking life and limb?" Hero stood up and started pacing. "Good heavens, Diana, one man is already dead. Those two in jail—unlucky blighters—are likely to be transported."

"I know." Diana's response was a near wail. "I am so sorry to be dumping this on your shoulders. It was selfish of me, but I suppose I was in a 'misery loves company' frame of mind."

Hero sat back down and hugged her sister. "Mama used to say 'a burden shared is a burden lessened.'"

"I thought perhaps you could at least talk sense into Jonathan. He always listens to you."

"Not lately," Hero said. He is still angry that I would not pressure Papa into letting him go to London."

"I did not want to trouble Papa with this," Diana said. "Not until we absolutely must."

"Oh, my Lord, no," Hero agreed. "His heart is not fully recovered from that last incident—in January. And there's the gout besides. But he will *not* slow down."

"Perhaps when Michael comes home…" Diana's voice trailed off, but her tone sharpened when she added, "Meanwhile, what do we do about our family being involved in the smuggling business? I hear the militia is getting tougher on 'the trade.'"

Hero patted Diana's hand. "I'll speak to Jonathan, but I am not sure he will listen to me. Can you and Milton forbid Anthony's involvement? Perhaps if Anthony is out of it, Jonathan will lose interest."

"I cannot see that happening unless Milton quits too, and I have a feeling Teague would never allow that. The roof aside, I think Teague threatened Milton."

"Threatened him? With what?"

"I don't know, but I think Milton is afraid of Teague. I know I am. He could evict us like he did the Thompsons."

"He is a terrible bully," Hero agreed.

"If only Lord Alexander Sterne would take more interest," Diana lamented, "but, obviously, that is wishful thinking." She rose. "I must go. Thank you. Mama was right about sharing burdens."

Chapter 11

That night, long after everyone else had gone to bed, Hero sat waiting in the library, listening for the sound of her brother's horse returning and for the door in the rear entrance to open and close. When she heard these sounds, she stood in the library door and caught him as he was starting up the stairs.

"Come in here, Jonathan. I want to talk to you." Aware of Adam asleep just across the hall, she spoke softly.

"Ah, can't it wait, Hero? I'm really tired." Jonathan did not bother to lower his voice.

"Shh." She closed the door as he came through it. "Yes, at three o'clock in the morning, I should think you would be tired, but, no, it cannot wait." She gestured to one of the chairs flanking the fireplace; he took it, looking sullen as he did so. She took the other one and gazed at him for a moment, taking in his attire: a black knit fishermen's cap, a black sweater, and black trousers. His boots and the cuffs of his trousers looked wet.

"So?" she said, jumping right to the point, "is this what fashion demands of the modern-day smuggler?"

"What? I don't know what you're talking about."

"Don't even think of dissembling with me, Jonathan Whitby. I know you've been out with Teague and his gang of bully boys."

He responded after a moment with something close to a sneer. "So?"

"Do you have any idea how dangerous smuggling can be? Are you aware that the government has increased the militia patrols tenfold?"

"Those chaw-bacons running around in their pretty red coats are so stupid they stumble over their own feet. We sent them chasing themselves ten miles and more up the beach from where we were before our boats came in."

Hero closed her eyes for a moment, trying to ignore this blatant display of adolescent bravado. "Bert Larson got himself killed a few weeks ago."

"He was just in the wrong place at the wrong time."

"And you do not think you could ever be in the wrong place at the wrong time yourself?"

"Those are the chances you take in this business," he said.

Hero suspected this idea was some sort of slogan among his newfound friends. "Jonathan, Papa and I treated Billy Jenkins and Jake Harrison. It would break my heart—Papa's too—if something happened to you."

"You needn't worry. I can take of myself."

There it was again: adolescent bravado. She changed tactics. "Have you seen your friend Trevor Prentiss since you came home?"

"That whey face? Yeah. I've seen him. Afraid of his own shadow, he is."

"Does it not occur to you that sometimes what looks like cowardice is just common sense?"

"No, it does not." The sneer was pronounced now. "Look, Hero, what harm is it to keep the government from getting its cut of honest men's business? Taxes are too high—I've even heard you complain about them."

"There have been five deaths that we know of in the last six months among smugglers on the coasts of Cornwall."

"Yeah. Sure. There is a certain amount of danger. But that's what makes it fun. Exciting. And God himself knows there is nothing else of interest going on in Weyburn!"

"Still—"

He rushed on. "Besides, I'm out there with Milton and Anthony. We look out for each other." He stood up and gave her an exaggerated bow. "Now, if you will excuse me, I am very tired."

"But it is dangerous for all of you," Hero insisted.

He looked down at her as she still occupied her chair. "You're not going to stop me, Hero. You're not my mother. And it wouldn't do any good if you were."

"Papa—"

"What can he do? Kick me out of the house? Disown me? So be it. I have friends—"

Hero stood and took a step toward him. "I was about to say Papa and I love you and do not want to see you hurt."

"Papa knows?"

"Not yet."

"Doesn't matter anyway." He strode to the door and jerked it open.

"Jonathan, please—"

"Just stay out of my business, Hero. Don't you have enough of your own to occupy you?"

He slammed the door shut.

Hero sank into the cushions of the couch and put her hands up to her face, unable to control her sobs. What on earth had just happened? This was her sweet little brother? *No, not little*, she told herself ruefully, *he towers over you by several inches now.* Never had she seen him so belligerent, so unwilling to listen to her. He'd been home less than a month! Had she truly been so involved in herself that she had not seen this coming?

She did not hear the library door open, but suddenly Adam, in a brown plaid robe and a pair of slippers, was standing in front of her, offering her a handkerchief and leaning on one crutch.

"I—I'm sorry we woke you," she said, swallowing a sob.

"I was awake before. I heard his horse when he came in, but I did not know at first that you were waiting up for him."

"You had another of those horrible dreams?"

"Yes. Any distraction is welcome, of course, but I am sorry about what happened with your brother."

"You heard it all?"

"Not all. Mostly just what he was saying, not your side of it. But I caught the gist of it. He's involved with the smugglers, is he?" He leaned his crutch against the couch and awkwardly sank down next to her, his injured leg thrust out before him. His robe fell open slightly, revealing an expanse of bare skin and dark hair on his chest.

Wiping her eyes and turning to half face him, she nodded. "But that is not the whole of it." Then, because she had been unwilling to worry her father with all that Diana had told her earlier, she found herself pouring it all out to Adam. "I am so worried," she ended, feebly, she thought.

"Of course you are," he said. "Does your father know?"

"No. I am afraid to tell him. He suffered a heart seizure last winter and neither Diana nor I want him to know, if we can keep it from him."

"Does your brother know how ill your father might be?"

"I don't think so. We did not want Jonathan to worry at school, and by the time he came home for the Christmas holiday, the crisis was over."

"You did not want to worry the son then, and now you are trying to protect the father." He took her hand in his and laced his fingers with hers. "The doc is tougher than you might think, but I agree with you—there is no need to burden him if you can avoid doing so."

She returned the pressure of his grip, grateful to be able to draw strength from him, feeling warmth emanating from him and spreading through her body to relax her, and, simultaneously, to set her whole being alert and tingling. She drew in a deep breath, steadier now that she had shared what she had been holding in for literally hours now.

Reluctantly, she disentwined her hand from his. "I—thank you for listening to me."

Now that she had regained control of herself, she expected him to take his leave. Instead, he put his arm around her shoulders and pulled her closer. "'Twas my pleasure, madam. My pleasure," he whispered as he lowered his lips to hers. At first it was a tentative, tender kiss to comfort, but it quickly turned into something more urgent, more exploring. She heard a little moan and was only mildly surprised to realize it came from her own throat as she eagerly returned the pressure of his lips. Her hand crept up his chest to caress his neck. She thrilled to the hard muscles, the soft hair on his chest, and the smooth, warm skin of his neck. His tongue caressed her lips, then his mouth moved to nibble at her neck and that tender place just below her ear. She felt the stubble of his beard brush against her face and neck; he smelled of soap and something that was just him. She was lost in sensation—but only for a moment. Suddenly, she felt almost panicky. Abruptly, she sat up straighter and turned away slightly, putting distance between them.

"That," he said with a chuckle, "was no hallucination."

She smiled nervously and shook her head, but held his gaze. "No, it was not. Nor was it at all wise, though I must admit you managed to take my mind off the quarrel with my brother. Temporarily."

He withdrew his arm from around her shoulders, but made no move to separate himself further. "What will you do about this situation?" he asked. "What *can* you do?"

"I don't know." It came out as a soft wail. "I do not want him hurt. Or Milton or Anthony, either. Or anyone else for that matter, but I am afraid if I notify the militia, that is exactly what will happen." She stood and reached to give him a hand up from the soft cushions. "In any event, it cannot be resolved here, tonight."

She handed him his crutch as he managed to rise from the couch. Fully upright now, he asked, "Are we still on for tomorrow?"

"Tomorrow?" she said blankly.

"You promised to take me about, show me the Abbey."

"Oh. Yes. Of course I will do so." She was standing so close she could feel the warmth of his body. She looked up and held his gaze, sure that they were both thinking of that kiss. "I—we had both best get some sleep."

"If you say so," he said lightly, and bent to kiss her cheek. He hobbled to the door.

"Good night, Adam," she said as she lit a candle to see herself upstairs, then extinguished the lamp by which she had been reading earlier.

* * * *

Alex chastised himself as he returned to his room. *You had no business doing that, my boy. But my, oh, my, it had felt so right, so good.* All he had wanted to do was comfort her, to remove that strained look about her eyes. When was the last time he kissed a woman simply to offer sympathy, comfort? As he crawled back into bed, he heard her close the library door and start up the stairs.

It was not his own ghosts and demons that kept him awake now, but the problems she faced. They faced. He was vaguely conscious of feeling a sense of ownership to those problems—not just because they affected people he had grown to treasure as friends and perhaps more, but also because he felt a sense of belonging, of responsibility. *Whoa! Where did that come from?* He reminded himself that it had been nearly fifteen years since he had last visited his uncle at Weyburn Abbey. And as he rode through the town some six weeks ago, he had hardly recognized the place as anything but another English town, grown from a country village since he'd last seen it. Certainly, he had felt little of this sense of "belonging" that seemed to be attacking him now.

Tomorrow's outing should be interesting.

* * * *

Alex looked forward to being able—at last—to see for himself some of the countryside about which he had been hearing for weeks now. He also looked forward to spending a few hours in Hero's company, though he cautioned himself against a repeat of last night's kiss, however much he might desire it. As he thought about that kiss—and it occupied his thoughts far more than it should have—he was troubled by her reaction. At first she had been responsive, even welcoming, but then she had pulled away, almost in fear it seemed. Fear of him? Or of herself? It was an issue that would bear exploring.

By the time Alex arrived at breakfast, Hero had already eaten and set about some task she wanted to deal with before her outing with Adam—or so her father informed him. Alex suspected she might be putting off facing him, but he pushed that thought from his mind as he engaged in small talk with her father, and then with her brother when he finally showed up for the morning meal.

Alex saw none of the sullen disrespect in the young man that he had overheard the night before. In fact, he was quite amiable with his father. He still pursued the idea of going to London, but Alex felt the boy was not so bent on the idea as he once was. Jonathan was politely correct in his conversation; it was hard to believe this was the same fellow who had slammed out of the library only a few hours earlier.

Two hours later, dressed in his own buckskin breeches, a new linen shirt, a blue coat, and wearing his own boots, Alex met Hero in the stable yard as she watched Perkins and Davey hitch a horse to the gig. Annabelle was there too, along with Nurse Henson, who was keeping a close watch on her charge. He exchanged hellos with everyone, then stood near Hero.

"So. What do you think?" she asked. "Will you have difficulty getting seated in this vehicle?"

Hero wore a dark green day dress printed with small yellow and white flowers; the low neckline showed an enticing hint of cleavage. White lace trimmed the neckline and elbow-length sleeves. She had donned a straw bonnet decorated with a strip of the fabric from which her dress was made, and she had a light woolen shawl which she tossed on the back of the seat of the gig. Alex thought she must have taken more care than usual with her attire for this outing, and he wondered if that had been for his benefit or that of the villagers they might meet. Regardless, the effect was delectable, he noted.

He leaned on one crutch and cocked his head at an angle to look at her. "I think I will manage. I can step up on the good leg, though I cannot comfortably put much weight on the other one yet."

"Let's see," she demanded and stood back to observe as he proved capable of maneuvering himself—albeit awkwardly—into and out of, then back into the gig. He noted that Davey had been positioned to come to his aid if he had needed it.

"There. Art thou satisfied, oh mistress of the horse—and me?" He smiled broadly and their small audience chuckled.

"Yes. You did that quite nicely. I would venture to say that the crutch will be superfluous in another week or so." She went to the other side of the carriage to climb in and take the reins herself.

Annabelle had followed, and stood looking up at her. "Can I come too? Please, Auntie H'ro?"

"No. Not today, Annabelle. The gig holds only two."

"But I'm little," the child begged.

"You will stay here and work on your numbers." Hero glanced at Nurse Henson, who nodded to confirm this and stepped forward to take Annabelle's free hand—the other arm awkwardly hugged the continuously growing Bitsy.

Hero shook the reins and clucked at the horse. She did not look back as they left the stable yard, but she sighed and said, "I hate refusing her."

"Those big brown eyes are hard to resist," Alex said.

They were both silent as she managed the horse until they reached the main thoroughfare. He was conscious of the woman at his side as their arms occasionally touched, and as he caught whiffs of a lilac-tinged scent that was hers alone.

He looked at her and said, "Do I owe you an apology for last night?"

She glanced up at him, meeting his gaze directly. She blushed, and he liked that she did so. "Good heavens, no," she said, looking away. "It would be rather hypocritical of me to take umbrage at what was, after all, a kindly gesture."

"Hmm. Kindness was perhaps not the only thing I had in mind," he said. "But we can take that up another time." Her blush deepened, but she did not say anything. He changed the subject. "How far are we traveling?"

"It is three miles to town from our manor, and the Abbey is about six miles beyond that."

"Tell me about the Abbey." He felt a bit dishonest, but his memories of visiting the Abbey as a child were rather vague, and during his last visit, when he was in his late teens, his interests had centered far more on his uncle's stable than in the property as a whole. Of course, at that time he'd had no idea it would all be his one day. He remembered riding and fishing with his uncle, who became then—if he had not been already—one of Alex's favorite relatives. The two of them shared long talks, often far into the night, during which Alex and his mother's brother discovered a mutual love of history and the classics. Both had excelled in those subjects at university, albeit a generation apart. They had also discussed history being made in their own time as Napoleon swept through North Africa and Italy and tried to kill France's fledgling democracy by declaring himself emperor.

Alex recalled that, as an adolescent, he had not wanted to make the visit, but his mother had insisted that he do so. Once there, he was surprised to find his Uncle Harwood treated him as an equal and, for the first time in his life, young Alex had felt confident that he might one day do something worthwhile. *Maybe that's why I did not protest more when Father bought my commission and sent me off to war and arms with Wellington—Wellesley, then*, he mused. He wanted to share these thoughts with Hero, but now was simply not the time.

Hero raised a hand in greeting to the driver of an oncoming carriage. "Hmm. Where to begin… Weyburn Abbey was originally built in the twelfth century by Norman clerics. It was a fully functioning, fully independent monastery until Henry the Eighth went on that rampage against all things Catholic in the fifteen thirties. The chapel itself was almost completely destroyed then. Two walls remain, and most of the cloister. There is still a magnificent garden there. As I'm sure you know, when Henry got desperate for money, he sold, to private parties, the church lands and treasures he had seized. That is how it came into the Harwood family."

"Were the Harwoods good stewards of the land?"

"For the most part they were. But now the whole estate has passed into the negligent hands of a son of the Duke of Thornleigh. The duchess was a Harwood."

Alex, of course, knew this history already, but he hesitated to interrupt her, though he winced at her "negligent" comment.

She continued her guidebook-like recitation. "Although the Abbey originated as a monastery, it was also a fortress against the native Celts and Saxons. It must have been truly magnificent in its day. Built on a cliff overlooking the sea, it was once surrounded on the other sides by a wall— thus it had protection from attack by sea or by land. After the destruction of monasteries all over England, the wall, along with the ruined chapel, became a quarry for Harwoods expanding the facility and for generations of tenants on Abbey farms. The monks' great hall had survived, and it as well their living quarters were turned into the spectacular country home we see today."

"Who lives there now?" Alex asked innocently.

"No one. That is, no one of any consequence. There is a caretaker staff, of course. A housekeeper and six or eight maids. The housekeeper's husband is the butler—he supervises the male staff, the gardeners and general maintenance men. A total of perhaps thirty or thirty-five staff members. It is well kept. I'll give the current owner that much."

"The ever-so-generous Miss Whitby," he teased.

She gave him a withering look. "You'll see."

"The housekeeper and the butler—are they long-time employees?" *Are they likely to recognize me and upset my little cart full of lies?* Alex had been apprehensive about this aspect of his "inspection tour," though he wondered if hired help would see that lanky, somewhat cocky teen in the hardened veteran he had become.

"I think Mr. and Mrs. Mullins have been there eleven or twelve years. Certainly they were hired before the deaths of Sir Benjamin and his wife."

Not recognizing the Mullins name, Alex breathed a little easier.

As they slowed down through the town, Hero raised her hand and smiled or called greetings to a number of people; Alex recognized and acknowledged a few of them as frequent visitors to Whitby Manor.

"We shall come back and have lunch at the inn," Hero said.

The road beyond was familiar to Alex and he winced inwardly at the spot where he had been attacked. Beyond the tree-lined stretch that paralleled the sea, the road veered away from the sea and they passed by several farms. Alex noted signs of neglect: a roof or a fence in need of repair, a ragged-looking herd of sheep that seemed untended. One farm seemed wholly deserted.

"That is the farm from which the Thompson family was evicted," Hero said.

"Evicted? Why?" he asked.

She told him the story.

"Seems a bit harsh," he said mildly, as he quelled his anger and chalked up yet another mark against the man Teague. What happened to the family?"

"They emigrated to America."

"But why was the farm not let to someone else?"

"Probably as a warning."

"A warning. I see."

"I hope you do, Adam," she said, turning her gaze to hold his. "This is precisely the sort of thing Lord Alexander Sterne needs to know."

"He will. Believe me, he will know."

Chapter 12

They turned off onto a long, straight driveway of about a quarter of a mile, which gave visitors a glorious view of the Abbey rising majestically from green, well-tended grounds surrounding it. Built of the same gray stone seen in any number of other buildings, including the farms they had seen along the way, the center of the house was a three-storied edifice with simple, powerful lines. A two-storied wing jutted from either side of the main structure.

"Good Lord!" he said, more in awe of the fact that this was *his* than in wonder at the size of the structure itself, but of course his companion could not know that.

"Quite impressive, is it not?" Hero said. "Weyburn people are very proud of this landmark. And you should know that Sir Benjamin was held in *very* high regard."

Alex did not respond as she guided the horse to a hitching post off to the side of the cobblestoned driveway. At the main entrance, they raised the lion-headed brass knocker several times. Eventually, a middle-aged woman answered the door.

"Miss Whitby. How nice to see you. What brings you way out here?"

"Mrs. Mullins, may I introduce Mr. Adam Wainwright? Mr. Wainwright, Mrs. Mullins is the Abbey's housekeeper." She turned back to the woman. "Mr. Wainwright voiced an interest in seeing such rooms of the Abbey as might be open to the public."

"Of course," Mrs. Mullins said. "Come right in. I'll show you around myself." Alex suspected she was already spending the gratuity housekeepers and butlers at great houses customarily received for this added duty. "Many of our rooms are shut off with holland covers on all the furniture," she explained, "but the main drawing room, the library, the ballroom, the gallery, and game room are all open."

"And the wine cellar?" Alex asked. "I am planning to expand the wine cellar of my property in East Anglia," he improvised as he handed his beaver hat over to a maid, "and I was told the Abbey's cellar is quite remarkable."

Hero, in the process of removing her bonnet, gave him a questioning look, which Alex ignored as he awaited the housekeeper's response. Earlier Alex had conjectured to himself that the smugglers would need storage space such as barns on tenant farms or, more likely, the huge cellar of the Abbey itself, which Alex knew had survived intact, despite repeated attacks on buildings aboveground over the centuries. Moreover, as a boy, Alex had explored the cellar thoroughly; he knew it was connected by a tunnel to a cave in the cliff below the Abbey itself.

Mrs. Mullins was surprised at his request, but she finally nodded. "Mr. Mullins keeps the keys to the cellar, but I am sure he will accommodate you, sir." She then began what seemed a practiced spiel about the Abbey, repeating much of what Hero had told him earlier, and ending with, "The last two or three generations of the Harwood family have been extremely conscious of the historical significance of the Abbey. Sir Benjamin was particularly reluctant to make serious structural changes. He always said quite enough damage was done in the sixteenth and seventeenth centuries—we needn't add to it."

"A wise position to take," Alex said in a neutral tone, though the housekeeper's words brought to mind that and similar remarks he remembered his uncle making.

She proceeded to show them the rooms she had named. They were as elegant as he remembered, though showing wear here and there—a much traveled spot on a carpet, worn upholstery on the arms of a couch or a chair. In the game room, one wall displayed a collection of stags' antlers, and one end of the room was dominated by a canvas-covered billiards table. The library, he was glad to see, still boasted one of the finest private collections in England. *Would a single lifetime be enough to do this room justice?* he wondered. It was decorated in subdued colors of earth and her natural glories: beige, browns, muted reds, golds, and greens.

When they reached the ballroom, Hero said, "I attended my first ball in this room—danced my first waltz here." She took a small spin under one of three crystal chandeliers. Watching her skirt whirl about, revealing her shapely ankles, Alex silently vowed that one day she would again dance the waltz here—in his arms.

It was the gallery on the second floor that caused Alex a moment of trepidation. Harwood portraits dating back to the sixteenth century faced a wall of windows that overlooked what had been the cloister garden of the original Abbey. Knowing full well that he resembled his uncle—had not his mother commented on the likeness often enough?—Alex made sure to stand behind the two women as the three of them viewed two centuries and more of family portraits.

Mrs. Mullins spoke affectionately of her one-time employer's ancestors just as though she had known them all personally. A jokester of the previous century had set a sack of mice loose in the midst of a church service. "Such a naughty boy," Mrs. Mullins said indulgently. A pretty young woman had drowned only days before her intended wedding. "'Tis said she did it a'purpose," Mrs. Mullins whispered, shaking her head. "Her bridegroom never married. So sad."

They moved on, and the housekeeper said, "These last two portraits are my personal favorites. This one shows Sir Benjamin's parents and five of their seven children—two were born after the portrait was painted—but here is Sir Benjamin as a young lad, his hand on his father's shoulder, and standing next to him, looking ever so pretty, is his sister Elizabeth. She is the Duchess of Thornleigh now."

"And mother of the current owner of the Abbey," Hero explained, glancing at Alex, then back at the painting.

"That is true," the housekeeper said. "A charming woman, though I met her only in Sir Benjamin's final days."

Alex tried not to seem overly interested in this picture of his mother as a young girl, but he thought he could see in the girl the alert, caring woman she became.

"And, here," Mrs. Mullins said, pointing at the final painting, "is our Sir Benjamin and his wife. Lovely, lovely people. Sadly, they had no children, though they were devoted to each other. He lasted only two years after she died. Tragic it was to see how he missed her."

Trying to seem only mildly interested, Alex hung back slightly, though Hero stepped closer for a better view.

"They truly were fine people, Adam," Hero said, turning to Alex. "Sir Benjamin was a particular friend of my father's. They used to play chess together..." Her voice trailed off in what seemed to Alex to be confusion.

"May we see the cellar now?" he asked abruptly.

They returned to the entrance hall, where Mr. Mullins awaited them with a large ring of keys in one hand.

"Get to the wine cellar through the kitchen," he said. "Kitchen and cellar are not usually shown to the public."

"I appreciate your kindness in making an exception," Alex said. Keeping up the pretense of this being his first visit to the Abbey, Alex held to the rear as they proceeded through a labyrinth of halls to the large kitchen. He noted that the kitchen was severely outdated, and that at least half of it looked to be little used. A heavy door of oak planks held together with black metal bands led to the cellar.

As he inserted a key into the lock, the butler eyed Alex's crutch. "The stairs are steep and narrow. You sure you want to do this?"

"I shall manage," Alex said, wondering if the man was deliberately trying to discourage him.

"As you wish," the butler said, accepting a lit candle his wife held out to him. "What about you, Miss Whitby? The cellar is not very clean."

"I'll come too," she said and added with a teasing smile at Alex, "I'll go first and catch you if you fall."

Mrs. Mullins chose not to accompany her husband and the visitors into the cellar. The stairs were, indeed, narrow and steep, but not excessively so. Alex went down more clumsily than the other two, but he did so without mishap.

At the bottom of the stairs, the butler used the candle to light a lantern that had been hanging on the wall. The wooden stairs and railing were sufficiently sturdy and set in the middle of the long side of a large rectangular room about eight feet wide and twenty feet long. A table of unfinished wood and two stools provided a workstation. A large barrel dominated one end of the room; smaller kegs were stacked at the other end.

"*Vin ordinaire* in the large barrel, ale in the kegs," Mullins said. "Special wines in bottles on the shelves facing us, brandy and champagne on the shelves either side of the stairs. As you can see, we try to keep everything properly labeled."

Alex made a pretense of looking over the shelves, even leaning on his crutch to reach for a bottle here and there, blowing off the dust and examining the labels. What he really noticed was that the back wall, facing the stairs, was new. The stone was old enough to blend in with the other three walls, but overall, the cellar was less than a third as large as he remembered. One section of the shelving on the new wall appeared to be movable; faint scrapes on the packed earth floor confirmed this conjecture, but he ignored the temptation to examine that area of the shelving more closely.

"A nice selection of wines and spirits," he noted.

"Yes," Mullins agreed. "Sir Benjamin was quite proud of his collection. Wanted it preserved for his nephew—his heir, you know."

"Let us hope that fellow appreciates Sir Benjamin's efforts," Alex said.

"We can only hope he does so," the butler said stiffly.

Later, gratuities paid to the Mullins couple, Alex and Hero were back in the gig and on their way to visit Abbey tenant farms.

"Why did you insist on seeing the cellar?" she asked.

He shrugged. "I like wine. Did you notice anything unusual about that cellar?"

"No. But I had never seen it before. Looked like any other I've ever known—including the one at Whitby Manor."

"Your father serves a fine table."

"Yes, he does. He and Sir Benjamin had a friendly rivalry going about the quality of their cellars. Ours is not terribly different from the Abbey's."

"Does that seem strange to you?"

"Why should it?"

"Whitby Manor has always been the domain of a single family, has it not?"

"Yes." A slight frown drew her brows closer together.

"But the Abbey originally served an entire religious community— perhaps as many as a hundred monks, plus servants and any number of visitors or men on religious retreats.

"True." The frown was no longer slight. Then she brightened and looked over at him. "I see what you are getting at—the cellar should have been much larger to serve so many."

He nodded, pleased at her perception. "Considerably larger, yes."

"Well, the entire Abbey has undergone considerable change in the last three centuries."

"I doubt the cellar would have suffered much damage. Its contents pillaged, certainly, but that vast underground chamber would probably have survived."

"So some Harwood in recent centuries decided to wall it up?"

"Perhaps." He let the matter drop as they approached one of the Abbey's tenant farms.

"This is the Tamblin farm," Hero said as they stopped outside a fence enclosing a neat flower garden.

"Your sister?"

"You remembered."

"And her husband, the smuggler."

"Oh! Don't mention that!" Hero jumped from the gig and tied the reins of the horse to a fence post.

"I had not intended to do so, but if the subject comes up—" He clambered out of the vehicle.

"You will just ignore it, of course," she warned, then seemed to realize he was teasing her. She gave him an exasperated look and turned to greet her sister just emerging from the farmhouse door.

* * * *

Hero had looked forward to the outing with Adam, but she had spent much of what was left of the previous night trying to think of excuses to avoid it. And reliving that kiss. She was frankly astonished by her reaction to it. She had submitted to being kissed by only a few men since her debut to society some eight years ago. Never before had she been an eager participant in the event. On those other occasions, she had mostly endured, trying to convince herself that she could overcome the past and embrace life as other young women did. But always fear and revulsion had managed to set her straight on that score. Last night was different, however. She had even, for a moment, quite lost herself in the sheer ecstasy of Adam's lips on hers—until memory asserted itself.

When morning arrived all too soon, she had still been toying with the idea of opting out of accompanying him to the Abbey. Perhaps Stewart could take him. She deliberately went to breakfast early to postpone their meeting again. Then she gave herself a mental shake. That was an act of sheer cowardice. Hero Whitby faced issues in her life head-on. *She* was in control. Was she not?

When they met in the stable yard, she was relieved to find him behaving entirely naturally. But, good heavens, why would he not? That he seemed somewhat uncertain about her reaction had bolstered her confidence and made the situation easier. Adam Wainwright was really a rather intriguing human being.

No. Not Adam Wainwright.

But who?

She had accepted his wish to be known by that name. It had even seemed logical; but now, in the midst of this tour of the Abbey and its environs, she was beginning to wonder. His demeanor as a "tourist" seemed—well, perhaps—a little too pat? Was he more familiar with those rooms than he pretended? Had he, in fact, visited Weyburn Abbey before? If so, under what circumstances?

In the gallery she had noted a certain resemblance between Adam and that portrait of Sir Benjamin, but it was not so pronounced as to be undeniable. He could be a distant relative coerced into performing a disagreeable task for the disinterested owner of the Abbey. Of course, he *could* be the errant Lord Alexander Sterne, but given what she had always heard of that one, she was inclined to dismiss that possibility. *What? He should suddenly give up the dubious attractions of the city to become a responsible landlord? Not likely. Not likely at all.*

Adam's interest in the Abbey's cellar and his comments afterwards had caught her attention, but before she could explore that line of thought, they had arrived at the Tamblin farm and then visited two others before going on to the copper mine. Diana and Milton received them politely, and proudly showed off their huge vegetable garden and a prize ram they hoped would be a start to a more splendid herd of sheep. Hero was pleased to see the ease with which Adam discussed such matters with Diana and Milton, and later with the Robertsons and the Carters as well. Nor did he try to avoid discussing matters like needed repairs here and there.

They drove to the copper mine, but could not get close as its aboveground structures were in a huge loading yard behind a forbidding stone fence topped with shards of broken glass. An iron gate was locked and the gatekeeper, a rather taciturn old man named Watson, refused Hero's cajoling pleas to allow them to look around.

"Can't do it, Miss Whitby," he said. "Got real strict orders from Mr. Teague. No one—no one—but miners gets through this gate. Ain't much to see up here anyways." He returned to his post in a small shack on his side of the fence.

Nevertheless, she paused the gig at the locked gate for a few minutes. She and Adam gazed at the stone buildings with rusted metal roofing and what appeared, even from a distance, to be cobweb-covered, dirty windows.

"I am sorry about this," Hero said. "I should have thought to contact Stewart's brother, who is a foreman on one of the shifts."

"Not to worry," he assured her. "It's not like I could actually go down into a mine. Managing those cellar stairs with a crutch was one thing, a mine would be quite another. There should be ledgers that will give a sufficient report."

"Do you think Mr. Teague will share those willingly?"

"Perhaps not willingly. And probably not with one Adam Wainwright, but..." His voice trailed off as he took a last look at the mine buildings.

They returned to the town where, as Hero had promised, they had lunch at the coaching inn. The lowest portion of the inn, like so many local buildings, was fashioned of stones, but the two upper stories were a later addition of dark wooden beams and whitewashed plaster. The roof was thatched. The main public room boasted a large stone fireplace, wooden walls, and heavy wooden beams on the ceiling. The bar and tables were of dark wood, highly polished by years of use. She introduced Adam to the Barkleys, the innkeeper and his wife, and to three other customers, a farmer named Manson and two of his laborers, Ryan and Spicer.

Hero and Adam took a round table nestled into the space of a bay window that looked out onto the town's main street, which had little traffic at this hour of the day. Mrs. Barkley had just set her meal of the day and two glasses of ale in front of them when Jeremy MacIntosh, holding a walking stick in one hand, emerged from a door Hero knew led to bedchambers above. Hero had met Mr. MacIntosh previously and she knew Adam had struck up a friendship with the man, who, like Adam, was a former soldier. Thus she was not surprised when Adam lifted a hand in greeting.

"MacIntosh. Do join us," Adam called and gestured to an empty chair at their table.

"Wainwright. Miss Whitby." The man bowed to both of them.

"Yes. Do join us, Mr. MacIntosh," she said. "We are having a late lunch."

He took the offered chair. "I've had me lunch, though I might join ye for a wee drink. But, please, miss, you must call me Mac. Ever'one does—even folks in Weyburn now." He raised a hand to the innkeeper, who promptly brought another glass of ale to the table.

"Here you go, Mac."

Hero smiled and said, "As you wish." She liked this man. He was friendly and down-to-earth. "Are you finding the sea air as invigorating as you had hoped, Mac?"

"Yes, ma'am. I am. Breathing much easier than when I first got here."

"That's wonderful," she said.

"I walk out every day," he said with a glance at Adam. "Even went out on the shore last night."

"Is that so?" Adam asked. "At night?"

"Well, now, it wasn't quite night when I started, you see. Sort of twilight. But I walked farther than I intended, and got caught in the dark. So I found me a big rock to sit against to wait for the moon to rise. Comin' on to full last night, you know."

"Did you have to wait long for the moon?" Hero asked.

"Not too long. Half hour, maybe. I had the sound of the surf—almost sang me to sleep, it did. Then I heard voices and I could see dark shapes moving along the edge of the sea. They were meeting a boat coming in. I figured I better just keep quiet and stay put for a while." He chuckled and took a drink of his ale.

"But you could see what was going on?" Adam asked.

"Oh, yeah. I tell you, Wainwright, made me think of San Sebastián when a supply ship was comin' in. All that hurly-burly."

"San Sebastián is a port in northern Spain the British army used," Adam explained to Hero.

She nodded. "I know."

Adam turned back to Mac. "You want to be careful wandering about at night, Mac. Getting caught between smugglers and militiamen would be like the worst of a battle with Spanish and French partisans."

"I 'spect you're right, sir, but it was mighty innerresting—an' I was pretty well hid."

"Good."

"It were real strange," Mac went on. "They had some pack animals. Unloaded barrels an' bags an' boxes from the boat an' put 'em on the animals. Drove 'em along the beach a ways, then turned right toward the cliff and—bang!—they was gone! Just disappeared. Strangest thing I ever seen."

"Caves," Adam said.

"How did you know that?" Hero demanded.

Adam glanced at Mac, then shrugged. "Just guessed."

"Yeah. That's what I finally figured," Mac said. "Thought I'd stroll around there this afternoon—in the daylight—see if I was right."

"I shouldn't think that would be necessary," Adam said. "Might draw attention in the wrong quarters."

"Ah. You might be right. Maybe I'll just go a different way." Mac drained his glass and rose to leave. "Nice visiting with you."

Adam and Hero were just finishing their meal—a tasty shepherd's pie and an apple tart—when the outer door to the inn opened and Willard Teague entered with Wellman, the owner of the mercantile store. Teague paused abruptly on seeing Hero and Adam. He motioned Wellman off in the direction of the farmer Manson and his laborers. It occurred to Hero that this might not be a chance meeting. Teague approached the table by the window.

"Well, well, look who's here," he said in a loud, genial voice. "Our Miss Whitby. And Wainwright, isn't it?"

Adam nodded, and Hero said in a guarded tone, "Hello, Mr. Teague."

"Now, Hero. I've told you about that 'Mr. Teague' stuff. Name's Willard, though most of my friends call me Will." He pulled out a chair and sat down at their table without waiting for an invitation. "Showing your patient our town, are you, Hero?"

Hero did not like his making free with her given name in such a public place, but she did not want to make a scene. "Yes, Mr. Teague. We have just come from visiting the Abbey."

Teague looked at Adam. "You should have said something. I would have shown you around myself, though I'd think once you see one of those fancy country houses of the quality, you've seen 'em all."

"Mrs. Mullins and her husband were kind enough to show us all that they could," Hero said.

"That so?" He was obviously waiting for her to elaborate, but she did not do so, not at all sure why it suddenly occurred to her that it might not be a good idea to mention seeing the cellar.

"Well, what do you think, Wainwright? Gonna trot right back to London and make his lordship an offer?" Teague continued to speak in a loud tone that demanded the attention of everyone in the room.

Adam leaned back in his seat, his expression hard for Hero to read. "Not tomorrow," he said, "but I do like the look of this area."

"I'll just bet you do," Teague said, with a leering look at Hero. She blushed at his innuendo, but said nothing.

Now Adam's expression was not hard to read at all. His mouth was grim, his eyes a hard cobalt blue as he said, "Miss Whitby has been very kind in helping me become acquainted with Weyburn and I quite appreciated seeing the Abbey. It is rather conveniently situated above the sea, is it not?"

"That depends."

"I assume there is a trail down that cliff?" Adam's tone, while not as ostentatiously loud as Teague's, carried to the other table, which suddenly became quiet.

"Oh, yes, but it is not kept up and can be treacherous after a storm."

"I should think part of the upkeep of the estate would be seeing that trail kept in pristine condition to allow access to the beach below," Adam said casually. Hero forced herself not to smile at this seemingly innocent dig at the Abbey's steward.

"Folks at the Abbey now don't need access," Teague said brusquely. "Nobody else needs it, either. Trespassing, if they tried it." Hero thought this was more of a warning than a simple observation.

Adam shrugged, and after a moment said, "Don't let us keep you from your friends, Mr. Teague."

Teague was clearly furious at being thus dismissed, and again Hero stopped herself from smiling. The steward scowled and rose abruptly. He strode over to the other table, calling loudly for a tankard of ale as he went.

"Adam," Hero said quietly, "we should be going. I have a patient I want to visit before we return home."

Chapter 13

The patient Hero wanted to see was Sally Knowlton's newest charge. The girl, who had turned up on Sally's doorstep after a long ride on a public coach, could not have had more than fifteen years, and she was slender to the point of emaciation. Her pregnancy, which she estimated to be six months along, hardly showed. She had blond hair, large blue eyes, and an oval face that brought an image of the Madonna to Hero's mind. Her name, appropriately enough, was Mary.

"I'm sorry, Adam, but I must ask you to wait here in the gig," Hero said as she stopped the vehicle in front of Sally's house. "I will not be long." She handed him the reins and stepped down.

"Take your time," he said. "Gertie and I will get along fine. It's not too hot today—I may even have a bit of a nap." Gertie was the name of the horse.

She smiled up at him. "You do that."

She rapped on the door and was not surprised when Sally herself answered the summons. "Thank goodness, you've come. I want your thoughts about Mary—as well as that other matter I mentioned in my note. I don't think her babe is doing as well as it should be. Far too small for the time she's given us."

"You know your girls sometimes miscalculate," Hero said.

"Yes. Yes. I have considered that."

Hero examined Mary, who seemed totally unconcerned about the health of the child she carried. "I'll just be glad when it's over," she said with a sigh and patted her belly. "When I'm shut of this, I'm off to London."

"London?" Hero controlled her reaction. "Surely you are not going to the city alone."

"Well, sure I am. Ain't got nobody wantin' to go wit' me. There's always gents willin' to help a damsel in distress."

"What about your babe?" Hero asked needlessly. She knew the fate of babies like Mary's: farmed out to be fostered, then off to a workhouse or onto the parish, which often enough dumped them onto the streets of some city to fend for themselves, vulnerable to every conceivable sort of exploitation. It was precisely the fate from which she had saved Annabelle.

"Miz Knowlton says I needn't worry overmuch 'til it gets here." *Trust Sally to try to be reassuring*, Hero thought.

While she was here, she briefly examined the other two current residents of the house and gave them her usual admonishments about diet and exercise. Then she looked for Sally and found her in her small office.

Hero remained standing. "I cannot stay long. Mr. Wainwright waits in the gig."

"I saw you drive up," Sally said. "He's a handsome man."

"Yes. I suppose he is."

"You 'suppose'? Something wrong with your eyes, my girl?"

"Don't tease," Hero said. "You have something for me?"

Sally's expression sobered. "Yes. Look at this." She picked up a letter from her desk and stood to hand it to Hero, who scanned the contents, then drew in a sharp breath. She closed her eyes briefly as though she could thus erase what she had just read. "A Bow Street Runner?" she whispered in awe.

"Right. He's come and gone already. I had no idea—but he must have been that man who came about—uh—three weeks ago. Said he was looking for a secluded place for his sister for a few months. You know, the usual story."

"Did he ask about Barbara?"

"He asked me about a Lady Barbara Gaylord. I told him I had never heard of anyone named Gaylord. Then he asked, had I known any Barbaras at all—five years or so ago? I had to admit I had. You know I'm never good at lying about anything. Besides, he could have asked in town and eventually learned that much."

"There is no need for you to develop your skill in lying." Hero handed the letter back. "Did he say anything else?"

"He asked what happened to her. When I told him she died in childbirth, he asked, 'Was she buried with her babe?' I couldn't tell him she had been, could I?" Sally was clearly distraught, twisting her hands together and rumpling the letter in the process.

Hero put her arms around the older woman. "Don't fret, Sally dear."

"But what are we to do? I know how fond you are of that child."

"*We* are doing nothing. If he—or anyone else—comes again, send them to me. Just tell whoever asks that I handled the disposition of Barbara's babe—which I did. Perhaps by then I will have figured out something."

"Oh, Hero, I'm so sorry—"

Hero hugged her. "Not to worry, Sally. I have to go now. You just do what you always do. Take care of our girls."

She returned to the gig, climbed into her seat, and said to Adam when he would have turned the reins over to her, "You drive, won't you? I'm sure that between the two of you, you and Gertie can get us home."

He gave her a questioning look. "Something wrong?"

"I—don't know. Maybe. Probably."

"Would you like to share?" he asked as he guided the horse back onto the main thoroughfare.

She sighed, and since she had previously shared Annabelle's story with him, she told him about this new development.

"What will you do?" he asked as they were forced to wait as a herd of sheep crossed the road in front of them.

"Fight like the hounds of hell to keep her," she said vehemently.

He reached to pat her hand, which gripped the edge of the seat between them. "That's my girl."

It was merely a casual gesture of support and kindness, she told herself. Nevertheless, she appreciated it and she felt a shred of relief at sharing. She thought she might be getting used to that little lurch of her heart whenever he touched her.

* * * *

Over the next few days, she dealt with a myriad of problems on the Whitby estate and in the clinic. The idea of a confrontation with some unknown faction over Annabelle was never far from her mind. Still, she found herself thinking often of the enigmatic Adam Wainwright. She readily admitted—to herself—her attraction to the man, and that such attraction was totally out of character for the usually self-contained Miss Whitby. She had long ago given up the conventional dream of becoming a wife and mother. To be honest, the idea of being a wife held little allure at all, and she supposed Annabelle fulfilled any latent need to be a mother. Certainly she could not love that child more if she had herself suffered through the pains of childbirth. *My God! What will I do if I lose her?*

She saw less of Adam in the days following the trip to the Abbey. He had taken to going out almost daily with Mr. MacIntosh, who had hired an open carriage and team to "see the countryside." Since the encounter with Mac in the inn, Hero suspected the relationship between the two men was more complicated than that of newly acquainted ex-soldiers of war. But it was really none of her business, was it?

She had other matters to concern her. Besides worrisome apprehension about Annabelle, she fretted about the continued involvement of members of her own family with those infernal smugglers. The moon, which some called "a smugglers' moon," though waning now, still shone brightly each night, and Hero's heart jumped when she heard Jonathan come and go. She could not allow herself to sleep until she knew he had come home each night.

A week after that awful confrontation with Jonathan, Hero sat in the library reading late into the night. A summer storm, complete with thunder, lightning, and furious winds, had hit just after supper. The worst had passed, but she could hear rain dripping from the roof. Her father had retired early and Adam had gone out again with Mac, but well after midnight, he poked his head into the library to bid her good night before going to his own room. She ignored her regret that he had not prolonged the encounter, or that she had not manufactured an excuse to have him do so. A few minutes later, she heard a horse literally galloping into the stable yard. Jonathan. But why was he riding so recklessly?

She met him in the kitchen as he came into the house. He looked distracted and—yes—afraid. She turned up the wick on the lamp Mrs. Hutchins always left on the kitchen's long worktable.

"Jonathan? Is something wrong?"

He visibly jumped. "Oh! You startled me." He closed the door and leaned his forehead against it for a moment. Then he straightened, his expression of fear and perhaps horror more pronounced now. He flopped down on the bench at one side of the table. He set his elbows on his knees and held his head. "You were right, Hero. You were right," he wailed through his hands.

"About what? Jonathan, you are scaring me." She touched his shoulder and he flinched. She moved to a stool across the table from him.

He raised his head to reveal tears in his eyes. "It was terrible—so bloody awful! I never thought—I can't believe—It was murder, Hero. People died! Died!" His words were punctuated with sobs.

Hero rose and got him a glass of water. "Here. Drink this and, for heaven's sake, tell me what happened."

He gulped the water, set the glass down, and calmed slightly. "There was a ship—but it was not at the usual place. One of us—I don't know who—had a lantern and signaled the ship that it was safe to come in." He paused, his face crumpling. "It—it came in and hit that mass of rocks up the beach from the Abbey cliff. The ship—it broke up, Hero. Just shattered on those rocks."

"Oh, no-o-o," she murmured, putting a hand to her mouth.

"He—we—deliberately lured that ship onto the rocks. Soon enough the surf began to wash up debris and cargo—and—and bodies!"

"Are you sure?"

"I saw them." He uttered an anguished moan. "A little girl. And a woman and a man. Two men tried to wade ashore, but our men turned them back."

"Turned them back? How?"

"C-clubbed them." He sobbed. "Hero, it was awful. I swear to you, sis, I never—never—wanted anything like this to happen."

"Why? Why did—"

"He said we couldn't leave any witnesses."

"Who said that?" she asked, but instinctively she knew.

"Teague." Jonathan's voice had gone flat.

"He planned to lure a ship to ruin?" Hero asked in horror.

"I—I'm not sure. I think something happened to the ship we expected—maybe lost in the storm—and then this one showed up. Lost too, maybe. Who knows?"

"A crime of convenience."

"I—I—maybe…" He drew in a deep breath. "I never thought anything like this would happen. Outsmarting the taxman is one thing. But innocent people died tonight." He ended on a strangled sob.

"Oh, Jonathan. We have to go to the authorities—"

"No! No! We can't. We can't!"

"But—"

"Hero, the magistrate is afraid of Teague. Hell! Everybody in Weyburn is afraid of him."

"Language, Jonathan," she said almost absently as she racked her brain for something to do that would not put her baby brother in jeopardy.

"Sorry. After—after he made us pick up as much cargo stuff as we could and take it away, Teague gathered us all together gave us and 'all-for-one, one-for-all' kind of speech. Said if anyone snitched to the militia, the rest would have to kill him. Most of the others agreed with him."

"But you did not?"

"N-not really. And then he looked right at me and Milton and Anthony and said, 'That includes family members too.'"

Hero drew in a deep breath. "Oh, good grief!"

"What am I going to do, Hero? If it was just me…but I can't let them kill Milton and Anthony."

Hero reached across the table to grasp his hand. "Of course you can't." She looked into his distraught eyes. "I have no idea what we will do." She squeezed his hand. "But we will do it together, Jonathan. You are not alone. Certainly we can do nothing now, tonight. You go on up to bed. We shall talk about it in the morning."

"I—uh—all right." He rose, then paused. "Hero, I'm sorry. I'm really, really sorry."

She jumped up and put her arms around him. "I know, Jonnie-boy. I know." They hugged each other tightly and Hero thought she had her little brother back. *But, oh, the circumstances of his return!*

When the kitchen closed behind him, Hero sat back down on her stool and, her elbows on the table, cradled her head in her hands. *What to do? What to do? What to do?*

She looked up as the door opened again, thinking Jonathan had come back.

It was Adam. His clothing—slippers, buckskin breeches, and a shirt opened at the neck and hanging loosely over the breeches—had obviously been donned hastily.

"Surely we did not wake you?" she said.

"No. I heard his horse when he came home. Just now I heard him go upstairs. I listened, but did not hear you go up. You were not in the library." He stood, his hands on his hips. "Is something amiss?"

"Oh, yes. Something is very much amiss'" She could not help the irony. "Same story, new page. And I just—I cannot—"

He sat on the bench where Jonathan had sat. "All right. I am a good listener. Tell me."

And because he knew so much of the story already, she did just that, ending with, "This has not happened before—not here, not at Weyburn. Deliberately luring a ship in, I mean. During the war, it occurred elsewhere on the Cornish coasts, but not here." She sucked in a deep, shuddering breath. "Jonathan. Milton. Anthony. What am I to do?" She felt the tears she had held in with Jonathan streaming down her face as she raised her head to hold his gaze.

He stood and reached to pull her to her feet and into his arms. She put her arms around his waist and clung to him, burying her face against his chest, welcoming the warmth and strength through the thin fabric of his shirt. He laid his cheek against her head and just held her for few moments, stroking her back, sharing her distress.

He leaned back and put a finger under her chin, forcing her to look at him directly. "Hero, this is not your problem alone. Nor is it just your family's problem. Everyone in Weyburn owns a piece of it."

He stepped away to lower the wick in the kitchen lamp and check to see that the outer door of the kitchen was locked, then he led her out of the kitchen, down the hall, and finally into the library. He gently pushed her onto the couch where she had been reading earlier, and he sat himself down close to her. He took her hand in a now familiar gesture and laced their fingers together.

"I was there tonight," he said.

"You were—what? You—?" Words failed her.

"Mac and I saw it—that is, we saw some of it. We were on the cliff at the Abbey. We were too late and too far away to see it all. The ship had already foundered on the rocks. We saw the gang hauling goods away."

"You were a witness? You saw—Oh, Adam, that could be so very dangerous for you and Mac. You heard what Teague said about trespassing. You must not embroil yourself in Weyburn problems."

"I already have," he said so softly she was not sure she had heard aright. In a more normal tone, one laced with anger and regret, he said, "We saw it, but we were too far away, and there were only the two of us. Twenty or more of them, all armed, I am sure. Even with the element of surprise..." His voice trailed off.

She sat for a moment, mulling over what he had just said. It did not make sense. She released her hand from his and turned a bit sideways to look at him directly. "Let me get this right: You and Mac just happened to be walking or driving along the top of the Abbey cliff late at night? When you knew very well you should not be there?"

"Walking. We left the carriage some distance away."

Now she was exasperated. "Oh, for goodness' sake. Adam! What were you thinking?"

"Actually," he said in a matter-of-fact tone, "Mac and I were thinking to see if we could find anything worth taking to the militia."

"Oh, really? And did you?" Her concern for him had produced that bit of sarcasm.

He nodded. "We did. Mac is going to visit Colonel Phillips at militia headquarters in Appledore tomorrow. But now I suppose I must see Mac before he leaves and add what Jonathan told you to the report."

She jumped up from the couch. "No. Absolutely not! I forbid it. I told you of Teague's threat to Jonathan and Milton and Anthony. You

cannot endanger them. I never would have told you anything if—if—"
She began to pace.

Adam rose and grabbed her about the waist in midstep. "Hero, stop."
He pulled her against him and kissed her. Just planted his lips on hers
and kissed her quite thoroughly. Moreover, she kissed him back—equally
thoroughly—her arms around his neck, her hands in his hair. A sense of
intensity, urgency, and simple need engulfed them.

Finally, reason prevailed and she pulled back, but not away. "Wh-why
did you do that?"

He grinned. "I might ask you the same thing." He hugged her tightly.
"The truth is I had to stop you—to make you listen and—*and* I just wanted
to kiss you. I've wanted to do this again for days now." He kissed her again,
but with less intensity this time, and released her.

She stepped back. "All right. I am listening." She folded her arms
across her chest.

He ran a hand through his hair. "This smuggling business must stop
before any more people are killed or injured. It simply has to stop. The
government turned a blind eye during the war years. It will no longer do so."

"I agree. But I cannot—I will not—be a party to seeing members of
my own family hanged or transported. Surely you understand that."

He gave her a look of sympathy and nodded. "Yes. I do understand.
And I promise I will do all in my power to protect them. Trust me, please."

"Trust you? I'm to trust you—you, who will not even trust me with
your real name?"

She knew this hit home, for he went very still for a moment. "I will,
Hero. I will. Just not quite yet. Meanwhile, can you trust this?"

He pulled her close again and this kiss was gentle, tentative in seeking
her response which, God help her, was all the affirmation he really needed,
but she whispered yes anyway.

* * * *

Alex asked himself repeatedly during the rest of that night and all the
next day, *Why didn't you just tell her? You passed up the perfect opportunity
to do so.* The truth was that he needed to be Adam Wainwright for a
while longer. Despite her response to his kiss, he was not at all certain
how she would respond if she knew it was Lord Alexander Sterne kissing
her. Nor was Hero the only person in Weyburn for whom he wished to
remain known as Adam.

He had spent the last several days trying to come up with solutions to problems that had been building up and expanding and plaguing Weyburn people—his people now—for over a decade. The linchpin of the entire situation was one Willard Teague. He knew Teague knew who he was, but Teague was unlikely to confront him directly. Should he do so, Teague would have to explain just how those henchmen of his had come to attack Alex on the way to the Abbey.

The broken leg was virtually healed now—Alex limped and resorted to a cane only when he was especially tired—so he set out to learn as much as he could about the land and environs that he was coming to recognize as belonging to him—or he to it—in every sense of the word *belonging*. This feeling was new to him, but he rather liked it. With Mac accompanying him, he made a point of visiting every place of business in Weyburn, from the blacksmith's forge to the bakery to the mercantile store, the combination bookstore and lending library, the cobbler, and the seamstress's shop. In each place, he bought something and commented on the convenience of having such wares and services available to people in less populated areas of the nation. By the end of a week, people were stopping him on the street to pass the time of day.

But they did not pass on information about the smuggling operation. In fact, townspeople—only a few of whom were actually involved in that endeavor—scrupulously avoided the topic. Alex felt that many of them were just plain scared—or at least intimidated by Teague and his gang.

He and Mac did not confine their investigations to the town itself. Pretending to be beachcombers, they also explored a long stretch of the beach, including a number of caves along the coastline. They were actually looking for stores of contraband goods. Late one morning, as they emerged from the third cave that day, Mac stood with his hands on his hips and pronounced himself ready to give up.

"There's no doubt they're using some of these caves to store goods temporarily. All that scraped earth in the cave floors tells us that much—not to mention the signs of traffic at the mouth of some of them."

"I'm sure you've the right of it, Mac," Alex said. "But their real storage places have to be first, the Abbey cellar, and second, barns on tenant farms. My money is on that deserted Thompson farm and the Abbey cellar— which could itself easily accommodate the cargo of at least two ships." He explained about seeing the cellar on his visit and described what it had looked like years earlier to a young boy seeking imaginary adventures.

"Ah. It is connected by a tunnel to the cave directly beneath?" Mac asked. "That sounds like a godsend to smugglers!"

Alex nodded. "No doubt it was originally intended as an escape route if the Abbey came under siege." He placed a hand on his brow to shade against the sun as he gazed up at the cliff and then farther along its face to that area just beneath the Abbey. Yes. They were still there: the guards he and Mac had seen at the mouth of that cave for the last three days. "It is perfect for their purposes. Just perfect." His tone conveying a note of resignation, he sat on a large boulder wedged in the sand and looked out at the sea. Storm clouds hovered on the horizon.

"Major, are you saying we're done with this recon work?" Mac squatted in the sand and looked up at his employer, his friend.

"I think so. But we cannot call in the militia until they have a chance of dealing with at least the greater portion of the gang. They need to catch them actually moving the goods."

"An' then what, my lord? You been talkin' some about settling in the Abbey."

"I am thinking of doing so, yes. What? You will not be happy as a country boy?"

"I did not say that, sir. I grew up in the country, you know. Up north. Border country. I like country life. I like it here."

"So do I, Mac. So do I."

"Well, sir, that presents a problem, doesn't it?"

"More than one, I'd say."

"Yeh, but if you see to the hanging or transportation of some of your neighbors, you ain't likely to be near so welcome here as what you are now."

Alex ran a hand through his already windblown hair. "Believe it or not, Mac, I have thought of that."

That night they had stationed themselves on the Abbey's cliff overlooking the sea.

Chapter 14

For the next few days Hero endured a vague sense of foreboding. Life bumped along as usual, but it seemed to do so in a suspended atmosphere, waiting for some cataclysmic action—but what? She found herself hugging Annabelle harder and wanting her near all the time. She was also keenly aware of the cloud that hung over the entire community because of recent activities by the smugglers. Everyone knew about the deliberately wrecked ship and everyone seemed to anticipate repercussions from that event. If people spoke of it at all, they did so in hushed tones marked by disapproval and fear. To avoid dwelling on such things, Hero donned an old day dress that had seen much wear, pulled on a pair of gardening gloves, and joined Stewart in weeding the herb garden. Physical activity, she reasoned, was therapeutic. She and Stewart talked of Weyburn problems as they worked.

"My bother said you did a fine job of patching up that miner he brought in the other day," Stewart said.

"Thank goodness we were able to clean the wound and stitch it up and send him home. He is sure to have a very sore arm for a while. He is so worried about losing his job," Hero said.

"Ah, my brother Kenny will cover for him, I'm sure. But you know, Miss Hero, that accident need never have happened. Kenny has complained often enough to Teague about safety in that durned copper mine, but he is just ignored. Teague always says 'costs too much' or 'next month' or some such. And this is not the first mishap there."

"I know. If only the owner would take more interest—"

"Miss Hero!" the maid Dorcas called. "There's a real fancy lady askin' to see you."

"A fancy lady?" Hero asked blankly.

"Came in a closed carriage with a crest, but I didn't reco'nize the crest. Not from anywhere near here. She gave me her card." Dorcas held out a salver with the card on it.

Hero glanced at the card and drew in a sharp breath. She had thought she would have more time. "Oh, dear. Show her to the drawing room and offer her tea or lemonade. I will be with her shortly." Her calm demeanor in front of servants belied the absolute terror clawing at her innards.

"Yes, ma'am."

Hero dashed up to her room, snagging the first maid she saw in the hallway to help her change into a more presentable garment. She washed her face and hands and tucked in stray strands of hair, then declared herself as suitable as she was likely to get on such short notice. She entered the drawing room to find a woman in her late sixties, sitting on the horsehair settee, imbibing a cup of tea.

"Hello," Hero said.

The woman, dressed in an expensive, stylish travel outfit of deep blue, rose as Hero entered the room. Her white hair was arranged in a style befitting a woman of her age. "I am Lady Renforth, Dowager Countess of Renforth," she announced. "My son is the Earl of Renforth. I shall get right to the point. It is my understanding that you delivered my granddaughter, Lady Barbara Gaylord, of a child, nearly five years ago. Is that correct?"

Hero curtsied to the older woman. "I helped a young lady I knew as Barbara, yes. Please do sit down, my lady." Hero gestured her back to the settee and seated herself on a nearby chair.

The woman murmured, "At last, a straight answer." She closed her eyes for a moment as she sat back down. "I am here about the child. Mrs. Knowlton informed me that you handled things in that regard."

"Yes. I did. But before I share those details with you, may I ask why over four years have passed with no one taking any interest?"

Lady Renforth sighed. "I am sure that seems strange to you. Indeed, it seems incredible to me. My son, Barbara's father, is a hard man—very like his father was. When his daughter fell in love with a young man and turned up with child, he more or less washed his hands of her. Mind you, his wife—his second wife—was instrumental in his doing so. Barbara was the child of his first wife, who, by the way, died giving birth to Barbara. The current countess simply could not abide the fact that Barbara was prettier, more personable and charming than her own daughter, Georgiana, who was scarcely three years younger. Her solution to Barbara's unfortunate condition was to just send the girl away! I still find it hard to believe they were so very cruel."

"You knew nothing of this?" Hero asked.

"No. I stayed in the country that year while the others went to the city for the Season. I had suffered a bout of influenza that winter and just did not feel up to the long journey from Lancashire. I missed my Barbara—we were always very close. Why, I think she spent more time with me in the dower house than she ever did in the main house. I hoped she was having a good time going to balls and routs." She paused, apparently dwelling on memories, then she sighed again. "Barbara wrote me regularly, but then her letters stopped. Eventually, my son wrote me that he had allowed Barbara to join a friend on the friend's father's Irish estate, but that the ship on which they traveled had gone down in the Irish Sea with no survivors. I cried for months."

"I'm so sorry," Hero said softly. "When did you learn the truth?"

"Only a few weeks ago. It pains me to tell you, but I had a terrible row with my daughter-in-law. I made the mistake of criticizing the wanton behavior of her daughter Georgiana, and she told me, 'Well! Your darling Barbara was no angel, either' and she blurted out the truth. My son was furious with her—and I must admit that I was furious with both of them. Why—why had they not sent her to me? They were quite self-righteous in their defense—trying to protect the family name, the effect of scandal on Georgiana and the younger children, and so on. All rather specious in my opinion. So here I am, trying to ferret out the rest of the truth."

"Why?"

Tears welled in Lady Renforth's eyes. "Because I loved Barbara as the child of my heart. I simply have to know what happened to her and her child."

"Does your son know you are on this quest?"

"He knows and he heartily disapproves. But I am my own person now. I was not always so. I married very young—an arranged marriage in which I had no say-so. But the marriage settlements left me rather wealthy in my own right—much to the chagrin of both my husband and my son. My husband was rather a cold, harsh man. So is his son, I am sad to say. It took me a long, long time to discover the strength I, as woman, had. I tried to pass that along to Barbara."

"If it is any consolation to you, I think you succeeded in that regard, my lady." Hero proceeded to tell her as much as she remembered of the young woman she had known only as Barbara.

"And what happened to her child?" the countess asked.

Hero squirmed in her seat and hesitated, but finally said, "The child is with me. I could not bear to see her go the way of so many abandoned children. She is a very bright, happy little girl. I would hate to see anything happen to change that."

"She is here? Oh! Please, m-may I see her?" The woman's lips trembled as she asked.

Again, Hero hesitated. "I would not want to see her upset."

"Nor would I, Miss Whitby. Nor would I. But, please, I beg you."

Hero rose to give the bellpull a tug and when a maid answered, she instructed her to have Nurse Henson bring Annabelle to the drawing room. A few minutes later Henson arrived with Annabelle in hand, and Hero dismissed the nurse.

"This lady would like to meet you, my love," Hero said to Annabelle, who had turned unexpectedly shy.

Lady Renforth gasped. "Why, she looks exactly as Barbara did at that age! Exactly." She extended a hand. "Please come and sit by me, my child."

Annabelle looked up at Hero for reassurance. Hero gave her a little nudge. "It's all right, darling."

Annabelle climbed onto the settee and sat very sedately, her hands in her lap, and looked up at this strange lady. "Why is the lady sad?" she asked Hero. "She's crying."

"I'm sure those are happy tears," Hero said. "She is happy to see you."

"Yes. I am very, very happy to meet you," Lady Renforth said, reaching to touch Annabelle's blond curls hanging down her back. "What is your name, child?"

"Annabelle."

"Ah!" The countess nearly choked and in a tearful voice said, "Why that is *my* given name."

"Annabelle knows that her mama gave her that name."

"My mama is in heaven," Annabelle explained. "She died when I was borned. That's why I live with Auntie H'ro."

"Oh, I see," the countess said. "And do you like living with her?"

"Oh, yes. We have fun. I have a kitten and a pony and we go to the beach and shopping in town and she shows me how to do things." Her face wrinkled a bit and she glanced at Hero. "But she makes me do my numbers and letters." Then her face brightened again. "She reads me a story every night."

"How very nice," the woman said, with an appreciative glance at Hero.

Impulsively, Hero decided to introduce the visitor fully to the child. "Annabelle, Lady Renforth is your mama's grandmother. She is your great-grandmother, and she came all the way to Cornwall just to meet you."

"Really?" Annabelle was obviously delighted with this idea. "Does this mean I am not a orphan? Freddie said I am a orphan."

"Freddie does not always get things right, though, does he?" Hero asked, sidestepping the issue.

"No, he does not," Annabelle said emphatically. "He told me Bitsy is a boy cat, but Mr. Stewart said that's not true. It isn't, is it?"

Hero shared a smile with Lady Renfort. "No, darling. Your Bitsy is a little girl, just like you."

"I thought so. Can I go play now?"

"May I," Hero corrected automatically.

"May I?"

"You must pay Lady Renforth a proper goodbye."

Annabelle jumped down from her seat and curtsied prettily to the guest. "I am very pleased to meet you, my lady," she said formally.

"And I, you, my dear," the countess said. "Could—could I give you a hug?"

Annabelle looked at Hero, who nodded. The countess hugged the child tenderly and Hero could hardly hold back her own tears at seeing those in the other woman's eyes. Still, she could not help wondering what was in store. Would the countess try to take Annabelle away from her? How could she—unmarried daughter of a country doctor in Cornwall—fight a member of the aristocracy? Her heart clenched in fear.

When Annabelle skipped out of the room, pausing to give Hero a kiss on the cheek, the countess said, "I believe, Miss Whitby, that you and I have much to discuss."

Hero replied bluntly. "Yes. I suppose we do. Are you going to try to take Annabelle away from me? I warn you, I will fight you tooth and nail. My father's brother is a London solicitor. And the scandal would exceed anything your son and his wife ever envisioned."

The countess gave her a wan smile. "Having seen how you deal with her, I would expect nothing less from you, Miss Whitby. The truth is that I just want the best for my Barbara's child—and for the rest of my family as well. Were I to create an uproar over Annabelle, my son would be absolutely apoplectic. The scandal would reflect adversely on his other children, whom I do love—including Georgiana. I cannot forgive what my son and his wife did to Barbara, but I cannot undo it, either."

"There is that," Hero said in a neutral tone.

"Over the last several weeks, I have given the matter a great deal of thought," the countess said. "A great deal, once I learned of the child's existence. My son wants nothing to do with her, and he is unlikely to change his mind. He is that self-righteous and he was that angry with his daughter and her young man. I want only the best for Annabelle—and I think you do too."

"Yes, of course," Hero murmured, wondering where on earth this was going.

"I want to be a part of her life," the countess begged. "She is my Barbara's child. If I must take legal action to do that, I will, but having seen how you love and care for her, I would not want to do that. But—I will, if necessary, scandal or not."

"What do you mean 'part of her life'?"

"I want to visit her occasionally—two, maybe three times a year— just to see how she goes on. I want to know her and her to know me. Perhaps when she is older, she can visit me in Lancashire. You could accompany her, of course. Ultimately, I will see to her education—including a governess immediately, if you agree. An exclusive boarding school later, of course." She paused for a moment. "As I said, I have thought this through rather thoroughly."

Overwhelmed, and not a little relieved, Hero nodded. "I have no objection to what you propose. However, I will never, ever have Annabelle subjected to slights of any kind. If your son were to create a fuss over what you propose, I would think it best that she remain right here in Cornwall until she is of age and can make her own decisions."

"My son," the countess said bitterly, "just wants to sweep Barbara—and her child—under the rug. Oh, yes, he knows there was a child. But he and his wife abide by the lie they fabricated. Is that not a terrible thing for a mother to admit about her son? It is sad but true. However, I cannot forget that sweet, sweet girl. I loved her so dearly. I promise you—*I promise*—I will see no harm come to her child."

Hero felt tears coming to her own eyes at seeing this woman's pain. They made plans to meet the next day for lunch at the inn, where Lady Renforth had already booked rooms. Hero would bring Annabelle, and the three of them would visit Barbara's grave and spend the day getting acquainted. And, yes, Lady Renforth would welcome the company of the ubiquitous Bitsy.

* * * *

Having seen Lady Renforth off, Hero practically danced back into the house; she was feeling absolutely exultant at the way things were turning out with Annabelle, and she wanted to share her euphoria. As she passed through the hallway on the ground floor, she saw that Adam's door was ajar.

She tapped on it lightly and called, "Anybody home?"

"I'm right here." His voice came from the terrace, but immediately he was opening the door to her and smiling down at her. "Do come in. You look as though something has gone well for you."

"Adam, you won't believe what just happened!"

He grinned. "So tell me then. I assume it has something to do with that elegant traveling coach I saw when I came in a while ago."

"That carriage belongs to Annabelle's great-grandmother." She stepped into the center of the room.

"And that is good—why? I know how anxious you have been about that sprite." He closed the door and leaned against it, just looking at her, waiting for her to go on.

"I was so worried. Terrified, actually. But it is going to be all right." She told him the whole story of Lady Renforth's visit.

"What a wonderful outcome," he said, coming to put his arms about her and give her a tight hug. "Wonderful."

She lifted her head to gaze into his eyes—those blue eyes that never failed to mesmerize her. There was a long pause, then he lowered his mouth to hers in what she later supposed had been meant as a casual congratulatory kiss. It quickly turned into something else. Her arms slipped up around his neck and she pressed her body against his, needing to be closer, ever closer. For the minutest fraction a second, some analytical part of her brain told her this was not real, that it was happening merely as an aftermath of the tension she had felt earlier. She ignored that and gave herself up to the sheer passion of the moment, opening to him as he probed for entrance, and their tongues joined in a primal dance.

He broke the kiss, but only to sprinkle kisses on her eyes, her cheeks, her nose, her neck, that tender, erotic spot just beneath her ear, the exposed flesh above the neckline of her dress. His hands played up and down her back, gripping her buttocks to pull her even closer. She could feel her whole body responding, straining toward him—her nipples hardening, a burning need in her groin. Both of them were breathing hard, and Hero could hear her own involuntary whimpers—pleas for more. Then she felt the hard evidence of his arousal against her belly, and she tried to jerk away in a panic.

He refused the separation, still holding her close. "Hero? What is it, love? What just happened?"

"I cannot do this. I-I thought I could. With you. But I can't. I just can't."

"You can't?" His voice was flat, with a hard edge to it. "What does that mean? Good God, Hero, you're no green girl given to teasing a man to distraction. You want it as much as I do."

"No. I mean—I don't know. Forgive me." She stifled a sob and tried again to jerk out of his arms. She wanted to flee to her own room. She wanted the comfort of his embrace. The memory of pain and humiliation assailed her.

He refused to release her. He merely held her closely for a few moments, until her panicky breathing turned more normal. Then he led her to the couch and sat the two of them down, still keeping her close.

"I think I may understand," he said quietly, tentatively. "Someone hurt you very badly, didn't he?"

She nodded, unable to look at him. "Y-yes. There was more than one."

"Oh, my God!" She heard his anger and disgust, but knew instinctively it was not directed at her. "Tell me about it," he said.

"I-I can't," she whispered. "I-I've never told anyone."

"Tell me, Hero," he pleaded. "I think you and I may have something wonderful and precious between us, but your fears are keeping us from realizing it. Tell me you agree."

She nodded, but still could not look at him.

"Tell me." With his arm around her shoulders, he gave her a firm shake.

"It—it's so ugly—so sordid."

"What happened may be so, but, Hero, *you* are not. You are beautiful and good and loving and lovable. *You* are a wonderful person, my dear girl." He kissed her on the temple. "Now just tell me. It's time you told someone. Get it all out."

She drew in a deep, shuddering breath. "I was almost fifteen. My mother was very ill—I did not know it at the time, but she was dying. Diana was married by then, Michael was away at school, Jonathan was about the age Annabelle is now, and Papa was very busy with his practice. Still, he and I cared for her. And then—" She stifled a sob and went on more calmly. "Then Mama decided I needed to get away. She insisted. She sent me away." This came out as a wail of despair.

"Where?" he prompted with a little jiggle of her shoulder.

"To visit her friend, the Baroness Portman in Somerset. I had been before. The oldest daughter, Marie, was my age and a special friend. Her brother was three years older."

"Oh, my God. I know where this is going," Adam said, his tone sounding anguished.

She nodded glumly and went on, almost in a monotone. "Reggie—his name is Reginald—was home for a school holiday and two of his friends had come with him. Marie and I went out riding with them often. We always had a good time on our rides and the visit was doing what Mother had hoped it would do—take my mind off troubles at home. Marie was not feeling well one day, so I—foolishly, perhaps—went alone with the three of them. I mean, they were gentlemen, were they not?" She glanced at Adam for corroboration of this point, but found his expression harsh and inscrutable.

"Then what happened?" he prompted.

"I did not realize they had tapped into Reggie's father's liquor supply even before the ride—and they were sharing a flask as we rode along. I was just so stupid—so naïve! They chatted and entertained me with tales of their exploits at school. We were all laughing. Then we stopped to rest the horses—as we always did—and that's when it happened."

"They raped you. All three of them?"

"Y-yes." She felt tears streaming down her face, and was drawing deep breaths. "I tried to run, to get to my horse, but it was useless—I needed help what with the sidesaddle and all, and they dragged me down—and—and—did it. I remember Reggie saying he got to be first because he'd never had a virgin before. How disgusting was that?"

"Disgusting is the mildest of things you might have said," Adam muttered, his jaw clenched in fury. "Why did you not tell anyone? Have them horsewhipped? Make them pay for what they did?"

She sighed in resignation. "I threatened to, and they just laughed. Said it would be my word against theirs. So what good would it do me—other than to ruin *me*? As though they had not already accomplished that little deed," she added bitterly.

"So you kept quiet?"

"I did. Reggie was the golden child in that family. His father doted on him as the heir to the barony. His mother thought him the handsomest, most wonderful creation God and she had ever achieved. I knew very well none of them would believe me, let alone support me."

"Then what happened?"

"I threw a tantrum and insisted on returning home the very next day. The baroness said I was a spoiled brat and Marie was not best pleased, but they did hire a carriage and sent a maid and a footman to accompany me home. I think I cried all the way. When I arrived back here, Mama had taken a turn for the worse. I think she must have known it was coming. She died within the week. Papa was prostrate with grief. I could hardly unload that burden on him."

"And all these years—you just kept it locked in?"

"Yes." She gave him a searching look. "Surely, you can understand that. Have you not kept all those horrors of the war locked away too?"

"I—maybe you are right," he admitted.

"But they come out in dreams—right?"

"Yes. Is that what happens to you?"

She nodded. "It's not as bad as it once was, but yes, sometimes I have bad dreams. I honestly thought I had dealt with it. Overcome it."

"Until I made you dredge it all up again."

She sat up straighter and gave him a tentative smile. "Yes, but you know—I think it *has* helped. Just to say it aloud to another human being—sordid as it was—is."

"It truly is a terrible story, Hero. I hate that you had to live through something like that. But *you*, my lady, are pretty damned wonderful. Perhaps you will be able to put it behind you once and for all now."

"I hope so." She glanced at the clock on the mantel. "Oh, my goodness. The time! Mrs. Hutchins will have supper on the table already."

He kissed her on the cheek, then stood and went to the alcove that held his washbasin and returned with a wet cloth. "Here. Wipe your face. Then we will go out on the terrace and return to the house via the front entrance as though we are returning from a short walk. 'Twouldn't do for someone to see you leaving my room."

Chapter 15

Later that night, Alex lay awake, unable to put that scene with Hero out of his mind. He knew how difficult it had been for her to bare her soul as she had. Dredging up such a devastating, painful experience had taken incredible courage. Were such an incident widely known, society would undoubtedly view her as—how had Teague phrased it?—ah, yes, as "damaged goods." Apparently she had accepted that opinion of herself. Why else would such a lovely, lively woman have remained unmarried in a country and time that saw the titles of *wife* and *mother* as the only viable choices for women—a social milieu that relegated single women to oblivion? Had he not heard his modern, progressive mother rail against the limited options for a lady of the gentry or the aristocracy? That is, honorable options: governess, nun, ladies' companion, dependent relative—barely tolerated so long as she stayed in the shadows. Yet this woman had forged a place for herself in a field that rejected those of her sex—as, indeed, did most fields of public endeavor. Shakespeare might produce a Portia as a woman of the law, but woe betide a modern woman who wanted to be a lawyer, or a doctor, or a politician on her own. *Nineteenth-century England,* Alex mused, *is truly a man's world, and God help the woman who tries to get a foothold in that world.*

As much as he might be sympathetic to the plight of women in general, that sympathy was vastly overshadowed by his admiration of—and attraction to—this woman in particular. Major Lord Alexander Sterne had had his fair share of women in his time. But never had he wanted another woman as he wanted Hero Whitby. Nor did he think this was just a passing fancy as others had been. The intense physical need was eclipsed by his desire just to be with her—in the same room, breathing the same air, to know always where she was, feeling a tie that extended beyond mere proximity.

Was he in love with Hero?

Well…perhaps.

Probably.

Yes.

Yes?

Yes…

Once before, he had fallen victim to this condition. As a young ensign in India, he'd thought himself in love with Madeline Henderson, the blond, pink-cheeked, blue-eyed daughter of a general. She had reminded him of a porcelain figurine, fragile and precious. He remembered—with chagrin now—manufacturing situations where he could gaze at her, wangling invitations to social affairs that he knew she would attend, even writing sappy love notes to her. But Madeline had come to India to snag a husband—and she had her eyes set on something more promising than a lowly ensign and a third son, much as she basked in *any* male attention. It had come as a distinct disappointment to discover that, rather than fragile and precious, she was brittle and cheap. However, the lesson had taken, and despite an occasional liaison, he had not again allowed himself to become quite so enamored of another woman.

Now Hero was playing havoc with his emotions and his judgment. But he could hardly do anything about that as Adam Wainwright, could he? No. His personal issues would have to await the outcome of this infernal smuggling business.

Knowing the locals as he now did, he was attuned to their concerns and worries—and intensely aware that there was much that he could do—should have done before—to alleviate some, or even many, of those. Townspeople were fearful. The smugglers among local folks perhaps regretted having wrecked that ship, though the word circulating was that people who had been most instrumental in that misdeed were the outsiders Teague had brought into Weyburn some years ago. Local people who had actually taken part were trying to fade into the background—playing least seen, as it were. Even Jonathan was staying close to home.

Alex knew the gang would have to do something soon about all that contraband they had hidden away. Yet there had been little noticeable activity on that front. Then, one night, there was. But it did not go well for the law-abiding, law-enforcing element. Word had reached the ears of the militia of a planned movement of goods at thus-and-such a place and time. It turned out to be a ruse—a deliberately floated rumor that sent the militia on yet another wild-goose chase.

Alex and Mac met the next day with Colonel Phillips and his aide, who had taken rooms at the inn while a contingent of their troops bivouacked on the beach near Weyburn. When Alex and Mac entered the main room of the inn, Teague and three of his bully boys were sitting at a table across the way. They sent sly glances at Alex and Mac, apparently sharing a huge joke. However, they did not linger, leaving the inn soon after Phillips and his aide came down from above. Alex wondered sourly when Teague ever managed to do any of his estate business, what with the way he was always turning up elsewhere.

Phillips, in his forties, had even features, gray eyes, and black hair that was graying at the temples. Alex had been favorably impressed with the man's apparent competence and shared his frustration at being outmaneuvered by the sort of men who would deliberately entice a ship to disaster. The aide was younger—a captain of perhaps thirty, with blond hair and a deferential attitude toward his commander. The militiamen wore their red-coated uniforms. It was midmorning and the four men were sitting at the same window table Alex and Hero had occupied so many days earlier, drinking coffee and commiserating over the last night's debacle. On the table, Phillips had laid out a map of their section of Cornwall.

"I cannot believe we were so completely bamboozled," Phillips said. "It was all a trick. And now we must play that infernal waiting game again—wait for them to move that contraband. But—by God!—this time we shall keep our own watch and not trust an informant!"

Alex leaned across the table to say to Phillips, "I think we should watch the Abbey itself, but more to the point, the entrance to that cave below the Abbey cliff. It will not be easy, but you should be able to position your men so they can see and not be seen. Goods from those cargos must still be in the ancient cellar of the Abbey—or in the barn of the deserted Thompson farm—or, more to the point, in both. It might be possible to move goods aboveground from the Abbey itself, but it is far more probable they will go through the tunnel to the cave."

"Likely they'll need as many as twenty mules and packhorses. That much livestock is hard to handle secretly," Mac observed. "Not to mention they will have to transfer the stuff to buyers' wagons. Now where they gonna do that?"

"Here? In town?" Phillips offered.

"Perhaps…" Alex's voice trailed off in thought. "That might be too risky, though."

"This little village of Trenton?" Phillips pointed at a location on the map. "Five miles along the coast, then—what?—another five miles inland. The Trenton road connects to a main highway."

The four of them sat in silent thought for a few moments, drinking coffee and nibbling at some scones Mrs. Barkley had produced. Then Alex sat up straight and snapped his fingers.

"I have it! The mine. It has a loading yard that would accommodate the kind of traffic we are talking about." He explained the situation as he and Hero had observed it, ending with, "There are enough trees and shrubs there to provide adequate cover for your watchers."

"I have a capable young lieutenant who can handle that task," Phillips said.

Later, as Mac and Alex strolled about the town, trying to appear their touristy best, Mac said, "Rather like old times, eh, Major?"

Alex knew exactly what he meant. "There do seem to be parallels between police work—which is what this is—and dealing with Boney and his troops."

Mac grunted. "With a lot of hurry-up-and-wait about both."

"There is that," Alex agreed with a chuckle.

For the next few days, there was little activity on the smuggling front. The militia remained in place in Weyburn, but Teague and his lot seemed to be playing a cagey game—or perhaps they were having difficulty lining up their buyers. Meanwhile, for Alex, life at Whitby Manor continued more or less as it had. Soon after it had been devised, he shared with Dr. Whitby and Hero, but not with Jonathan or anyone else in the household, the general plan he and Phillips had developed. Now they too were committed to the temporary "wait and see" approach to life in general.

He had worried that Hero might turn shy and withdrawn after finally admitting to another person what had happened to her as a girl. To his delight, that had not happened. At first she did seem a little subdued, with an expression of wariness in her eyes when they chanced to meet his. He thought she was merely unsure of how he was reacting to what she had told him. She knew very well how others might react—had not Teague reiterated that view only a few weeks ago? His own deepest reaction, which he tried to keep from her, was anger. Rage, actually. In London, Alex had known the present Baron Portman. Not well, but he knew who Portman was—and what he was: a brash braggart who tended to drink to excess and gamble recklessly. The baron was a womanizer who made no secret of the fact that he was out to bargain his title for a rich wife—even if said wife came with the smell of trade about her. Alex hoped fate would provide a suitable reward to the man for what he had done to a young, vulnerable

Hero, but if fate failed to do so, Alex silently swore that, if ever their paths crossed, he would achieve that end himself.

Three days after his meeting with Phillips, Alex and the doctor had, as usual, been playing chess in the library in the evening. Hero had put Annabelle to bed and Alex had waited for her to appear in the library, for only with her settled into her customary place on the nearby couch would he feel complete and at ease.

She came in waving a letter in the direction of her father. "Papa. I have been rereading Michael's letter. What can he possibly mean, saying he is bringing us a surprise?"

"I have no idea, my dear," her father answered absently, concentrating on his game. "A new horse? That boy has always appreciated fine horseflesh."

"A Belgian tapestry, perhaps," she offered. "One might fit nicely in the drawing room."

"Hmm. Why not just wait 'til he gets here and you will know," her father said, moving his bishop into a precarious position. "Aah," he groaned as Alex swept up the bishop. "I should have seen that coming."

"I'm sorry, Papa. I distracted you," Hero said.

She picked up the last volume of a novel by Sir Walter Scott, but her sighs and occasional comments to the chess players suggested to Alex that her heart was not into the book.

When the match ended, the doctor gathered up the chess pieces to consign them to their box.

Alex glanced in Hero's direction and held her gaze. "Knights and deeds of chivalry and derring-do not so fascinating this evening?" he asked.

"Not really. I keep thinking about Jonathan—"

"Stop fretting about the boy," her father said. "Young fellows of a certain age don't like to have their mothers—or sisters—always concerned about what they are doing. I know. I was one once."

Hero smiled at her father. "I know, Papa, but—"

"No buts," he replied. "Leave the boy alone. He said he's spending the night with Anthony. Accept it: He's spending the night with Anthony."

"I know that is what he *said*, but—"

The doctor snapped the lid shut on the chess pieces and set the box on the board. "Sometimes, Hero, you simply have to trust that people will be honest with you—even younger brothers." He picked up his cane, came over to her, and bent to kiss her on the forehead. "Not to worry, my dear. Now don't stay up too late."

"Yes, Papa. Good night."

Having stood as the older man bade them both good night and left the room, Alex turned his gaze on Hero again. "He's right, you know."

She carefully marked her page in the book and set it aside, then looked up at him, one eyebrow lifted. "I do not need the two of you ganging up on me."

He slid onto the couch next to her and put an arm around her shoulders. "Wouldn't dream of it," he murmured and kissed her.

Later, he tried to tell himself it had been meant as a simple kiss good night, but he knew that was a lie. He had dreamed for days now—not to mention nights—of fulfilling the promise of those earlier kisses they had shared. From the way she immediately responded, he thought she might have had the same dreams, for she welcomed him enthusiastically, angling her head to give him better access as his lips moved from hers to her neck and to the swell of her breasts above the neckline of her dress. Cupping his hand around the firmness of one breast, he felt the bud of the nipple harden as he teased it with his thumb. Again, she moved to allow him better access to that portion of her anatomy. He placed his mouth against one cloth-covered nipple and allowed his hot breath to stimulate it as his hand continued to tease the other.

Pleased at her little moans of pleasure, he slipped his hand under her skirt and felt the smooth flesh of her inner thigh. His fingers brushed against the most intimate folds of flesh at the apex of her legs.

"Adam?" she murmured in awe.

"Open for me, sweet," he urged, surprised and pleased when she did so immediately. His fingers probed and caressed until she was fairly writhing in his arms. Both were breathing hard and his erection was already throbbing. He withdrew his hand and pulled back from her slightly.

"No-o-o," she moaned in protest.

Grinning, he stood and pulled her to her feet. "Come, my love. We need to finish this across the hall."

"Across the hall?" she asked dumbly.

"Yes." He chuckled at her tone. "Across the hall."

He quickly doused the lamps in the library, grabbed Hero's hand, and maneuvered her around the furniture and through the door of the library and then the door of his bedchamber. She seemed a bit dazed as he achieved all this, but murmured not even a whimper of protest as he locked the door.

Earlier he had left his bedside lamp turned low, and now, in that soft light, he gave her a piercing look. "Are you all right with this—with us?" He pulled her close and whispered against the smooth skin of her neck, "I want you—I want you desperately—but I would not have you against your will, Hero. Even your hesitation. You must want it as much as I do."

He felt her swallow. "Yes. Yes, I do."

"Well, then—the first order of business is to divest ourselves of this excess clothing."

"Oh." She began to pull at the sleeves of her dress.

"No. Let me," he said. He slipped the cap sleeves off her shoulders and, his hands touching, caressing all the way, shimmied the dress down her body until it pooled about her feet and she stepped out of it.

He drew in a deep breath of anticipation. "The shift, too," he said.

"A-are you sure?" she asked nervously.

He laughed softly. "Oh, yes. I am sure." He marveled at the utter perfection unfolding before him and bent his head to kiss each breast as it was exposed. He felt himself growing even harder, and nudged her toward the bed and pulled back the cover.

"In you go," he said.

She scooted over to allow him room and gazed openly as he removed his shoes, then his shirt, and finally his breeches. She gasped, but did not turn away at seeing him in all his nakedness.

He took her in his arms again, exulting in the sheer ecstasy of skin against skin, but he paused in caressing her to say again, "Are you sure, Hero? You can still change your mind. At the moment—"

She arched her body against his. "I'm sure. I promise. I will have no regrets."

He kissed her deeply and again brought her to that peak of pleasure before positioning himself between her thighs. He entered her slowly, letting her adjust to him, but then it was she who needed more—faster— deeper—until he finally collapsed on top of her.

After a moment to collect himself, he propped himself on his hands and asked, "Are you all right? Did I hurt you? Please, God, don't say I hurt you."

She laughed softly. "You did not hurt me. I had no idea that could be so wonderful."

He grinned. "Next time it will be better."

* * * *

Retreating to her room some time later, Hero relived every moment of that encounter. Days earlier, she had surprised herself by confessing to Adam the trauma of that incident in her youth. Afterwards, she had determined that what she felt for Adam had nothing to do with what had happened to her all those years ago. That had been about overbearing boys seizing an opportunity to exert power and control—to prove their masculine "right" to do whatever they wanted, with no regard for anything or anyone but their own selfish desires of the moment, and egged on by the excitement of her refusal and the urgings of their partners in crime. She would never forgive them, but she would no longer allow them to own even a small portion of her very self.

She knew that, tonight, she had moved beyond, that never again would she be insensible to anything life had to offer, never again would something outside herself make her afraid to embrace the wonder—the joy—of her own life, her own self.

Adam had given her this incredible gift. Adam. No, not Adam. Yes, Adam. This man. In this place. He was gentle, giving, and infinitely tender. What did it matter if that was not his name? It was the *man* with whom she was in love.

In love?

She closed her eyes against this realization. It was true. She loved this man calling himself Adam Wainwright. Moreover, she trusted him. She cherished him for his understanding, for the way he fit in with her family and her friends and neighbors.

She loved him.

But she hugged this knowledge to herself, not willing to share it yet—even with him.

Three days later, she found herself wanting to repudiate every nuance of this discovery, although there had been two nights of incredible bliss in between.

Chapter 16

The entire Whitby household eagerly awaited the return of its prodigal son. Alex suggested that perhaps he should remove to the inn, but both Hero and her father assured him that would not be necessary. Alex knew that Captain Whitby had sent word, upon his arrival in London and then from his last overnight en route to Cornwall, of the expected time of his homecoming. Thus Hero, her father, Jonathan, and Alex had repaired to the library after the midday meal, where they would have tea and wait, for a large window in the library looked out on the circular driveway in front and would afford the first glimpse of the captain's arrival.

Jonathan seemed unable to sit quietly and kept pacing around the room, spinning the huge standing globe, and generally wearing a trail in the carpet from the window to the platter of biscuits that had accompanied the tea tray. Hero, her father, and Alex continued their threads of conversation that had begun in the dining room, namely discussions of the latest news from London newspapers, the main topics of which were the social unrest resulting from a downturn in the nation's economy—and the Prince Regent's marital difficulties.

"The truth is that it never was what anyone would call a marriage made in heaven," the doctor said. "Prince George and Caroline of Brunswick disliked each other from the moment they met—and they met at the altar!"

"No, that was a marriage concocted by politicians," Hero said, "but that is no excuse for his having treated his wife so abominably. After all, he did agree to what those politicians suggested."

"Perhaps he learned something from his experience," Doctor Whitby replied. "He allowed his daughter some say in her choice of husband, and the gossips tell us Princess Charlotte is quite happy."

"Let us hope they are right," Hero said.

"The royals and their marital bliss—or lack thereof—aside," Alex said, "those latest reports of labor unrest in the Midlands are very troubling."

"If the men who own most of the land and the manufactories in this country would take more responsibility for the people in their care, I daresay there would be less unrest to be troubled about," Hero said flatly.

"I say, Doctor," Alex said facetiously, talking around Hero, "has your lovely daughter always been so reticent about voicing her opinion on matters best left to the male half of the species?"

"Adam. You know I am right," she said. "Why, just look what's happening right here in—"

"He's here!" Jonathan announced from his position at the window. "Good Lord, there's enough luggage piled on that coach for the whole army! Wha—? You won't believe this! He's got a woman with him."

"A woman?" Hero rose to move toward the window, but almost immediately they heard Stewart in the entrance greeting Michael and telling him the family were in the library.

The door opened to reveal the red-coated army captain, and at his side, her hand on his arm, was a pretty, dark-haired young woman dressed in a stylish travel costume, looking very nervous.

"Michael!" Hero gave a small squeal and flung her arms around her brother's neck. Their father and his younger son were quick to reach for his hand to extend their own welcome.

The army man hugged them all, but then quickly pulled his companion close and said, "Allow me the pleasure of introducing Monique LaPierre Whitby." He paused dramatically. "My wife. And this lot, my love, are your new family."

Utter silence followed.

Monique smiled tremulously and held tighter to her husband's arm even as she executed a deep curtsy that included all of them.

"Your *wife*?" Hero squeaked in a shocked tone and returned the other woman's curtsy rather mechanically.

"Well, well," the doctor murmured.

"Oh, jolly good!" Jonathan said. Alex could not tell if this was in praise of the woman, the marriage, or the coup Michael had achieved.

"Michael, you horrid, horrid man," Hero said through surprised laughter. "You might have let us know."

He kept his arm around his bride as he explained, "We were married only a month ago. I could not bear the idea of leaving Monique in Belgium while I came home to settle things and then return for her. I knew we would probably beat the news home, so—"

"B-but you never once let on—we had no idea—" Hero turned to the woman. "Oh, my dear, I do not mean to be so boorish—of course you are most welcome. Michael's choice will be our choice as well."

"*Merci*," Monique said in a soft voice. "Michel, he tell me so."

"Welcome, my daughter." The doctor enfolded her in a gentle embrace and Jonathan bowed over her hand.

Alex had stood when the newcomers entered the room and simply observed this family scene. Suddenly, Hero caught his gaze and said, "Oh, I am sorry, Adam. Michael, let me introduce our friend, Adam—"

Seeing the man's eyes widen in recognition, Alex listened helplessly as Michael stepped closer, extending a hand in greeting. "Major Lord Alexander Sterne. What a great pleasure to meet you under happier circumstances, sir." Alex took the extended hand and murmured an appropriate pleasantry as Michael went on to tell his family, "I attended several of the wounded from the major's regiment, though he may not have been aware of that—there were so many wounded and things were so chaotic in Brussels then."

"Yes, they were," Alex agreed, kicking himself mentally for not having recognized *Whitby* as the name of one of McGrigor's medical team. In the aftermath of Waterloo, he had focused on his own men—and those awful letters he had to write to grieving families. He looked at Hero and his heart sank as her expression changed from shocked surprise to embarrassment and then to fury.

"M-major Lord—My, my. This day is just full of surprises, is it not?"

He took a step toward her. "Hero. Please. I—"

"Not now, *Adam*." She gave the name an ironic twist. "Not now." She straightened her shoulders and said to the room at large, "If you will all excuse me, I shall speak with Mrs. Hutchins to ensure we have adequate accommodations for Michael and his bride." With a catch in her voice, she hastened from the room, refusing to make eye contact with Alex, but he thought he saw a glint of tears in her eyes.

Michael looked bewildered. "What just happened here? Did I say something wrong?"

"No, son, you did not," his father replied, "but our—uh—major here has some explaining to do. So, let us sit and hear what he has to say."

Michael and Monique sat very close together, holding hands on the couch from which Hero had had command of the tea tray earlier. Alex and the elder Whitby took the overstuffed chairs they had occupied previously, and Jonathan turned a straight-backed chair around and straddled it. All looked expectantly at Alex.

Alex drew in a deep breath. "First of all, I apologize for being the instrument of dampening your homecoming, Captain. I never intended this to happen. And"—he paused to look at each of them in turn, focusing especially on Jonathan—"I would ask that what I tell you remain in this room." He waited for each of them to murmur or nod acquiescence, then proceeded to explain why and how he had come to be in Cornwall and the circumstances of his having become a patient of the Whitby father-and-daughter medical team. The elder Dr. Whitby offered an occasional comment of clarification, but mostly Alex felt it was rather a long monologue.

When he finished, the captain looked at his bride and then at Alex and shook his head. "An amazing tale, Major. Sounds like something out of a gothic novel. Complete with ready-made villains in these smugglers."

"I will let your family fill you in on that part of the story," Alex said, wanting to avoid embarrassing the Whitbys, especially Jonathan, unnecessarily.

"We can do that later," the older man said. "I must say that I am disappointed that you were not willing to be honest with us before now, my lord. And I find myself wondering, where do we go from here?"

"I'm not sure, either," Alex said. He had not anticipated this turn of events—at least not yet. "However, I do want to reiterate my apology for deceiving you and ask your indulgence for a while yet."

"You want to go on being Adam Wainwright? That seems rather impractical now." The doctor's tone was skeptical.

Alex stood and ran a hand through his hair, still trying to work through the logistics of the immediate situation. "No, I think not. That shot has been fired. I think I should probably remove immediately to the Abbey and begin to try to set things right there."

The older man emitted a sympathetic sigh. "That might be best, my lord."

"Alex. Please, Dr. Whitby. My family and my friends call me Alex and I should like us to continue to be friends." He offered his hand to the older man, who took it in a warm clasp.

"That should not be too difficult, my son—Alex. Making your peace with Hero might be another story, though."

Alex immediately excused himself to do just that.

* * * *

Hero had rushed out of the library in what she herself might have described as a high dudgeon. She walked down the hallway several feet before pausing. She bent over, put her hands on her knees, drew in a deep, shuddering breath, and leaned against the wall. No. She took another deep breath and straightened, bracing her shoulders. She did not have time for this now. She really did need to speak with Mrs. Hutchins. She found that good woman in the kitchen, where she and Cook and the kitchen maids were all in a dither, planning a grand homecoming supper for Michael.

"Mr. Stewart said Mr. Michael brought a lady with him," Mrs. Hutchins said.

"Not just 'a lady'—his wife," Hero announced.

"His *wife*?" Mrs. Hutchins said in wonder, and the whole kitchen staff paused in what they were doing.

Hero smiled. "I had the exact same reaction. But, yes, indeed: his wife. They were married a month ago."

Mrs. Hutchins clasped her hands in front of her breast. "Newlyweds. So this is, as it were, a wedding supper."

"You might say that," Hero agreed. "Stewart did send a footman to notify my sister and her family of Michael's arrival and invite them for supper, did he not?"

"All taken care of, Miss Hero. And Davey just finished hauling all that luggage up to Mr. Michael's room, though that room seems rather small for a married couple, you know."

"It will have to do for tonight," Hero said. "We'll work out something more appropriate tomorrow."

"Yes, ma'am."

Mrs. Hutchins clapped her hands. "Back to work, girls. This is to be a very special meal."

Hero made her escape, but now that the domestic details no longer demanded her attention, or she no longer used them as an excuse, she had to face that revelation about this man who had dominated her thoughts—her life—in recent weeks. She just needed to be alone for a while, but she knew if she retreated to her room, someone would be sure to be knocking on the door forthwith. Without really thinking or planning her movements, she made her way to the clinic rooms—blessedly empty now—and through the outer door to the terrace there. She sank onto the bench at the wooden table and gazed out at the sea, hardly aware of the clouds scudding across the blue sky or of the blue-green sea below. Afternoon shadows were lengthening, but it would be daylight for several hours yet.

Her elbows on the table, she placed her hands on either side of her head and began to take herself to task. How could she have been so stupid, so blind? No. Not entirely blind. She'd had inklings of who and what Adam Wainwright might be. His manners, his language, his casual references to matters of history or literature. And especially after that trip to the Abbey. Oh, what a fine show he had put on there! How he must have been laughing at her—at all of Weyburn. He who could have done so much and who had done so little! She felt such a fool.

But that was the least of it, wasn't it? She had fancied herself in love with him. In love! Hah. Years ago a schoolgirl crush had ended disastrously. Marie's brother and his friends had violated her physically, but this was so much worse: Adam—Alexander Sterne—had ravished her spirit, her soul. Even worse, she had been a party to it—welcomed it, in fact. Welcomed those kisses, those caresses, loved what he did to her body, what she did to his. What she had thought of as beautiful and good had, in an instant, turned ugly and sordid. She closed her eyes against the humiliation of it all.

"I've been looking all over for you." His voice. He crossed from the terrace in front of his room to this one off the hospital rooms. He sat down across from her. "We need to talk, Hero."

She refused to look at him directly, fearing that she might lose herself in the depths of his blue eyes. "There is nothing to talk about. I made a mistake. Not my first, as you well know."

"Hero, look at me. Look me directly in the eye and tell me you are not seriously likening what happened to you years ago with what you and I might have."

She forced herself to raise her eyes to his. The anger and pain she saw disconcerted her. She looked back out to the sea and shrugged, refusing to respond verbally.

"I know you are hurt—that I have hurt you—and for that I am truly sorry. Please let me explain—"

She cut him off. "There is nothing to explain. You are who you are."

He ignored her interruption and went on. "At first I thought Weyburn people might be more open with Adam Wainwright than with someone they already disliked. I would learn much more as Adam, you see."

"In other words, you lied to them—to me." She heard the bitterness in her own voice.

"I wanted *you* to see *me*—not that image you had built up in your mind."

"It is not the first time I have been profoundly wrong in my estimation of someone," she said. "I'll get over it."

"If you are so sure of that, then perhaps we were both mistaken," he said, his tone turning cold and angry.

"Perhaps we were."

He stood and placed his hands on his hips; she felt him looking down at her. "I came to tell you goodbye," he said.

She looked up at this. "You're leaving? Back to the joys of London, I suppose."

"Eventually, perhaps."

"I wish you well."

"I wish I could believe that." He turned on his heel and left.

She sat for a long while staring out to sea, feeling totally bereft, tears streaming down her face.

* * * *

Alex packed his few belongings and persuaded Perkins to drive him to the inn, where he found Mac tucking into the evening meal.

"Ah—uh—Wainwright. Won't you join me? Mrs. Barkley turns out a very tasty lamb stew."

"Thank you, no. I'm not hungry. I'll have a drink, though." He signaled the innkeeper. "Whiskey. A large one," he said.

Mac raised his eyebrows as Barkley left to get the drink. "Something wrong, Mr. Wainwright?"

"You might say that." Alex waited until Barkley had brought the drink and he had taken a large, burning swallow before answering. "To start with, you can drop that Wainwright business, Mac. I am back to myself."

"Very good, sir."

"I doubt it is all that good, but it's happened." He explained the arrival of Captain Whitby and the captain's inadvertently blurting out Alex's name and title.

"I take it Miss Whitby did not react well," Mac said.

"Not well at all. But then she has never made a secret of the regard she has for the owner of the Abbey. Lack of regard, that is." He took another swallow of the drink and felt its warmth all the way down.

Mac finished the last spoonful of the stew, pushed the bowl aside, and reached for his glass of ale. "So now what, sir? Are you taking a room here?"

"No. You and I, my friend, are taking up residence at the Abbey. Now. This evening. Before I have time to talk myself out of it."

"Do you think it is safe to do so?" Mac asked.

"Safe enough with you along as an extra set eyes and ears," Alex said.

"Very good, sir. I need a few minutes to gather my things." Mac finished his ale and rose.

"While you do that, I shall pen a note to the Abbey's steward, who, I'm sure, has long been expecting something of this sort." Alex signaled Barkley again for a refill of his drink and asked for writing materials. He merely sipped at the drink this time as he composed the note.

Mr. Teague:
You are to report to Weyburn Abbey no later than 8:00
tomorrow morning. You will bring with you any
ledgers you may have in your possession that pertain
to the maintenance of the entire estate and be
prepared to explain any and all discrepancies. Also,
please bring with you any keys that may be needed to
examine any of the properties of the Abbey.
A. Sterne

Alex put the date and time beneath his signature, then signaled Barkley again. He gave the innkeeper the note and a coin to see the missive delivered immediately to Teague.

"I shall see it done, my lord," Barkley said.

Ah, Alex thought, *the word is out already.* But he had not sworn Perkins to secrecy, had he?

Chapter 17

An hour and a half later, having hired a coach and driver at the inn, Alex and Mac presented themselves at the front entrance of the Abbey. The butler, Mullins, answered their knock after a long while. He carried a lamp, which he held high.

"I beg your pardon, sir. The Abbey is closed to visitors at this hour."

"Not to me," Alex said brusquely and pushed past the man.

"Sir! I shall summon help and have you thrown out if you do not leave at once." His raised voice brought the sound of footsteps rapidly approaching from the rear of the building.

"He owns the place, you twit," Mac muttered as he too shoved past the openmouthed butler and set down two large bags before returning for the last two.

Alex turned and faced Mullins just as his wife joined him. "Mac is right: I own the place. I am Lord Alexander Benjamin Sterne, and if you will direct me to the nearest room that is not shrouded in hundreds of yards of holland linen, I will be happy to supply you proof of that statement."

The housekeeper and butler looked at each other and, with the kind of silent communication found in long-lasting marriages, seemed to come to agreement, nodding to each other before shifting their attention back to Alex.

"I am afraid that would be the kitchen at the moment, my lord," the housekeeper said apologetically. "Mr. Mullins and I were just having a cup of tea. Would you care to join us?"

"Mac and I will be happy to do so," Alex said as Mac set down the last two bags.

They followed the Mullins couple into the kitchen, which Alex was pleased to see was clean and neat. A white cloth covered one end of the central worktable, and tea paraphernalia had been set out there. Both the husband and wife were nervous, but did not appear to be frightened. They directed Alex and Mac to a bench on one side of the table. Mullins sat on the other side while his wife added more hot water and more tea to the pot, then procured two more sets of cups and saucers before sitting herself. After checking the strength of the brew, she poured and passed the tea and a plate of lemon biscuits.

Alex retrieved from an inner coat pocket the papers Mac had brought with him from London. "These documents should establish my identity adequately," he said. He sipped the hot tea as the couple held the papers closer to the light and studied them intently.

Finally, Mullins handed them back to Alex. "Yes, my lord. They seem to be in order."

There was a long, heavy silence as Alex tapped his fingers nervously on the table. Then he announced, "I intend to open the Abbey immediately and to take up residence here."

"Oh, very good, my lord," Mrs. Mullins said with a welcoming smile. "The staff will be so pleased."

"Yes. Well, I will need to know much more about the staff than I do presently," he said bluntly. "Beginning with the two of you."

They looked at each other apprehensively, but merely waited for him to go on.

"Miss Whitby indicated when I visited here earlier that you have been fulfilling housekeeper and butler duties here for several years."

Mullin nodded. "That is true."

"Who hired you?"

"Who—?" Mullins seemed confused by the question.

"Who actually employed the two of you? Sir Benjamin? Or Mr. Teague?"

"Oh. Sir Benjamin," Mullins said.

His wife added, "Atkins, the previous butler, wanted to retire. Mrs. Jennings, the housekeeper at the time, decided she wanted to go and live with her daughter, so the two positions became available at the same time. We were very lucky."

"Who recommended you?"

Mrs. Mullins drew herself up like a pouter pigeon. "We came with very good references, my lord. But Mrs. Jennings is my husband's cousin."

"So Mr. Teague did not employ you?"

"No. As a matter of fact, he had suggested a connection of his own, but both Sir Benjamin and his dear wife were very fond of Annie—Mrs. Jennings—and they accepted her recommendation," the wife answered.

Her husband added, "Later, Sir Benjamin wrote it into his will that we should stay on after he passed. We like it here. I—uh—I hope you will find our services satisfactory, my lord."

"I see," Alex said, stalling before asking his next question. "Who built the wall in the cellar?"

The two looked at each other for a moment, then the husband answered, "It was built after Sir Benjamin took ill."

"Why?"

Again, it was the husband who answered. "Mr. Teague said it would prevent dampness coming from the underground portion of the house and he convinced Sir Benjamin it would be an economizing measure."

"I see," Alex said again, and finished his tea. "I am sure that in time, I will get to know all of the staff, but for now, I should like you to rouse a maid or two to the task of preparing bedchambers for Mr. MacIntosh and me. It need not be the master suite for tonight. We'll look everything over tomorrow and decide on more permanent arrangements."

"Very good, my lord." The Mullinses rose immediately to do as he bade.

Alex looked at Mac when they were no longer within hearing. "What do you think, Mac?"

"They know more than they are saying, but I'm not sure they are in Teague's pocket."

"Neither am I."

* * * *

Hero steeled herself for the family gathering. She would simply present herself as though today had not turned out to be the most devastating day of her life. She could pretend to be normal—had she not had years of practice already? She gave herself a mental shake. *Do stop feeling sorry for yourself. Wallowing in self-pity is the way of madness. Now, for heaven's sake, just carry on. You've already put a damper on Michael's homecoming!*

She went to her room and called for a maid to help her out of the cotton day dress and, after she had washed away any residual evidence of tears, into a teal-blue, high-waisted silk gown with a wide, scooped neckline and cap sleeves. She dismissed the memory of how, in choosing that garment earlier, she had imagined Adam's removing it. No, not Adam. Never again Adam. *What was that again about self-pity?* She squared her shoulders as she drew on elbow-length gloves.

She reported to the nursery to gather up Annabelle, for this was to be truly a family gathering, with all the children as well as the adults. Annabelle was dressed in a sunny yellow frock that seemed to suit the child's excitement at being included in an adult affair.

"Ooh, Auntie H'ro, you look like a princess!" Annabelle squealed as Hero entered the nursery. The little girl sat on a child-sized couch, petting her kitten beside her.

"And so do you, my darling. Your new dress is very pretty." Hero mouthed a thank-you to the nurse.

"Nurse Henson says I must leave Bitsy here when we go down to supper. Do I really got to do that? Bitsy will get lonely."

"Yes," Hero said firmly. "You must leave Bitsy here. And she will not be lonely because Nell will be coming to play with her while we have supper." Two-year-old Nell, Diana's youngest, would be given over to the care of Nurse Henson while the rest of the family dined.

"Oh. Aw right, then." Annabelle jumped down from the couch and turned to admonish the kitten. "Now you be good, Bitsy. No scratching."

Hero, Annabelle, and Nurse Henson went down to the drawing room, where Annabelle was introduced with proper curtsies to her Uncle Michael and her new Aunt, Monique, who promptly became "Auntie 'Nique." When the toddler, Nell, had departed with the nurse, there ensued one of those awkward silences that sometimes occur in any gathering of people.

Annabelle, standing at Hero's knee after everyone was seated, looked around the room, then up at Hero. "Where is Mr. Ainrye?"

All eyes focused on Hero, and she could tell that the Tamblins had been informed of the afternoon's bombshell news. She leaned closer to Annabelle and said, "He had to be somewhere else this evening."

"Oh. Where?"

"I—I'm not sure," Hero said, accepting the glass of sherry her father handed her. She watched as Annabelle was given a glass of lemonade— only half-filled, as a precaution against spills.

"But he's coming back, isn't he?" Hero knew that Annabelle, despite being firmly ensconced in the Whitby family, had latent memories of the first three years of her life—and feared being abandoned by new people who appeared. *Drat that man!* She chalked up yet another mark against him. "Uh, not tonight, he's not," she said to Annabelle. "Now, why don't you tell Freddie about your new trick with your pony?" She gave the child a gentle shove in the direction of Diana's younger son.

"You handled that well," Diana, who sat next to Hero on the horsehair settee, said softly, and touched her glass to Hero's. In a more normal tone, she announced, "Michael, it is wonderful that you have given us an excuse to have us all together. What with Anthony and Jonathan at school so much of the year, it is rare for us to have this pleasure."

Michael and his bride occupied another settee set at an angle to the one on which Hero and Diana sat. Dr. Whitby and his son-in-law, Milton, occupied winged chairs that had been moved to be part of the conversational group. Anthony and Jonathan and Diana's two daughters, Juliet and Portia, sat on straight-backed, cushioned chairs behind the Tamblin parents; the girls, aged twelve and nine, were obviously awestruck by the stylish young woman Michael had brought into the family's midst. Hero had noted that others had been given glasses of sherry or lemonade as appropriate to their ages.

"So—Michael—tell us the story of you and Monique," Diana demanded in an "older sister" kind of tone.

Michael grinned and glanced at his wife before responding. He set his glass on the table in front of him. "It was just after the Battle of Waterloo."

"But that was over a year ago!" Hero said. "And all this time, you never said a word?"

"Let him finish," Diana admonished.

"Yes, allow me to tell *my* tale *my* way, Hero. This lovely woman came to the hospital looking for her brother. She was dressed in fine clothes and seemed totally out of place in that environment. Many citizens of Brussels fought beside the allies, you know."

"My brother, Andre, he no come home after the battle. Not the next day, either. I so hoped he merely injured, but—" Monique shrugged and looked down at her hands in her lap.

Michael slipped a comforting arm around his wife's shoulders. "I helped her look for him, but we did not find him. I think I fell in love with her during that search." He looked at his wife, who smiled at him. "But I was sorely afraid I would never see her again. You simply cannot imagine what chaos reigned in that city. I mean there were wounded everywhere, in our hospital, of course—we had taken over the cathedral, I might add—in private homes, and even lying in the streets."

"It truly was 'orrible," Monique said.

"But to my surprise," Michael went on, "she came back the next day, donned an apron, and started washing dirty bodies with ugly wounds. She was great with patients, especially with those speaking French."

"Did you find your brother?" Diana asked gently.

"No," Monique answered. "He had died in the first onslaught at Quatre Bras. H-he was buried with his comrades."

"I'm so sorry," Diana murmured, and the rest of the Whitby clan nodded their sympathy.

"So the two of you worked together, eh?" Dr. Whitby asked.

"We did. But she was a real woman of mystery." Michael grinned teasingly at Monique. "She'd appear at the hospital each day in a fine dress, put on an apron, and get to work, but she refused to let me take her home or even send one of our orderlies with her."

"They were all needed right there," Monique interposed.

"Turns out," Michael went on, "her family had no idea what she was doing. Her father is a lawyer, one of the city's best-known judges, actually."

"Papa has very strict notions of what women should do," Monique said. "Tending wounded foreign soldiers was not something he approved of."

"Nor did he approve of her walking out with a foreign soldier—officer or no," Michael said. "You won't believe what I went through to convince first the daughter and then her father that I am a worthwhile sort of person!"

"Hmm. Perhaps they sensed the truth," Hero teased.

"But I persevered and finally won her, and then him, over."

Stewart appeared in the doorway to signal Hero that supper was being served. Conversation during the meal was lively. Hero was pleased to see the ease with which they all seemed to slip back into the sort of family interaction they had been used to, though Michael had been away for over four years. Monique seemed rather quiet, but surely that was to be expected when a bride was meeting her new family for the first time.

After supper, at Hero's suggestion, Diana sent her two daughters to the nursery, where they would help entertain Freddie and Annabelle who were to remain in the playroom until the Tamblin family were ready to return home. The children would have their own tea there. The rest of the family retired to the library where Stewart delivered a heavily laden tea tray. From one end of the couch she shared with Diana and Milton, Hero had command of the tea tray. Her father and the two young boys sat in scattered chairs. Michael and Monique sat in winged chairs across from Hero. When the tea had been poured to everyone's satisfaction and her father had offered his eldest son and his son-in-law brandies to accompany it, Dr. Whitby, as the family patriarch, spoke.

"I have filled Michael in on what has been going on in Weyburn recently," he announced. "I think as a family we need to be prepared for what the future might hold."

Hero saw the others all nod and that Milton had instinctively reached for his wife's hand.

"Smugglers are hardly a new phenomenon for any coastal town in all of Cornwall," Michael said.

Trust Michael to jump right to the heart of things, Hero thought.

"That is true," her father agreed. "However, since the war, the government's pursuit of such activities has intensified profoundly. And, heretofore, no one in our family has been directly involved. But now—"

Milton sighed heavily. "You must know I never intended—I had no idea things would get so out of hand."

"Mr. Teague threatened to evict us if Milton failed to help him after he lost those other members of the gang," Diana said. "And after what happened to the Thompson family..."

"Anthony and Jonathan?" her father prompted.

Milton gave his father-in-law a bleak look. "Bad timing. They just happened to be there when Teague came to the house. Had I been able to keep them out of it, believe me, I would have," Milton added, and Hero heard the anguish in his voice. "All I wanted to do was save my family's home. And I'm not the only one."

"No, I don't suppose you are," his father-in-law said.

"At least half the locals involved are there because Teague has some threat hanging over our heads," Milton said. "Those thugs he brought in from Bristol are very efficient at keeping people in line too," he added bitterly.

"The question is, what now?" Michael said. "Can the Abbey's steward make a threat of eviction stick?"

"He certainly did with the Thompsons," Diana said.

"That was months ago, though," her father said. "Now that the owner has shown some interest—"

"I shouldn't put too much stock in that," Hero said. "Alexander Sterne managed to ignore the situation for years. Sir Benjamin died eight years ago. Sterne has allowed Teague free rein for all that time."

"Well, now, Hero, in fairness," her father said, "Sterne probably did not know what was happening. I'm sure he thought things were being handled properly."

"It was his *duty* to know," she said, setting her cup and saucer down with a clatter. "It was his responsibility, and now it is all his fault."

"Be fair, Hero," her father admonished. "People make choices in life based on matters they see at hand. Isn't that right, Milton?"

"Yes, sir," Milton responded glumly and reached for his brandy goblet.

"For what it is worth," Michael said, "the major has been out of the country for God knows how long. He was in India with Wellington and then on the Peninsula. Injured several times. Men in his regiment practically worshiped him."

"I have no doubt he was a good soldier," Hero conceded. "But as a landowner, he abrogated his responsibilities."

"I'm just saying," Michael went on, "that a man does not command that kind of respect without showing genuine concern for his people. He earns it."

Diana brought them back to the topic at hand. "But what are we to do now? I cannot stand the idea that my husband or my son or my brother may b-be killed in a fight with the militia." Her voice caught.

"I know one thing for sure," Milton said, patting her hand. "Neither Anthony nor I—nor Jonathan neither—will be parties to luring another ship to disaster." He looked at the two boys for corroboration of his statement and they both nodded.

"I'd say do nothing for a while at least," the patriarch of the family said thoughtfully. "Just go along as before. I cannot believe that Lord Sterne has been here in Weyburn all this time without learning a thing or two. Let us give him a few days at least…"

"I suppose eight years later, a few days more will make little difference," Hero said grudgingly. She knew she was being stubborn, but she was not ready to entertain forgiving thoughts about one Alexander Sterne.

"What about the militia?" Jonathan asked, but no one seemed to have a response. Soon afterwards, Diana and Milton gathered up their brood and departed for home before it got too dark to travel safely.

Chapter 18

By the time Teague was expected at the Abbey, the housekeeper and butler had been up for a good two hours supervising the staff in subjecting the library to a thorough dusting and polishing. Alex found that whatever oil the maids had used on the furniture imparted a pleasant, woodsy smell, and they had left the French doors that looked out onto the garden open, so the fresh outdoors blended with the tangy cleanness. In his comfortable buckskin breeches, his shirt open at the neck and sleeves rolled up, Alex sat at a huge oak desk awaiting the arrival of his steward. He was not at all surprised that the man had chosen to try to assert command of the meeting by arriving late.

When Mullins finally announced Teague's arrival a good quarter past the hour, Alex stood to greet him. He thought the steward somewhat overdressed for the occasion, in black wool trousers, a silver embroidered waistcoat, and a bottle-green coat. His neckcloth would have made Beau Brummel proud, Alex observed sourly. Teague removed his hat and held it in one hand; the other held the ledgers against his chest, and a large ring of keys.

"Good morning, my lord. I say, I was glad on receiving your message that you have decided you no longer need the protection of Hero Whitby's skirts in dealing with us Weyburn folks." His affable tone belied the insult of his words.

Alex sat back down and said in a carefully controlled, deceptively calm tone, "And may *I* say that an insult is hardly the wisest way to begin this conference."

Teague made of show of stacking the ledgers on a corner of the desk. He ignored Alex's comment. "Your ledgers, my lord, just as you requested. I trust you will find them all in order. The keys too." There was a great jangling of keys as he laid these on top of the leather-bound books. "Can't see why you wanted all those at once—we cannot possibly inspect every building and enclosed area in a single day."

"Please, have a seat, Mr. Teague." Alex gestured to a chair he had himself placed in front of the desk. "We shall not be inspecting property today. And I should expect to find that these books align themselves fully with these that Mr. MacIntosh brought from my solicitor in London." Alex pointed to a similar stack of ledgers on the opposite corner of the desk and felt a twinge of satisfaction at seeing an expression of surprise on his employee's face.

"Ah, well, I cannot say what another man's books will have in them, but I guarantee you that mine are in order," Teague blustered, and sat, casually leaning back in his chair, draping an arm along its back and crossing his legs, either perfectly relaxed or trying hard to appear so.

Alex had previously studied the solicitor's ledgers at great length, and now he opened first one and then another at random and compared certain entries with what he found in those Teague had produced. He ignored Teague's signs of growing restlessness, shifting in his chair and drumming the fingers of one hand against his knee.

Finally, Alex nodded and said, "Yes. They do line up quite nicely."

"I could have told you they would, that this is a waste of time—mine and yours." Alex looked up to see a smug sneer on Teague's face.

"I expected nothing less, given the fact that Mr. Montague merely recorded for me information you sent him." Alex paused and held the other man's gaze for a long moment. Then he reached into a drawer of the desk and extracted several sheets of notes. "Perhaps you were unaware that Mr. Montague visited Weyburn some months ago." Alex watched closely as Teague tried to hide his alarm and calculation in absorbing this information.

"Seems I might have heard something about some stranger nosing around, but he did not show the simple courtesy of contacting *me*." Teague sounded aggrieved, but Alex could not tell if the grievance was real or feigned.

"Mr. Montague's notes coincide almost precisely with those I made after Miss Whitby and I inspected the properties very recently."

Teague sat up straight; his face was flushed with anger. "Now, see here—"

"No, Mr. Teague, *you* see here." Alex tapped the ledgers with a forefinger. "There are too many instances of expenses listed in these books for things like a roof on a farmhouse, an enlarged barn, new windows on outbuildings of the copper mine, labor for fencing, and so on—improvements here and there that were simply never made."

Teague gave him a condescending look. "You've been listening to too many whiners, my lord. Lazy rascals always expecting something for nothing."

"I *have* talked with a number of people—but I also have Montague's report, and I have eyes in my head. What Montague and I have actually seen simply does not add up with recorded expenses. It is called embezzlement, sir. And for that reason I am terminating your employment, effective immediately."

"You're what? Terminating—? You can't do that." Teague raised his voice in surprise and fury; his face took on an even deeper shade of red. His hands fisted on his knees. "I've been steward here for fifteen years, for God's sake."

Alex held his gaze in an accusing glare. "For at least half that time, you seem to have been far more interested in lining your own pockets than in tending to the needs of the people and property of Weyburn Abbey."

"Sir Benjamin found no fault with my work."

"In his last years, my uncle was a sick old man. He liked you and he trusted you. You abused his goodwill. And he's been gone for a long time—during which you have abused mine. It's over."

"You can't get away with this. I'll sue. I have a contract—"

"I can and I am." Alex was adamant. "The contract was with Sir Benjamin. Both my solicitor and I have studied it carefully. I am giving you twenty-one days to vacate the steward's house that you currently occupy. If you are still in the area after that, I shall bring suit against you in a court of law. As it is, you are getting off easy—far too easy for what you've stolen, first from Sir Benjamin and then from me."

Teague jumped to his feet and bent over the desk. "You rotten son-of-a-bitch. You'll pay for this day's work, let me tell you! Nobody—nobody!—treats Willard Teague in such a high-handed fashion and gets away with it!"

Alex stared at him, one eyebrow raised. "Save the threats."

A single hard knock sounded at the door. Mac poked his head around the edge and asked innocently, "I say, my lord, do you need anything?"

"Mr. Teague is just leaving. Show him to the door, will you?"

"I know the way." Teague jammed his hat onto his head, mussing his perfectly coiffed blond hair in the process, and stomped out of the room, brushing by Mac as he did so.

Mac came in and, at Alex's gesture, took the seat Teague had vacated. "I heard that discussion only when he started yelling. I must say, Major, you ain't lost your touch in dressing down some miscreant." Mac grinned broadly, then asked, "Now what, sir?"

Alex reached behind him to give the bellpull a tug. "Now, we call a meeting of Abbey people."

Mullins answered immediately.

"Guess you heard him yelling too, eh?" Alex asked, knowing full well Mullins had probably been hovering in the hallway.

"Yes, my lord."

"Well? What did you think? Are we well rid of him?"

"I—uh—that is not for me to say, my lord. Did you need something, my lord?"

Alex sighed inwardly at the man's continued caution around his new employer and said, "Yes. I should like you to send one of the grooms around to all the farms and the homes of the mine foremen and their deputies, if such exist, calling them to a meeting here in the ballroom tomorrow morning at, say, ten o'clock. That should give them time for morning chores and such."

"Very good, my lord." The butler turned to leave.

"Oh! And say they are to bring their wives as well. Wives always seem to have a great deal to say about any matter at hand."

Mullins grinned and nodded. "Mine does, at least."

"I want you and Mrs. Mullins at this meeting too—as well as the entire indoor and outdoor staff here at the main house. You will need to arrange chairs and benches in the ballroom. Maybe bring up one of those kegs of ale from the cellar, and provide some lemonade—whatever Mrs. Mullins thinks. This is a meeting, not a party, but people deserve a drink, at least, for their efforts."

"Very good, my lord."

When the butler had closed the door behind him, Alex said, "Now, Mac, let's go and look at the master's suite and find more permanent bedchambers for both of us."

* * * *

Several miles away, Hero was also involved that morning in the allocation of bedchambers. It had started when Hero joined her father, who sat at the head of the breakfast table before any of the others had come down yet. Whitby waited until his daughter had filled her plate from the sideboard, taken a seat on the corner at his right, and poured herself a cup of coffee from the carafe on the table.

"The topic of the day," the doctor announced with mock solemnity, "is bedrooms. More specifically, who's to be in which bedchamber."

"I'm quite satisfied right where I am," Hero said, sidestepping the topic she knew her father was broaching.

"I am not talking about you, and you know it. You have been in your corner room ever since you left the nursery—well, except for those years you were away at school. Even then, that room was yours—with Michael just across the hall. No, my dear, I am talking about Michael and Monique."

"Yes, Papa." She recalled Mrs. Hutchins's comment on the same subject.

"His room is too small for the two of them. They should move into my rooms, and I will take the room down here, now that Adam—Sterne—has vacated it. After all, I designed that room for just this eventuality. Just not this soon, perhaps."

"Michael should have the master's suite?"

"Why not? He will be the master in due time. He will take over my position at the clinic. Relieve you some. Lord knows you have carried the practice in the last year what with gout and arthritis and general attacks of old age that have bedeviled me."

Hero laid down her fork and reached for her coffee cup. She smiled. "Do stop, Papa. You are not so decrepit as all that."

"I'm getting there, though." He shoved his empty plate aside and relaxed more casually in his chair. "Mind you, I intend to fight the good fight all the way. And the two of you will just have to put up with my meddling."

"Your meddling? Papa, *you* are the mainstay of this clinic. When Weyburn people need to see a doctor, they think immediately of Dr. Whitby—Dr. Charles Whitby—you."

"Perhaps. But we—and they—have always known that Michael would take over one day."

She looked down at her plate. "I—uh—yes, I suppose they have." *She* had always known it too, but it had been years since it had been said so baldly in her presence.

He sat up straighter and reached for her hand. "Hero, I meant no slight to your medical expertise. You do wonderful work. Wonderful. You make all those naysayers about women in medicine seem the fools they are. We are. Sad to say, I once thought the way they do. But you taught me otherwise."

Hero felt tears welling at his sincere compliment of her work, which was so integral to her sense of self. Had she not buried herself in this work for years and struggled to learn and learn and learn? "Thank you, Papa," she whispered and squeezed his hand.

He still gripped her hand and gave it a little shake. "But you know as well as I do that England is not ready, Cornwall is not ready, and I very much doubt Weyburn is ready, for a woman to head an important medical clinic—even if it is that woman's innovations and dedication that have made much of its reputation. But be assured, my daughter, so long as I am alive, you have a place right here. And Michael feels the same way."

"Michael feels how?" Michael asked as he entered the room right behind his wife.

"I am just assuring your sister that her place in our medical facility is assured," the elder Whitby said, releasing Hero's hand. "And in our home," he added with a direct look at her.

"Of course it is." Michael held a chair for his wife and gave Hero a piercing look across the table. "Good Lord! Don't tell me you doubted that."

"Um, not really," she lied, "but it *is* pleasant to hear it said aloud."

Michael grinned at her and raised his voice to shout, "Hear ye! Hear ye! Hero Gwendolyn Whitby is ours! She belongs to us—whether she wants to or not."

"Michel…" his wife chided with a laugh.

Mrs. Hutchins came running into the dining room, a footman following. "What on earth?" she asked, her hand on her chest.

"Sorry, Mrs. Hutchins," Michael said with a chuckle. "Just a little family clarification, if you will."

"Goodness. I had quite forgot how chaotic things can get with two young men in residence. I'll send in more coffee," the housekeeper said, and left just as Jonathan entered the dining room.

"What was all the shouting about?" he asked, making a beeline for the sideboard.

As the three latecomers filled their plates, the doctor said, "Would you believe it started with a discussion of bedrooms?"

"Bedrooms?" Michael echoed as he and Monique sat down.

"I'm not moving out of my room," Jonathan said around a mouthful of scrambled egg.

The elder doctor explained his plan.

"Oh, no, no," Monique said, placing a hand on her husband's arm. "We would not dream of putting you out of your *chambre, mon père.*" Hero found her mixture of French and English charming. She was sure Michael did too.

Michael said, "My old room *is* crowded for the two of us, but why don't we just knock out a wall between it and the guest room next to it?

Or, Monique and I can move to the room on this floor. That room is quite spacious, as I remember it."

"Ridiculous," his father said. "That is just postponing the inevitable. I built this room for me. I intend to enjoy it. Now you and Monique finish your breakfast and then take a look at my suite of rooms and see what changes you would like to make."

"Yes, sir."

Later in the morning, as she reviewed that scene in her mind, Hero was glad to see the issue handled so amicably, and she was heartily warmed by reassurance from both her father and her brother of her place in their world of medicine. She had no doubt there would have to be accommodations made from time to time. It was apparent that Monique and Michael had worked together well in Belgium and it was equally apparent that they both intended to continue working together here.

But what changes would have to be made in the family dynamics if—when—Michael and Monique had children? At the moment, Annabelle was the darling of the household. Would she still be so treasured when there were other children in the house—children who were known to be truly Whitby children? Hero wondered if she shouldn't just set up her own household—in town, say. Her mother had established small legacies for both her daughters, so such a plan was financially feasible, though she knew it would cause quite a stir for a young single woman to live apart from her family. Or perhaps she could remove to Sally Knowlton's establishment and help enlarge it.

Stop it. Just stop, she admonished herself. *You are already borrowing problems from a future that is not even showing itself yet. Have you learned nothing about enjoying what you have at any given moment?*

Her mind immediately, and unwillingly, shifted itself to Adam—Alex, as her father had said he preferred to be called. She had certainly enjoyed that interlude in her life, had she not? But it had been no more real than one of Annabelle's fairy tales. *Oh, come now*, she chastised herself. *At least be honest with yourself. His lovemaking was the most real experience of your entire life.* As she delved further into what had been between them, she was forced to admit, though only to herself, that it was not merely the physical passion that had awakened a long hidden need in her—real and wonderful as that had been.

No, what first occurred to her was the comfort, the feeling of contentment, of completion she had felt in his mere presence. She recalled their laughing together, sharing stories of growing up, talking about books and history and politics. Arguing, disagreeing, but cherishing the other's views too.

That afternoon at the beach, reading Wordsworth had been one of the most pleasant of her life; she knew she would treasure it forever. Would she ever again encounter another human being with whom she felt so "in tune," so at peace?

You need to remember, she told herself sharply, *that this is the man whose selfish indifference has created so much pain and suffering in the lives of people you love.* He may have proved himself brave and courageous on the battlefield, but that war has been over for a year. What's more, there had been that interlude from April of 1814 until Napoleon had escaped the following March when the nation had lost itself in the delirium of victory. Where had Lord Alexander Sterne been then? In London indulging himself. She'd heard the rumors and seen the newspaper gossip columns. And where had he been all those months prior to his arrival as a patient in the Whitby clinic? Nearly a whole year after Waterloo? Also in London, still unaware and indifferent.

How *could* she love a man like that?

Chapter 19

That afternoon Hero found the whole town abuzz with the news not only that that the amiable Mr. Wainwright was really none other than Lord Alexander Sterne, heretofore the absentee owner of Weyburn Abbey, but that he had only that morning fired his steward. She had gone into Weyburn to pay a call on Sally Knowlton's three patients, then she stopped by the vicar's household to deliver a book her father was recommending to the churchman. The vicar, Archibald Cooper, was not at home, but his wife, Dorothy, welcomed the break in her routine that a visit from Miss Whitby offered, insisting that Hero join her for a cup of tea in the vicarage drawing room. Mrs. Cooper was a plump, fussy kind of woman, in her midfifties, well-meaning and with a generous spirit. Her drawing room reflected her personality with its proliferation of knickknacks, framed profiles and watercolors of her children when they were young, deep-rose-colored overstuffed furniture, and hand-crocheted doilies all about. She was eager to elaborate on the news that Hero had already heard from Sally.

"I cannot tell you how surprised Mr. Cooper and I were to hear that that nice Mr. Wainwright was really Lord Alexander Sterne—owner of the Abbey, no less! My goodness gracious! Such a surprise. He'd had tea right here in this very room not a week ago. A duke's son! And just as normal and down-to-earth as you please." Having waited for the tea to steep, she now paused to pour for Hero and herself.

Hero accepted the proffered cup. "Yes, that news was a surprise to many of us."

"Some folks really do not know what to make of it all. I mean"—Mrs. Cooper leaned forward in a conspiratorial manner—"why did he pretend all that time to be someone he wasn't? Did you have no idea, what with his being at the Manor all that time?"

"I am sure he had his reasons." Hero was determined to avoid discussing his lordship's motives, especially since she still had so many questions about those herself. However, it came as something of a surprise to find that she did not want others thinking ill of him. "Are others condemning him then?" she asked.

"Some are. Mr. Wellman, who, as you know, likes to be first with such news, was rather annoyed that the Barkleys knew this before he did. He says now that he always suspected 'something fishy about that fellow.' But most folks are more tolerant, taking a wait-and-see attitude. Which I personally think to be the wiser course. Wouldn't you agree, Miss Whitby?"

Hero nodded. "Withholding judgment on another is usually a sensible approach." She set her cup down, finding the tea too hot to drink.

The other woman prattled on. "Now that he has dismissed Mr. Teague, there is sure to be a great deal of controversy over that. Mr. Teague has quite a following in this town, as you well know. On the other hand, he does come in for his share of resentment too. People haven't forgot what happened to the Thompsons. And his general demeanor is not exactly engaging, though some do consider him quite handsome."

"Handsome is as handsome does," Hero said absently, her mind still preoccupied by what Teague's dismissal might mean for the people of Weyburn. She deliberately turned the conversation to what she knew to be Mrs. Cooper's pet project: the establishment of a nursery school for very young children in the town.

On her way home, Hero could not stop her mind from returning to the news of Teague's being fired. Before leaving the town, she had stopped briefly to say hello to Samuel Porter, the blacksmith-mayor.

"I'm not sure what to make of any of it, Miss Hero," Sam had said, "but Willard Teague—he's been drinking some over at the inn this afternoon, along with a couple of those fellows he brought in from Bristol. You know the ones I mean?"

Hero nodded. "Teague's bully boys."

"Yeh. Them. Teague's been ranting about how 'that fancy boy from London has not heard the last of this.' Swears he will get even."

"Perhaps someone should warn his lordship."

"The Jacobs lad did just that. Said he don't want his and his da's savin' a good man to go to waste, 'Specially at the hands of someone like Teague."

Hero started to smile, then bit her lip. "I hope young Jacobs does not bring the wrath of Teague down on his family with talk like that—especially if Teague is feeling resentful and abused. Who knows what he might do?"

"It was just me and his da heard 'im. And he rode out right away to the Abbey."

Hero tried to convince herself that her only real concern in this turn of events was for her neighbors, that she was actively putting behind her whatever might have been between her and Adam—her and Alexander Sterne. She would simply refuse to let one act of caring for his dependents override the fact that he had continued to live his lie far beyond any need to do so.

But late the next afternoon Diana arrived with news that set her mind in a whirl again. Michael had gone off after the midday meal to show his bride around the countryside. Jonathan was off to the beach with several friends in what Hero was certain was perfectly innocent play. Her father was busy with a footman, moving favorite pieces of furniture from the master's suite and arranging things to his satisfaction in his new quarters. With Annabelle presumably still napping under the nurse's watchful eye, Hero had escaped to the terrace, where the sea and her own muddled thoughts managed to hold her attention more than the book that lay on the table beside her.

"Stewart told me I would find you out here," Diana called as she came around the corner of the house.

"Diana! You startled me! What are you doing here at this hour? Has something happened?"

"I have had a very interesting morning, dear sister mine, and I just had to share it with you." Diana sat at the table across from Hero and folded her hands.

"I'm listening."

"Lord Alexander Sterne—whom you may know," Diana began teasingly, "called a meeting of the Abbey's farmers and the shift leaders at the mine this morning. And you will not believe what he has done."

"Dismissed Teague, is what I heard," Hero said.

"He did that too. But he also gave us a list of things that he is going to see done immediately on Abbey properties—including our roof! Is that not just absolutely wonderful?"

"'Gave us'? You were at this meeting?"

"Yes. He insisted that wives come too. And everyone did. There must have been fifty or sixty people in that room, what with all the servants at the Abbey proper. It was in the ballroom. I'd quite forgot how elegant that room is."

"Is that all? He told you about improvements?"

"Heavens, Hero. Is that not enough? But, no, it was not all. He asked everyone to tell him things they would like to see done in their area of the Abbey holdings. And he had that Mr. MacIntosh write everything down. Then he said he would take them all into consideration, though he cautioned us not to expect all this to be accomplished yesterday."

Hero smiled at this detail, and asked, "Why did he include the women? That seems most unusual."

"One of the men asked him that same question—that old curmudgeon, Stevens—and his lordship laughed and said he thought the wives would keep both his and their husbands' noses to the grindstone to see that matters improved. We women all agreed with that, of course!"

"So the owner of the Abbey has managed to redeem himself in your eyes," Hero observed.

"Well, yes. To some extent, at least. Hero, we have waited eight years— eight years!—for someone to see to the needs of this estate. Actually, more than that, for after he lost his wife, Sir Benjamin really lost interest in keeping things up, let alone making real improvements. But you know that. You saw it. And you have seen the devastation that resulted."

Pleased to see her sister so energized and optimistic, Hero hesitated to respond.

Diana went on. "And it's not just been the neglect of buildings and fields and crops and herds. It does something to the spirit to see that one has so little to look forward to. I wish you could have been at that meeting this morning—to see how truly hopeful people were for a change."

Hero reached across the table to grip her sister's hand briefly. "I am truly glad to see you so cheerful, Diana, and I do most sincerely hope that your optimism is not misplaced."

"Why are you so negative about his lordship?" Diana asked. "I thought you liked him. In fact, I wondered if your feelings for him might be much deeper. I hoped they were."

"Ah, Diana. Ever the romantic, aren't you?"

"Was I so wrong, then? Be honest, Hero."

"I—I don't know. Maybe for a while. But, Diana—he lied. He kept from us—from me—the most basic information: who he was. I find it hard to forgive that deception."

"Perhaps he had his reasons," Diana said.

Hero recognized the very line of reasoning she herself had used with Mrs. Cooper, but she refused to dwell on that. She redirected the conversation. "I suppose the whole town and half the countryside will be beating a path to door of the Abbey to greet the new owner now that he is known to be in residence."

"That will do them little good. He will not be there for the next week or so."

"What? Why? How do you know this?"

"He told us as the meeting ended. He is going to London to find a new steward and settle other business matters, he said."

"Hah! I should not be at all surprised if he just stays in his London playground and sends his new steward to act in his absence, just as he did with Teague all these years."

Diana gave her a look of exasperation. "Hero—"

Hero threw up her hands in a mock defensive gesture. "All right. All right. I shall hope for the best."

"As will I."

* * * *

Alex had felt good about the meeting with his Abbey people. He knew this was not the best of times to be heading off to London, but he had two pressing reasons for doing just that. He really did need to find a new steward who would be able to keep track of the details of the huge business of the Abbey, someone with knowledge of logistics and experience in handling such matters. And he knew just the man: a former army captain named Alistair Gibson, who had been discharged from the army after losing an arm and having a leg severely injured in the Battle of Vitoria. The trouble was, Alex had no idea where the man might be these days, but he knew a good place to start was the Horse Guards, army headquarters in London.

His other reason was the Abbey's urgent need of an infusion of ready cash. Alex had invested his own money wisely during his army years, but he had not nearly what would be needed. He knew—and he knew he could demonstrate—that the Abbey could be made profitable, but the people he would have to convince of that were bankers—in London.

He hated leaving Weyburn when things were in such turmoil for both the town that depended on the Abbey and for the people directly connected to the estate. Despite his assurances at that meeting of Abbey people, he knew they still felt a great deal of uncertainty. How would they react to his dashing off to London after making grandiose promises to them?

There was also that unfinished business of the smugglers operating so close to home. He desperately wanted to be on the scene when that issue was settled once and for all.

And, finally, he hated leaving the area now because of the unresolved situation with Hero. He knew she was not indifferent to him, that a woman of her integrity would never have responded to him as she had without a sense of commitment—whether she was ready to admit to that or not. Somehow, he had to convince her that he truly was worthy of her trust—and her love. But he could hardly do that in London, could he?

So—best get this over with.

Knowing he could not yet endure a long journey on horseback, he traveled by post chaise, the fastest mode of travel available, but also the most expensive, what with the hire of coach, driver, and post boy at each leg of the trip. Even so, the journey would take two-and-a-half or three days, depending on the weather. *No wonder so few people travel much*, he grumbled to himself. He congratulated himself on having filched two books from what was now his own library to occupy the travel time.

On arriving in London the third afternoon, he was surprised to see the knocker in place on the door of Thornleigh House, and then delighted to find his parents in residence. After a quick hello to them, he went to his own room and freshened up, torn between a desire to lie down and perhaps have a nap until time for supper and a wish to greet his parents properly. The latter won out and he found them in the family drawing room, his father immersed in a newspaper and his mother doing some sort of stitchery.

"I must say, I was surprised to find you here," he said, taking a seat at one end of the settee on which his mother sat. "I have been imagining you still soaking up the history and culture of the Roman Empire or the Renaissance artists."

His father laid aside the newspaper. "Your mother decided three months had satisfied her desire for foreign history and culture for a while. She missed her children and grandchildren."

"But we are going again sometime," she said. "To Greece or perhaps Egypt. Perhaps we shall persuade some of you lot to accompany us." She patted his knee.

"We've been home only a week and she's already thinking of dragging me off again," his father said in mock weariness.

"Pish-tosh," she said. "You enjoyed the journey as much as I did." She turned to face her son. "We were told you were off to Cornwall. I hope you found all well there."

"Not exactly." Glossing over his injury, the mere mention of which alarmed his mother, he told them of how matters stood in the Abbey and its environs.

"I am so glad that you met Dr. Whitby," the duchess said. "He and Benjamin were friends, but there was enough of an age difference between him and me that I did not know him well. By the time he had come home from medical school in Scotland, I had gone off to school myself. But I always admired him. Had a bit of a girlish crush on him, as a matter of fact."

"Here, now," her husband growled.

She ignored him and went on. "And the Coopers are still there. How wonderful."

"This business of smugglers operating so openly is a bit worrisome, I would imagine," the duke said, changing the tone of the conversation.

"Very worrisome," Alex replied. "And that is the big reason I need to return as soon as possible."

"But not the only reason?" His mother raised an eyebrow.

"Well, there is always something with a large property, is there not?" he equivocated.

She gave him a knowing look, but did not pursue whatever line of thought she was toying with.

He told of them of his intent to search out Alistair Gibson and offer him the job of steward at the Abbey, and of his need to obtain funding for his plans for the Abbey.

His father nodded his approval. "Horse Guards should be able to put you on track for locating this Gibson fellow. If that does not work out, I could send you Nelson to help until you can find someone." The Duke of Thornleigh paused, seeming almost shy as he added, "And if you'd like, I could accompany you when you go to visit the bankers."

Alex snorted softly. "If I'd like? I had intended to drop your name, but having you there in the flesh, so to speak, would be even better! Never hurts to have a peer of the realm on one's side."

"Or," his father began in a measured tone, "I could just lend you the sum outright."

"I appreciate that offer, Father. Truly, I do. But I'd rather do it more or less on my own. Besides, you will have a trip to Greece or Egypt to pay for." He grinned at his mother.

He saw his parents exchange a knowing glance and then each nodded affirmation of their silent communication.

"Right." His father rose to ring for a servant. "Tomorrow we shall go shopping for money, but for now, let us all have a drink before we go down for supper."

They spent the rest of the evening chatting about family, and Alex went to bed later feeling more at ease with his parents than he ever remembered being since becoming an adult. He was aware anew of the intensity of the relationship between his mother and father and he thought about it with a sharp degree of envy. This turn of thought immediately brought a vision of Hero to mind. He drifted off to sleep reliving those three glorious nights he'd had with her.

But at some point in the earliest hours of the morning, he woke abruptly from yet another journey to yet another battlefield. Scenes of beautiful young men dying, body parts and abandoned weapons strewn about, blood and mud and confusion, the moans of the wounded blending with the screams of injured horses. *God! Will it never end?* he asked himself. He got up, grabbed a robe, and sat beside the window, mindlessly watching as the darkness gave way to something resembling daylight over the rooftops of the city.

The next day, as he and his father had conjectured, the bank was more than willing to lend a sufficient sum to the son of a duke for whatever purposes that son might have in mind. Although he had had little doubt of the outcome—especially after his father had offered to accompany him—Alex breathed a sigh of relief just to know that hurdle had been conquered. He also met with his solicitor and apprised of him what had transpired at the Abbey.

The following day, he set out to find Alistair Gibson.

This task proved to be more difficult than he had expected. Army headquarters had no current address for Gibson himself, though they did have an address in Richmond for a sister, a Mrs. James Reeves, who had been listed as "next of kin" to be notified in the event of his death on the battlefield. Alex returned to Thornleigh House for a proper mount and rode out to Richmond to find Gibson's sister, who turned out to be the wife of a butcher. She was waiting on customers as her husband prepared cuts of meat behind her. Alex waited politely in line to speak with her, and when it was his turn he handed her his card and introduced himself merely as Alexander Sterne. She took the card and, without looking at it, put it in a pocket of her bloodstained apron.

When he asked about her brother, she was guarded in her answer. "My brother is not here, but I will see that he gets your card."

"I should like to contact him in person, Mrs. Reeves. It would be most helpful if you could just give me his direction," Alex replied.

She sighed. "If he owes you money, I am sure he will pay you just as soon as he can. His wife has been ill recently and the family are having a difficult time."

Alex gave her what he hoped was a reassuring smile. "He does not owe me anything, and I was rather hoping he would be able to help me with a difficulty I am facing."

She pulled the card out of her pocket and looked at it, turned halfway toward her husband, and said in a louder voice, "*Lord* Alexander Sterne? What would a lord want with my brother?"

Her husband slammed a cleaver down on his cutting block and came to look over her shoulder at the card. "Hmm. I seem to remember Al talkin' 'bout a Major Sterne." He looked up at Alex.

Alex nodded. "The same. Can you help me?" He was aware now of people behind him.

"That depends," Reeves said. "Don't know as Al would want us giving out information on him."

"I assure you, sir," Alex said, "that I mean Mr. Gibson no ill at all. In fact, I have a proposition for him that he may very well wish to consider."

Reeves looked at his wife, who shrugged in an it's-up-to-you sort of gesture. "He's working as a scrivener for some lawyer in the Inns of Court," Reeves said. "Walker or Walter—something like that."

It was obvious that the Reeves couple were parting with no more information than that, so Alex took his leave. As the door closed behind him, he heard the shop already buzzing with the news of a lord's having visited there.

By the time he arrived back in London, it was far too late to visit Gibson at his place of work. Alex fumed at the Reeves couple for not giving him any more information, but he resigned himself to an extra day in the city. That evening he accompanied his father in visiting White's, the duke's choice of the gentlemen's clubs, where Alex played several hands of vingt-et-un while his father visited with old friends. Late the next morning, Alex presented himself at the law office of Walker and Sons, where his card caused a slight stir and a good deal of curiosity when he asked to see not one of the solicitors, but one of their scriveners. But soon enough Alistair Gibson came from a back room. Gibson, in his midthirties, had dark red hair and worried brown eyes. He wore dark trousers held up by suspenders and a white shirt rolled up to the elbow on the right arm. His left sleeve, which was pinned up just above the wrist, was stained with ink, as were the fingers of his right hand. He walked with a limp.

"Major!" Gibson said in surprise, and wiped his hand on his trouser leg before offering it to Alex in a warm grip.

"Is there somewhere we can talk?" Alex asked.

"If you will give me time to finish the document I am working on, I will meet you at the pub around the corner, though I cannot be gone long."

Alex nodded and left. Since it was nearly noon, the pub was serving a number of lawyers and their clerks. Alex found a corner table and ordered both the set lunch and small ales for himself and Gibson. A quarter of an hour later, Gibson, wearing a black coat over his shirt, hurried in and sat across from him.

He looked down at the plate and drink. "I usually have a sandwich in the park."

"I am hoping to put a stop to that," Alex said with a smile.

"Sir?"

"I am in sore need of a steward in Cornwall, and it occurred to me that you might be interested in such a position."

"A steward? As in an estate steward?"

"A steward as in an estate steward," Alex affirmed.

"B-but I have never—I'm not sure—Cornwall? Except for school and the army, I've always lived in the city. And I've not had any experience managing anything." Gibson looked dumbfounded.

"Yes, you have," Alex said. "You were the best quartermaster officer in the entire Peninsular army. It strikes me that a steward does the same sorts of things—only he does them in a set location and he does not have to scrounge among foreign locals to obtain proper materials."

"But, sir, I've no experience," Gibson protested.

"Neither do I." Alex explained about his inheriting the property and leaving it up to his solicitor and steward to oversee matters while he was in the army and the situation as he had found it recently. "Now I am taking more direct control—but I need help. The kind I think you can give me."

"Sir, I—I don't know what to say."

"I understood your sister to say your wife has been ill," Alex said. "Have you children too?"

"Two. Timmy is three and Beth is eight months. Alice had trouble with the second babe—but she's much better now, though I was worried for a while there."

"I do not mean to pressure you overly much, but the steward's house on the estate would certainly accommodate your family," Alex said, and named a salary that he was certain exceeded what the man made copying legal documents all day. "*And,*" Alex added, "if either of us finds this does not work for us, I will ensure the expense of your returning to the city."

"Well, sir, if you are willing to take a chance with me, I'd certainly like to consider your offer. I would need to talk it over with my wife, though."

"I would think the less of you if you did not," Alex said, "but, at the risk of contradicting myself and pressuring you a great deal, I need an answer soon—like tomorrow. I must return immediately to Cornwall, but I am prepared to advance you the funds to make your way there in due time with your family—say three weeks? I should think that would be sufficient for you to give notice at your current employment."

"I'll have a definite answer for you tomorrow morning, sir, but I'm quite sure Alice will be excited about moving to the country." Gibson glanced at a pocket watch and grimaced. "Right now, sir, I have to get back to the office."

"I'll drop by here tomorrow morning, then," Alex said, standing to shake Gibson's hand again.

The next day, after meeting with Gibson, Alex started the return journey to Cornwall, secure in the knowledge that he had hired a new steward.

Chapter 20

For Hero the days dragged following her sister's visit and the disclosure of Lord Alexander's plans for the Abbey. Her own life seemed in a state of suspension even as the atmosphere in the town had taken on a more positive, cheerful note. But beneath the more buoyant morale, there was a strain of apprehension, of people waiting for a catastrophe. The smugglers seemed to be lying low for the nonce, but there was an expectation, a fear of something to come. Hero noted that many were still wary of being totally candid in conversations. The uncertainty was like a festering sore on the body politic. Hero and Diana privately consoled themselves with the fact that at least Anthony and Jonathan were out of it: The boys had returned to school—reluctantly—five days after his lordship's departure.

Swearing publicly and repeatedly that "no one was going to tell Willard Teague what he could do and where," Teague had vacated the steward's house on the estate as he had been ordered to do, but he had not left the town. In fact he, along with his children and a servant to care for them, joined the household of Jessie Howard, a soldier's widow with whom everyone knew he had been carrying on an on-again, off-again affair for several years. Mrs. Howard had two half-grown children of her own, so the addition of six people put a strain on her household. She was a rather brash, blowsy sort of woman, who supplemented her widow's jointure by taking in laundry and mending. She helped with the laundry for the inn, for instance. She had brown hair, which was helped to that color by a regular application of henna; she was rather buxom, but not unattractive. Her cheerful personality and live-and-let-live demeanor allowed her to shrug off the gossip she knew very well swirled behind her back.

Hero saw Teague in town occasionally. She usually tried to ignore him, but one morning as she stepped out of the mercantile store, where she had gone to buy sewing thread for Mrs. Hutchins, there he was, right in front of her. He had obviously been waiting to accost her. She smelled alcohol about him.

He lifted his hat. "Good morning, Hero. Allow me to walk you to your carriage."

"I-I have other errands to run," she said evasively.

"Ah, well, then I shall escort you."

"That is really not necessary."

"Indulge me." He gripped her elbow. "I suppose you have heard that I may be leaving Weyburn in a few weeks or so."

"I had heard something to that effect, yes," she replied, not looking at him.

"I want you to come with me."

"You—what?" Flabbergasted, she stopped and stared at him, and then just babbled the first thing that popped into her mind. "But Mrs. Howard—"

He snorted. "I want you, and I want you to come with me. I find myself still very much attracted to you. I have enough money stashed away in the bank in Bristol. We could have a good life there."

"Mr. Teague—" she began, but he ignored her.

"Surely what with your brother's returning with a wife, you must be a bit *de trop* in the Manor. Let me be clear: I am no longer offering you marriage. Don't know what you had going with his precious lordship, but he's gone now, isn't he? Back to London where he probably has a mistress. What's good for the goose is good for the gander, eh?"

She shook herself free of him and fairly hissed her response. "You, sir, are a scoundrel of the worst sort. That you would even dare to offer me a slip on the shoulder—it—it is simply beyond comprehension."

He made a gesture as though he would take her arm again. She flinched. "Don't touch me!"

"Oh, come now, Hero. You're no schoolgirl innocent. There is no need for you get so high-and-mighty with me."

She brushed him off and took a step to put distance between them. "And I have *never* given you permission to use my name." She was furious with herself for honing in on such a triviality. "Now get away from me or I will scream, and you know very well that someone in this town would come immediately to my aid."

He did not step closer, but he did lean toward her and say in a hoarse whisper, "Have it your way, bitch. I could have given you a good life. We would have had a great time together."

"I saw the 'good life' you gave poor Letty," she said, and turned on her heel to stomp into the nearest place of business, the bookshop–lending library. She merely stood inside the door for a moment trying to regain her composure, but the bell had rung when she opened the door, and the girl who tended the counter came from the back room.

"Hello, Miss Whitby. May I help you with something special?"

"Uh—no, not right away, Carolyn. Just let me browse for a few minutes." She was surprised that she sounded almost normal.

"We have that new novel, *Emma*, by the author of *Pride and Prejudice*. I did not like it so well as her other works, but do have a look at it."

"I shall. Thank you." She did not think to tell the girl she had already read it.

Carolyn returned to her task in the back room and Hero made a pretense of looking at several books, until she was sure she really could walk down the street relatively calmly. Her fury was all the more intense because there was no way she could tell anyone what had happened. If her father or Michael knew, one of them might feel obligated to call the bounder out, and she could hardly risk a duel that might result in the death of a beloved family member! But of course, that despicable excuse for a human being knew that, didn't he? She ground her teeth in frustration.

Nevertheless, as she stepped out of the shop, she saw that Teague had disappeared, and she smiled and greeted warmly the red-coated Colonel Phillips, who was still lodged at the inn. The militiaman's continued presence, along with that of his men, who were frequently seen about the town, was at once both a reassurance for the townspeople and a cause of apprehension. Everyone seemed on pins and needles, waiting for something—anything—to happen regarding that smuggling business.

As she drove the gig home, glad now that she had come to town alone, she could not get that awful conversation with Teague out of her mind. His comment about her being *de trop* had hit home. Hero knew that her sense of ennui lately stemmed largely from uncertainty that bedeviled her in spite of those assurances she'd had from both her father and Michael. As the days wore on, Monique was establishing a firm place in the household—and making subtle changes in such things as the placement of furniture in the drawing room or in menus the kitchen staff prepared. Hero was forced to admit—grudgingly and only to herself—that most of the suggestions her brother's wife made were good ones, and Monique did them in such a diffident manner that one could hardly object, could one? But Hero was feeling less at ease than she had ever been in her own home. In the clinic too, Michael's wife had taken over certain tasks such as cleaning instruments after a procedure and seeing to their placement on a tray just as *Michael* was used to having them. Hero told herself that this was only natural as the husband and wife had worked so closely together for so many months, but she still felt a bit left out. No—pushed out.

Also, for her there was the unresolved matter of his lordship, Alexander Sterne. She had to admit that she missed him. She conceded now that she had even missed having him in Whitby Manor during those two days he had still been in the area. Now that he was gone so far away, the sense of longing was more acute. She tried to convince herself that Diana's faith that he would return was misplaced, that he had gone to the city to escape Weyburn and all its problems. But she fervently hoped that was not true— and chastised herself for wanting him to return, for wanting him to prove her wrong, for wanting *him*.

Then, suddenly, he was back.

That very day, when she arrived back at the Manor, Stewart commented that Lord Sterne had returned late the previous afternoon. He'd been gone eleven days and, despite her vow to ignore his absence or presence at the Abbey, she had felt every one of those days—perhaps every one of those hours. And now she could hardly ignore what she felt, for his return was the subject of every casual encounter with patients, tradesmen, neighbors—*and* her family. Even Annabelle was given to asking her constantly about "Mr. Ainrye."

* * * *

Alex had seen that encounter between Hero and Teague on the sidewalk in front of Wellman's mercantile store. And he'd seen her dash into the bookshop. He had arrived in town only minutes before and was sitting in that favorite window seat at the inn, waiting for Colonel Phillips. When he saw Teague take her arm so possessively, he had stifled a fit of jealousy, and when he saw her shake him off decisively, he wanted to jump up, tear out there, and plant a fist in the man's face. Before he could act—civilly or otherwise—it was over, and he told himself she might not appreciate having him intercede. Then Phillips arrived.

"Sorry to keep you waiting," the colonel said.

"Coffee?" Alex pointed at a carafe on the table and two mugs along with a plate of fresh-baked scones.

"Yes, thank you."

Alex poured the coffee and shoved a cup over to Phillips. "I see Teague is still in town."

"Blustering some, but mostly rather quiet. Something is definitely afoot. There has been some activity out there at the mine, and at those caves below the Abbey. We think they have moved the contraband down to the mouth of the cave—ready to be loaded on pack animals quickly. Unfortunately, we cannot verify that."

"I can," Alex said, reaching for a scone. He explained that he had asked Mac to check on the cellar while he was gone. Immediately on his return, Mac had informed him of that activity. Mac also reported that he had been careful to keep this bit of spy work from the watchful eye of the butler, Mullins, just as Alex had instructed. Alex was not sure why he was wary of Mullins, but he decided on the side of caution.

"There's more," Phillips said. "There are two large wagons sort of hidden behind the largest outbuilding out at the mine. They've been there for two days. Another two in the barn on that abandoned farm."

"Definitely something going on." Alex brushed crumbs from his coat.

"The weather has been rather overcast the last two or three nights," Phillips said, twisting to look at the sky through the window. "They are sure to move with the first clear moonlit night. Maybe tonight. Or tomorrow night. My men are ready. Actually, getting a bit restless with all this delay."

Alex nodded. "I can certainly relate to that. Mac and I will keep watch, and the moment we see any action below that cliff, we will report to the mine. I think most of the transfer will take place there."

"I agree. I'll accompany my main force to the mine area but send Captain Howell out to that farm with a small contingent as well."

"Good idea." Alex rose and took his leave of the colonel and made his way back to the Abbey. He thought he was probably as restless and anxious as any of those militiamen.

Nothing happened that night, but the next night all hell broke loose.

Alex and Mac lay on the grass at the edge of the Abbey cliff overlooking the sea. Although gossamer-like clouds streaked the sky, the moon shone brightly. The sea looked silvery. They kept their heads down lest they be seen from the beach below. The night was chilly and the grass damp with dew—autumn was definitely in the offing. They had been there about an hour when they began to see activity below. It was eerily quiet with only the occasional whack of a bit of harness, a muffled call, or the loud snort of an animal drifting up to them, but they could see the dark forms of men and pack animals, going into the cave unladen, and heavily burdened coming out. They watched until the traffic dribbled to nothing, then inched their way from the edge of the cliff, stood, and mounted the horses they had left some distance behind. They knew it would take the smugglers, with their slow pack animals, far more time to get to the transfer area at the mine than it would take the two of them on swifter mounts.

Alex and Mac, each armed with a rifle and a pistol, were cautious in approaching the fence around the yard of the mine entrance; having tied their horses in a clump of bushes, they walked the last hundred yards or so, hitting the ground and crawling as they got closer. The bare ground was warmer than the chilly night air and the dusty, earthy smell more pronounced as they neared the fence on their bellies.

As they got closer, they could hear the smugglers and their customers as they talked and argued about the loading process, and they could see in the muted light dark red forms of the militiamen on their own side of the stone fence—along with even darker forms of a few of the townspeople who had been trusted to join them. Colonel Phillips was in charge of this operation; knowing that the longer the delay, the more likelihood of losing the advantage of surprise, Alex waited none-too-patiently for him to call the attack.

Finally the signal: A sharp whistle sounded and the militia team jumped to their feet outside the chest-high fence and aimed their rifles across it.

"Halt!" Phillips shouted. "You are surrounded and you are under arrest."

The immediate response was rifle shots coming from guards stationed on the roofs of the buildings. The shots panicked both the pack animals and those hitched to wagons. Mayhem ensued. The militiamen had been trained to pick their targets carefully, but many shots went wild as they tried to use the stone fence to shield themselves. Moonlight was hardly conducive to making targets clear, and the poor visibility was worsened by dust stirred up by panicked animals. Animals and men alike screamed as they were hit. Shouted directions and cries of pain and fear added to the melee.

It flashed across Alex's mind that this scene was but a repeat of previous experiences, experiences that he relived on a nightly basis. He ignored that thought and concentrated on the task at hand: capture, not killing, was the goal he and Phillips had agreed on.

The gate had been unlocked and one wagon tried to make a run for it, the driver whipping his team into a frenzy. But it halted just outside the gate, when two militiamen grabbed part of the harness and stopped the team. The driver and his guards were quickly subdued. But the fight went on.

"Oh, sweet Jesus!" Mac called out near Alex. "I'm hit."

"Hang on, Mac. And stay down!" He crawled over to Mac's position.

Soon enough, the shots became sporadic and it was over. Alex conjectured that it had been only a matter of minutes, but it seemed far longer than that. The smugglers were forced to surrender. Alex turned instantly to Mac, who had his right hand pressed against his chest just below the left shoulder.

"How are you doing, Mac?"

"Bleeding, but I'm still breathing."

Alex took off his own coat and wrapped it awkwardly around Mac's injured shoulder, tucking in a sleeve to help stanch the flow of blood. "Keep pressing on it," he said. "Just stay still until we get things in order here."

"Yes, sir."

Lanterns materialized, probably from the mine buildings, and Alex and Phillips, with the help of two of Phillips's junior officers, made quick work of assessing the damage. Militiamen stood guard over smugglers who were uninjured or had suffered only bruises and scratches. These were bound hand and foot and put into the mine's largest outbuilding, which became a makeshift jail for the time being. Guards were posted.

Of the perhaps forty or fifty men involved in the fight, there were four dead: one on the side of the militia, and three of the smugglers. Besides Mac, seven others had been wounded: three militiamen and four smugglers. Alex and Phillips, directing others, made quick work of trying to tend to wounds, ripping shirts to form makeshift bandages, and taking care of a broken leg and a broken arm. A wagon was quickly divested of its half-loaded cargo, the wounded replaced the cargo, and a young militiaman was commandeered to drive it to the Whitbys' clinic. Alex retrieved his and Mac's horses and, leading Mac's mount, he rode beside the wagon, which necessarily maintained a slow pace. Alex could see that Mac was in a great deal of pain, but he was conscious, and aside from an occasional groan, did not complain.

Alex had seen Teague among the group loading goods onto the wagons, but he had not seen him among those incarcerated in the makeshift jail and he was not on this wagon. Alex fumed silently over this, and he wondered how many others had managed to escape. He could not be concerned about that now, though. The task at hand was getting these men proper medical care.

"Mac, you hang on now, you hear?" Alex said to man who had seen him through so many similar situations. "I am going to ride ahead and prepare the Whitbys for what's ahead."

"Right, sir." Mac winced as the wagon hit a rut on the road.

Ten minutes later, Alex knocked on the door of Whitby Manor. It was well after midnight, so it was a very sleepy Stewart who answered. Alex quickly explained the situation, then waited in the entrance hall as Stewart roused the Whitbys. The elder Whitby was the first to appear, then his son, Michael. A few minutes behind them was Hero.

"Let's step into the surgery as you tell us what's going on," the elder doctor said.

The five of them—Stewart had rejoined the group—retreated to that room and stood around the operating table as Alex briefly explained the events of the evening. He thought Hero seemed a bit subdued, but she listened as carefully as her father and brother did as he described as best he could the nature of the wounds they would be dealing with. Nor did she avoid eye contact with him. Forcing himself not to just stare at her hungrily, he nodded his acknowledgment of her presence. He wondered if she had got over being angry with him, but now was not the time to pursue that thought.

Her father sighed. "We knew it was coming, did we not? Eight wounded, you say?"

"Yes, sir. From the encounter at the mine entrance. There may be more from those at the abandoned farm—but that group was not so large."

"Stewart," the eldest Whitby said, "you'd best wake Mrs. Hutchins and have her keep plenty of hot water available. And have Nellie Matson join us too."

"And my wife," Michael added. "She is already awake and probably dressed by now."

"Yes, sir."

Stewart disappeared for several minutes and the others waited for the sound of the wagon. For the first time Hero asked a question of Alex. He was glad for the excuse to direct his attention to her. She was wearing a blue dress of some sturdy fabric, and her single night braid had been twisted and pinned up. He wanted to jump over the table and enfold her in his arms.

"Was Milton Tamblin there tonight?" she asked a bit hesitantly.

"I did not see him," Alex said, "but he could have been at the farm. The other two Abbey farmers involved before were there, so I am guessing that Teague put pressure on Tamblin too."

"And Mr. Teague himself?" she asked. Alex wondered why she asked about the former steward. That altercation he had witnessed the other day had not shown her to have undue interest in the man.

"He was there, but somehow escaped capture," he answered in a neutral tone.

Nellie and Monique joined them just as the wagon arrived. Suddenly everyone, including Alex, was busy either moving wounded or attending to their injuries.

Chapter 21

As Hero went about helping with the injured, she was keenly aware of her own physical reaction to the presence of Lord Alexander Sterne. Without his coat, his shirt sleeves rolled to the elbows, he exuded masculinity, and she had to remind herself that this was the absentee owner of the Abbey: He who had ignored the needs of Weyburn folks for so long was now pitching in to help move wounded from the wagon to litters and cots. The mere fact that he did so was impressive, but equally noteworthy was the care and tenderness he showed in the process. Nor did he arrogantly push for his friend Mac to take precedence over a man—a smuggler, at that—whom the Whitbys considered to be more seriously wounded, a man shot in the chest, the bullet lodged dangerously close to his heart. Mac himself was handling his pain stoically and Adam—no, Alex—was attentive in wiping his brow with a damp cloth and murmuring soothing encouragement to him. Here—this—was Adam, the man who had shown *her* such tenderness and empathy.

She did not like having to reevaluate her long-held aversion to the owner of Weyburn Abbey. And at the moment, she welcomed the need to concentrate on other matters—like sewing up a ripped scalp, or where a bullet had torn a three-inch gouge in the fleshy part of a man's forearm. The patient, one of the militiamen, was a big fellow, but young—only in his teens—scared, and far from home. As her father, brother, and Monique worked on the man with the chest wound, Hero tended her own patient, who sat upright in a wooden chair in a corner of the surgery. Blood had soaked through his red jacket, which she helped him remove, and into the white shirt beneath. Nellie Matson had moved a small table nearby to hold a basin and cloths and the instruments Hero would need. Nellie helped hold his arm steady on the table as Hero cleaned the wound and prepared to stitch it closed. The wound continued to bleed as she worked. The fresh, redder blood frightened him even more and he winced with every stitch.

"I'm sorry," she murmured. "I know this hurts. If it is any consolation to you, the scar will fade in time, though your arm will be quite sore for a while and you will need to keep it in a sling. The girls will be impressed with how brave you are."

He grinned feebly at this.

She kept up her nonsense chatter to try to distract him not only from his own pain and his obvious aversion to the sight of blood, but also from the blood and pain of the other patient nearby. She finished by gently washing his entire arm as well as his face and neck. She and Nellie wrapped a bandage about the wound and fashioned a sling for him, then they escorted him to one of several cots that had been set up in the hallway.

"You may feel a little dizzy, so you just lie here quietly until someone comes to take you back to your quarters," she said.

"C-could I have a drink of water?"

"Of course. Nellie?"

Nellie nodded and went to fulfill that request. Hero turned to attend the next patient—and found herself staring into the blue depths of the eyes of Alexander Sterne. Mac lay on his side on one of the cots; Alex squatted next to him, apparently trying to keep his friend distracted from the pain he must be feeling.

"Oh," she said, startled.

"I assume Mac is next in line," Alex said, standing.

"I think so. But let me check to see that the table has been cleared."

She seized the chance to postpone confronting her own conflicted feelings about this man. Having carefully transferred the smuggler with the chest wound to one of the wheeled beds, both Drs. Whitby were washing up as Nellie and Monique laid a clean sheet on the table. At the doctors' signal, Alex and Stewart lifted the cot to use it as a litter to transfer Mac to the table, and, with the help of the doctors, place him so he lay on the table on his uninjured side. This done, Alex stood back.

"The shot came from the roof, so it entered just below Mac's shoulder at an angle. I believe the bullet is lodged in his upper back," he said. "Right, Mac?"

"Yes, sir." Mac was breathing hard with the exertion of the move from cot to table, but even this brief conversation reinforced for Hero what she had observed before: These two men, from distinctly different classes, had a great deal of respect and affection for each other.

"Hero," her father said, noticeably favoring one of his feet and leaning on his cane, "you and Michael are on your own with this one. Michael has more experience with bullet wounds than I do. Stewart and I will see what we can do about those broken bones. Monique, you stay with Michael and Hero. Nellie, you come with me."

"Yes, Papa," Hero responded, but added, as she was already gently loosening the extra coat around the patient and Monique was unbuttoning his waistcoat, "You must try to sit for a while, Papa. Tell Stewart and Nellie what to do—they can handle it."

"She's getting to be really bossy, isn't she?" her father said in mock umbrage to the room at large.

"Yes," her brother agreed, "but she's right."

"*Et tu, Brute?*"

As the elder Dr. Whitby and his two assistants left the room, the others turned their full attention to the patient on the table. With Alex's help in lifting and holding Mac so that Hero and Monique could remove the coat and waistcoat, they undressed him down to his shirt. In the process, Hero felt it acutely whenever her hands came in contact with Alex's. Her body had not forgot the sensations his touch generated.

"Not to tell you professionals your business," Alex said, "but why don't you just cut the shirt off him? Save him some pain, perhaps."

They readily agreed to that, though Mac protested. "This shirt cost me a whole quid!"

"I'll buy you another," Alex said.

"Sorry about that loss—and our abusing your modesty so," Michael told him. "Not to mention the pain—but we have to strip you to the waist."

"I have endured worse," Mac said with a hoarse grunt.

"Indeed you have," Michael said as the bare flesh of Mac's upper torso was revealed.

Numerous scars crisscrossed his body, including some from what appeared to Hero to have been a flogging. She drew in a sharp breath on seeing these, and her eyes locked with Alex's. He nodded in response to her unasked question. "Mac is a man with principles. When he protested the abuse of a young soldier, he ran up against an officer who had none."

"Good grief," she murmured.

She and Michael both examined the entry wound, which still bled but not profusely. They probed to ensure that no bones had been nicked, leaving splinters to cause problems later, then they ran their hands along his back and found a bump that they determined was the bullet under flesh and skin. Mac flinched when they touched that area.

"That bullet will have to come out," Michael said, and looked to Hero for her agreement.

"Just do what you gotta do," Mac said. Alex gave his uninjured shoulder a gentle pat of encouragement.

Brother and sister working together, the entire procedure was accomplished in a matter of a few minutes. Hero was impressed with the quiet efficiency with which Monique assisted her husband by having the exact instruments ready for incisions, and then somewhat surprised that she just as unobtrusively helped *her* in stitching the two incisions closed and bandaging them. Monique had also periodically wiped the sweaty brow of the patient, who endured all these ministrations with very few gasps and moans. Hero could tell that such stoicism came at a price: The man was exhausted when it was over.

"Unless you need me for anything else," Alex said, "I will take Mac home—free up some of your hospital space. That is, I will do that if you will lend us a blanket and a carriage and team. I will return them within an hour or so and retrieve our mounts then."

The elder Dr. Whitby came into the surgery as Alex made this request. "Of course. You are welcome to whatever you need. Captain Howell arrived a few minutes ago with two more patients from the altercation at the Thompson farm and with several militiamen who will guard the prisoners among the wounded. We have plenty of help now. And none of the remaining wounds is truly serious. We should be finished by the time you return."

"Later, then." Alex looked at Hero directly and held her gaze for a long moment, then nodded to her and to the others. Then he was gone. And she was no nearer to dealing with her mixed feelings about one Major Lord Alexander Sterne than she had been, say, almost two weeks ago.

* * * *

Alex saw Mac safely tucked into his own bed and assigned a male member of the Abbey's skeletal staff to keep constant watch over the injured man. He then returned to Whitby Manor, hoping that he could manage some time alone with Hero and try to resolve the situation between them. He was determined to fight for whatever they had had. If only he could convince *her* that it was worth fighting for.

However, that notion had to be postponed.

He found the Whitbys at breakfast, along with Captain Howell and Colonel Phillips. They invited him to join them and informed him that the patients who had been enforcing the law had, if they were mobile, been taken home or to their temporary quarters in town. The others, along with those under arrest, were in the rather overcrowded clinic under the watchful eyes of militia guards. Quickly accepting their invitation, Alex realized he had not yet eaten. He filled a plate at the sideboard and turned to sit, but to his disappointment, Hero sat farther up the table, near her father, and the others sat between him and her on either side of the table. She poured him a cup of coffee and passed it down to him, offering him a tentative smile as she did so. Well, it was a start, he told himself. In answer to their questions, he reported that he had left Mr. McIintosh sleeping rather soundly under the influence of the laudanum they had sent with him. Phillips had been giving them an update on the night's events and now filled Alex in on what had happened after he left the mine with the wounded.

"So what is to happen now?" Michael asked.

With a glance at Alex, Phillips responded, "The jail here is inadequate for such a number of prisoners—twelve today and those two from before. We cannot leave them in that shed at the mine. We are transferring them to our headquarters in Appledore this afternoon. We shall hold them there until the court of assize meets here in Weyburn."

"Which is when?" Hero asked.

Again Phillips glanced at Alex before answering. "They meet only once a year in most English counties. Local magistrates handle lesser issues, as I am sure you know."

"Yes, of course," she said. "But waiting for the assize court could take months."

"That would ordinarily be true," Phillips said. "But in this instance, I think not. Lord Sterne arranged for it to meet here in a special session this year. A judge will be sent out from London as soon as I notify the proper authority. I shall send the letter today—so it should not be more than two, maybe three weeks."

"Ah," the elder Dr. Whitby said, "that should give you time to get those that escaped, then."

Phillips looked uncomfortable. "I do not hold much hope of that, sir. If they are smart, they will already be long gone from Weyburn—from Cornwall." His voice became more confident. "The good news is that this gang of smugglers has been dealt with. That is, disbanded. I doubt Weyburn will see much of that kind of activity in the future."

The increasingly closer sound of a team and carriage being driven at a furious pace reached the ears of those around the table. Then it halted. A few minutes later Diana burst into the room.

"Papa! Michael! I need your help! It's Milton. He did not come home and there was that awful fracas at the mine last night and—and—he may be dead!"

Seeing the two uniformed militia officers at the table, she stopped abruptly, her hand at her mouth, tears running down her cheeks. Her shoulders slumped and she dissolved into sobs. Those sitting at the table jumped to their feet and Hero dashed over to put her arms around her sister.

"Shh. Stop, Diana. Milton is not dead." Hero shook Diana gently when she continued to sob hysterically. "He is *not* among the dead."

"Then where is he? Why did he not come home last night? Mr. Teague came to the house. He had those awful men with him and—and Milton went with them, and—and now—" She drew a deep, steadying breath and stared at Hero. She seemed to read something in Hero's eyes, for she moaned, "No-o-o. No."

Hero nodded. "He was arrested—along with several others."

"Arrested?" Diana was outraged. "M-Milton is no criminal. Teague—"

On her other side, her father put an arm around her and kissed her temple. "Milton did what he had to. But he knew the risks. Now do stop crying. Let us figure what we can do for him, for you, for the children."

Hero said, "Have you had breakfast, Diana?" When she received a negative shake of the head in response, she led her sister to the head of the table. "Here. You sit by Papa and I shall get you a plate. Just sit. I'll get it for you." Hero picked up her own place setting and carried it down the table to an empty spot next to Alex. Then she reached for the bellpull and busied herself filling a plate with sausage and eggs and a muffin for Diana. When a footman answered the bell, she instructed him to bring more coffee and to see that someone dealt with Diana's horses and carriage. Finally, she sat in the chair Alex was holding for her.

She gave him a long, questioning look as she sat down, but he could not read her expression very well. Still, he relished having her so near—and that she had voluntarily chosen to sit next to him. He caught a whiff of the lilac scent he always associated with her. An image of burying his face in her hair spread on a pillow flashed into his mind, but he managed to put it aside. Hero seemed determined to pick up the conversation from before Diana's entrance.

"So—there is to be a special session of the assize court." She turned slightly toward Alex. "How on earth did you manage that?"

He shrugged. "When one's father is a duke, many things are possible. And if that duke happens to have the ear of the prime minister on a regular basis, things are even more possible. Colonel Phillips and I thought—and my father agreed with us—that the sooner this matter is resolved, the better."

She gave him a look of disgust and he groaned inwardly when she said, "*Resolved* means putting our people in jail and perhaps having them transported? Is that it?"

Diana choked and cried out, "No. Please, no."

Hero quickly said, "I'm sorry, Diana. I misspoke."

"Yes, you did," her brother said accusingly and reached to pat Diana's hand. "You need to stop and listen to others once in a while, Hero."

Alex saw that her brother's rebuke had hit home with Hero, and for a moment he felt sorry for her even though he had been the intended target of her outburst.

"All right, then. I'm listening."

"The truth is," Colonel Phillips said, "we cannot be certain of the final outcome until there is a trial. Ultimately, sentences will be up to the judge."

"So we just sit on our hands and twiddle our thumbs for two or three weeks?" Hero asked.

"Well, that would be a neat trick, would it not?" Michael asked. Everyone laughed at that impossible image; the whole mood lightened for a bit at least.

Hero smiled weakly. "You know what I mean."

Alex looked down the table at the colonel. "Colonel Phillips, may I speak with you privately for a moment?"

"Of course."

The colonel rose and followed Alex into the hall. Alex waved a hovering footman away and led Phillips into the Whitby library. He closed the door and, with both of them still standing, said, "You and I both know how Teague was terrorizing local people."

"Some of them were in it for profit."

"True—but not all of them."

"I should think that is for the court to sort out," Phillips said. "I'm just a glorified policeman here."

"This is a busy time of the year for farmers," Alex said. "Trying to get in a final crop of hay, harvesting other crops, taking animals to market, and so on."

"What is your point, Sterne?"

"I need Tamblin and those other two farmers to be tending to business on my land. If I stand surety of their reporting for trial, would you consider releasing them to me until the court convenes?"

"This wouldn't have anything to do with the other sister, now, would it?" Phillips wore a knowing grin. "I've watched you tiptoeing around each other."

Alex gave a weak smile and knew he must look a bit sheepish. "Well, yes, I suppose it does—some. But those farms—those families—will suffer if those crops and animals are not cared for properly."

"I see your point. But I feel I must warn you: If they cut and run, it's on you, not me. I am not risking what's left of my career for a few Cornishmen."

"Understood."

"Well, let's go tell that poor woman she can have her husband back. At least for a while. What happens at the trial may be a very different story."

* * * *

Talk at the breakfast table continued in a desultory fashion as the family and Captain Howell awaited the return of Lord Sterne and Colonel Phillips. Hero thought the family were reluctant to be too frank in their conversation in front of the remaining militiaman; thus they did not openly conjecture about what might be taking place in that private meeting, but all were anxious about it. *What could they possibly be talking about?* Powerful men in London made the rules; people in the country as a whole—even people like his lordship and the colonel—had to abide by them.

Diana sipped her coffee and moved her fork around on her plate, but she did not eat much. "Where is Milton now?" she asked.

The others looked at Howell for the answer. "A number of prisoners are still at the mine. We will be moving them to our headquarters as soon as Colonel Phillips can arrange the transportation."

"Do you think I will be able to speak with my husband before that happens?"

"That is something you will have to ask the colonel."

"I do hope Mr. Teague is not being kept in the same room as my Milton," Diana said. "Abbey farmers are not very fond of that man."

"Teague and two of his special cohorts seem to have escaped," the captain said glumly.

"Escaped?" Diana dropped her fork onto her plate with a clatter. "You mean that man is not to pay for forcing good men to go along with his bad acts? That is so unfair!"

Howell nodded. "True. And, believe me, we would like to track them down and see them properly punished, but we simply haven't the manpower to conduct a hunt all over Cornwall and Devon—and God knows if they are even still in this part of the country. They could be anywhere."

They heard footsteps in the hall signifying the return of Phillips and Sterne. Hero moved to stand behind her sister and gripped her shoulder. When the two men entered the room, the others sat staring at them as though in a tableau.

Phillips quickly explained the plan for temporary release of the three farmers into the custody of Lord Sterne.

"Oh, thank God," Diana cried even before he had supplied the details. Scarcely paying attention to the conditions of her husband's release, she glanced up at Hero and mouthed, "I told you so." Hero took this to be an affirmation of her faith in his lordship. The tension in the room all but disappeared.

All that remained was to settle the details. Lord Sterne, riding his horse and leading Mac's, both of which had been left in the Whitby stable all this time, would ride beside Diana in her carriage and see to getting the three farmers home where they were to remain until time to go to court.

Realizing now that she had half formed a plan to talk privately with Alex this morning, Hero felt frustrated in knowing that was not going to happen—and in not knowing whether he would welcome such. He cocked his head to the side and gave her a rueful glance.

Chapter 22

For the next three days, Hero tried to keep up a good front as she went about what were mostly routine aspects of her life. She was still adjusting to sharing medical duties with Monique. Monique readily bowed to Hero's expertise in the field, and Hero readily admitted that her sister-in-law was a most competent assistant. Nevertheless, just sharing that aspect of her life—even with Michael—was proving more difficult than she had anticipated.

For years she had schooled herself to the fact that Michael would eventually return and take their father's place. She had accepted that. After all, Michael was the one who had been to the best medical school in the kingdom. And there was the small matter that, as a male, he commanded an immediate position in this male-dominated world. But she also knew that her own knowledge and skills were nothing to look down upon. True, she was self-taught as far as book knowledge was concerned, but she had also been more or less apprenticed to one of England's most respected doctors—Charles Whitby—for nearly ten years. Visiting medical dignitaries had often praised her work, surprised though they might be initially to find that Dr. Whitby allowed her so much authority in his very fine clinic.

She was finding anew that there was a huge difference between having accepted something intellectually and actually living the reality. *But I can do this. I know I can*, she assured herself. *I just need to get beyond here and now.*

Getting beyond here and now, though, meant facing up to her feelings for Alex. Yes, he was *Alex* in her thoughts now. And Alex truly was the man Adam, with whom she had fallen in love.

Another hurdle conquered: She now admitted, if only to herself, that she truly loved this man she had disliked from afar for so many years. "From afar"—ah, there was the telling point! Up close was another matter.

She had hoped he would return to Whitby Manor after he had delivered Diana and the three prisoners to their farms, but he had not done so. Nor had he come the next day. Or the next. She tried to put the matter out of her mind.

What will be, will be.

Putting it out of her mind was not so easy. By late that afternoon, the whole town was talking of what a marvelous thing his lordship had done. Young people praised him for standing up for his own; older folks nodded and said they had expected nothing less of Sir Benjamin's heir. Nor was it only neighbors who sang his praises. Her father made no secret of his admiration for the man, and Michael added that what "the major" had done today was completely in line with his reputation as a soldier. And then there was Annabelle.

"Is it true?" Annabelle demanded the instant Hero entered the nursery. The little girl stood in the middle of the room with her hands on her hips and gave Hero a challenging stare.

"Is what true?"

"Was Mr. Ainrye here?"

"Yes, he was." Hero was not about to start lying to Annabelle now.

"Why didn't he come to see me? Did you make him go away?"

Hearing the hurt in Annabelle's tone, Hero nudged her toward a chair and pulled the child onto her lap. How she treasured this little person! "No, I did not make him go away." She smoothed Annabelle's skirt and kissed her cheek, trying to think where to begin.

"Freddie told me Mr. Ainrye is not Mr. Ainrye, but I told Freddie he most certainly is! And I'm right, ain't I? Freddie's always telling me big fibs." Hero knew that the children had spent time together on more than one occasion since the big revelation. She kicked herself for not talking about it with Annabelle before now.

"This time Freddie is not fibbing."

Annabelle looked up in disbelief. "Wha—No! That can't be."

"Mr. Wainwright's real name is Lord Alexander Sterne, but he is the same man, Annabelle. The same person." Even as these words left her mouth, she thought, *Listen to yourself!*

"If he's the same, why didn't he come to see me? Don't he like me anymore?" Again, Hero heard Annabelle's hurt, her latent insecurity.

"Of course he still likes you! How could he not like such a nice little girl as you?" She hugged Annabelle closer. "But he is a very busy man at the Abbey. He has to take care of much land and many people."

"Is that what a lord does?"

"Many of them do."

Annabelle's shoulders slumped. "Does that mean he can't be my friend anymore?"

"It's just that he might not have time for us now."

"Time." Annabelle sat up straighter, and said in a very authoritative voice, "One makes time for what is important."

Hero had to smile at hearing one of her own familiar maxims being repeated to her. She wound a strand of Annabelle's blond hair around her fingers. "That is true, but sometimes people just get very busy, you see."

"Maybe he just forgotted." Annabelle mused for a few seconds, then said brightly, "I know, we should invite him to come and visit us!"

She jumped down and dashed over to a cupboard where pencils and papers were stored. She carried several papers and some pencils to the table in the center of the room. "Come on, Auntie H'ro," she called, as she climbed onto a chair and pointed to one next to her. "You sit here and just write what I tell you. All right?"

Hero laughed. "All right. I shall be your secretary."

"Sec-uh-tary? What's that?"

"Someone who writes letters for other people."

"Oh. I gots a sec-uh-tary then." She giggled, and pushed herself up to sit on her knees and rest her arms on the table.

Hero picked up the sharpest pencil and said, "All right. What do you wish me to write, my lady?"

"Dear Mr. Ainrye," she intoned, then looked at Hero. "That's not right, though. How should I talk to him now?"

"Dear Lord Sterne."

Annabelle wrinkled her nose. "That's his name now?"

Hero nodded. "Or, you could say 'Dear Lord Alexander.'"

"I like that better." She began dictating again. "Dear Lord Alexander. I miss my friend Mr. Ainrye, and I hope he will come and visit me. Bitsy wants him to come too." She paused and then added, "So does Tootie."

"Is that it?" Hero asked.

"Yes. Read it to me." Hero did so and Annabelle said, "Yes. It's a good letter. Are you sure you spelled everything right?"

Hero laughed and gently tweaked the child's nose. "Yes, I am sure, Miss Know-All."

"Good. Then I can write my name."

This was a skill that Annabelle had mastered only very recently. She still could not write the entire alphabet without an error or two, but she knew the letters of her name. Hero handed over the paper and, in a mixture of lowercase and uppercase letters of various sizes, Annabelle laboriously wrote out the nine symbols of her name.

"There. Is that all right?"

"It is perfect," Hero assured her.

"Can you have someone take it to him right away?"

Hero did so, but not before taking the letter downstairs and adding her own postscript to it. *Lord Sterne: Please do consider Annabelle's invitation, to which I sincerely add my own and those of my family. Today is Tuesday. I shall arrange for Annabelle to join the Whitby adults for supper on Thursday evening, and I hope you will be able to join us as well.*

She signed the missive and sealed it with wax, then called for a footman. Davey answered the call. Hero gave him the letter and instructions to deliver it to the Abbey and wait for his lordship's response. Davey returned within two hours. Lord Alexander Sterne would be most pleased to accept Miss Annabelle's kind invitation. And that of her Auntie H'ro as well.

Hero delivered the news to Annabelle as the child was preparing for bed. Annabelle squealed with delight, and all the next day she pestered anyone who would listen with the news that she was to dine with the "big people" the next night and that her friend Lord Alexander would join them.

Hero tried to tell herself that her own reaction was just that Annabelle's excitement was contagious, but she knew that was not the full story as she anticipated the visit with as much—albeit more subdued—excitement as the child. She spent a good deal of time on Wednesday mulling over what she would wear the following evening. It couldn't be too formal, but she wanted to look her very best. She finally settled on an apricot Indian muslin which she'd had made in London last year when she visited her friends Harriet and Retta. It was designed very simply with a deep V-neckline and elbow-length sleeves.

After the evening meal that night and after Hero had seen the excited Annabelle to bed, she joined her father and Michael and Monique in the library. Hero and the two men were engaged with whatever authors had captured their attention this night; Monique was doing some fancy needlework. Her father retired about an hour and a half before midnight and soon afterwards Monique yawned politely and announced that she would do so as well.

"I shall be right up, my dear," her husband responded. "As soon as I finish this chapter."

"And another and another," his wife said indulgently.

"You know me too well, my love."

Monique had scarcely had time to get up to their room when there was a loud knocking at the front door. Hero heard Stewart rushing from the back of the house to answer the door. There was muffled talk, then Stewart knocked at the library door and entered as Hero called, "Come."

"That boy, Trevor Prentiss, is here, Miss Hero, Dr. Michael. He insists that it is urgent that he speak with you."

With a glance at Michael, Hero put aside her book. "Show him in."

Stewart opened the door wider and the boy came in, shyly holding his cap in his hand, but he seemed rather agitated. And his clothes were wet, for it had been raining off and on all afternoon.

"What is it, Trevor?" Hero asked, rising from her chair.

"I didn't know what else to do, so I come to tell you," he said.

"Tell us what?" she asked.

"It's about Mr. Wainwright—I mean Lord Sterne."

"What about him?" She felt a chill of apprehension. "Has something happened to him?"

"I-I ain't rightly sure, miss. Probably not yet." The boy looked distraught and twisted his cap furiously.

Michael too had risen. "Here. Sit down and tell us what is going on."

When they were all seated, Trevor said, "I know I wasn't s'posed to be there, but I had a terrible row with my ma and my sister this afternoon. I just had to get away, you see. So I went out to the Thompson farm. Ain't been anyone living there for months, don't you know?"

"What has this to do with Lord Sterne?" Hero asked impatiently.

"I'm getting to it," Trevor said.

"Don't rush him, Hero," Michael said.

She gritted her teeth and kept quiet as the boy went on.

"We used the barn there—you know—when I was with Teague's gang." He seemed embarrassed at admitting this in front of Michael. "So I thought I'd spend the night in the loft there—just let my ma and sister worry a bit, you see. I know it was wrong, but I was just that mad at them."

"So you are in the loft of the barn on the Thompson place," Michael prodded.

"I thought the place was deserted after that mess with the militia an' all." Trevor gulped. "But pretty soon, it wasn't. I'm up in the loft and I hear these horses and men come in the barn. I'm real quiet, because it's Mr. Teague and two of those men he brought from Bristol. Those fellows can be real mean. I think they'd been drinking, too. They was talkin' real loud."

"And—?" Hero could not help herself; she motioned for him to get on with it.

"And they were planning to hurt Lord Sterne. 'Teach that bastard a lesson once and for all—tonight, then we head out of here,' Mr. Teague said. Sorry about the language, Miss Whitby. 'How you gonna do that?' one of the others asked. 'Yeah. That house is a fortress, Will,' the other one said. Mr. Teague, he just laughed an' said, 'You'll see.' Then he said something about getting some food first and all three of them went into the farmhouse 'n' I lit out o' there. I guess they been hidin' there all this time, 'cept they went somewhere to get that drunk today."

"But you don't know how they plan to storm that fortress?" Michael asked.

"No, sir. I ain't never been in the Abbey. Only that farm an' some caves."

"I know," Hero said. "Michael, we have to stop them. We can't let them harm him. Again. These are the people behind that awful beating he took. They could kill him this time."

"I'll take care of it," Michael said. "You just tell me how they are gaining entrance. Stewart and I will warn him." He went to the bellpull to summon Stewart.

"I am coming too," she said.

"Hero, this could be dangerous. It's no place for a woman."

"I am coming," she said adamantly. "You cannot stop me."

Stewart arrived and addressed Michael, who was still standing. "You wanted something, sir?"

Hero jumped to her feet. "Stewart, we are going on a rescue mission." She explained the situation much more briefly than Trevor had. "Will you help us?"

Stewart said, "For Lord Sterne? Anything."

"Have Perkins prepare mounts for us—a regular saddle for me—and ask him to come along. We will need lanterns. And weapons. Michael, those are in the gun safe in Papa's office."

"My God, Hero, just tell me what you have in mind and I'll do it. There is no reason to put yourself at such risk."

"Please, Michael, this is no time to argue with me. I. Am. Going. I cannot lose him." She scarcely realized what she had said.

Something in her manner convinced him. "Just let me tell Monique what's happening."

"Hurry."

Michael and Stewart left the room.

"Miss Whitby," Trevor asked, "can I come too? I-I sort of owe his lordship."

"Yes, you do, Trevor," she said gently, "but actually what I would like you to do is ride back into town and tell Mr. Porter what is happening. Ask him to get some trustworthy men to come out to the Abbey and take

Teague and his bully boys into custody. Colonel Phillips and his men all left Weyburn yesterday."

"Yes, ma'am. I can do that."

Hero did not take time to change into a riding habit, but she did slip on a pair of pantaloons under her skirt to protect her legs as she rode astride. She grabbed a cloak, and within minutes, she and Michael met Stewart and Perkins in the stable, and they distributed lanterns and weapons.

"We are heading for the beach below the Abbey," she told them.

"Whoa!" Michael said. "Why don't we just approach the Abbey directly? It would be quicker."

"And those scoundrels might see us coming a mile away and do something drastic," she said. "Now—please—let's just go!"

They headed for the beach.

"We will ride to the bottom of the Abbey cliff," she explained. "The cave there has a tunnel that leads up to the cellar of the Abbey. That's how Teague will get in. He should be already through the tunnel by the time we arrive, but let's hope he has not done any real harm to Alex or any of the Abbey staff."

"You missed your calling, little sister," Michael told her. "Wellington could have used you among his staff officers."

That was the last talking they did until they reached the cave. They took the horses as far into the cave as they could, then dismounted. Hero was not surprised to see three other animals tied up in the cave at that point. She conferred with Michael and they agreed to strip all the mounts of saddles and bridles and simply turn them loose. Perkins assured them that the animals would all likely find their way home. He would send a stable boy to retrieve the gear the next day.

From that point, crude stone steps led steadily upward, until they encountered a door into what had once been an immense storage area for an abbey that served a small community of religious brothers. It was virtually bare now, with only some empty sacks and broken boxes lying around.

"There's a door along one wall," Hero said softly.

They held the lanterns high to search for the door, but actually muddy footprints showed them the way.

Chapter 23

Alex had had a busy day. Somehow the word had leaked out that he was hiring men to do such things as mend leaky roofs, rebuild damaged fences, lay cobblestones around the entrance to the mine, and myriad other tasks, large and small. Moreover, the applicants seemed to have learned that Lord Alexander Sterne—formerly *Major* Lord Alexander Sterne—was likely to give priority to former soldiers. Alex had caught two would-be roofers and fence menders trying to pass themselves off as veterans merely to obtain a job. One had been so stupid as to confuse Brown Bess—the nickname of the army's muzzle-loading musket—with the name of a cow! Alex and Mac had laughed heartily over that, even as they recognized the desperation of men seeking work—any paying work.

He had also met with Sir James Horner, a man with more money that wit, whose imprudent loans to the Prince Regent had brought him an undeserved knighthood—and the position of local magistrate. Apparently Teague had intimidated the poor man to the point that the judge automatically released any of the former steward's cronies who happened to be caught at cross-purposes with the law—regardless of the severity of the charge. Alex assured him that his life was not in danger, and his comely young granddaughters would be perfectly safe while visiting their grandparents, and therefore he could begin to uphold the law properly. And—Alex had gone into the mercantile store to drop a hint to Mr. Wellman that it might be a good idea if he no longer tampered with mail to or from the Abbey. Wellman seemed perfectly agreeable to that plan.

Thus his lordship had that night gone to bed early, though not before looking in on Mac to ensure that the Abbey's impatient patient was faring well. Alex awoke sometime after midnight with a vague feeling of unrest that he somehow felt was not tied to his usual round of reliving battlefield scenes. He had gone to sleep with his lamp still burning brightly and his book across his chest. There! He heard it again. Something, or—more likely—someone moving stealthily in his dressing room. The only person besides himself who would have reason to be there was Mac—and he knew Mac to be sleeping soundly, for Alex himself had delivered the dose of laudanum.

He pushed the book aside and raised up enough to reach for the pistol that he kept by habit in a drawer of his nightstand. Before his fingers fastened on the weapon, the dressing room door burst open and Teague strutted through it with a pistol in one hand. He stepped into the middle of the room and pointed the weapon at Alex.

"Don't even think of completing that move, your ever-so-noble lordship," Teague said with a sneer. Without taking his eyes from Alex, Teague called out, "Bring them in here. I want them to see what happens to those who cross me, who are disloyal to me." Mr. and Mrs. Mullins, both clearly scared out of their wits, were shoved into the room.

"Meet my in-laws," Teague said with a nasty laugh. Alex raised an eyebrow at this information and Teague added, "Hah! Didn't know that little detail, did you?"

"Please, my lord," Mrs. Mullins cried. "He said we would never see our grandchildren again if we didn't help him."

"I told you to keep quiet," Teague said and backhanded her in the face with the hand not holding his pistol. She cried out and staggered. Her husband tried to go to her aid, but one of the other men touched a gun to his brow and the butler went very still. Alex quickly swung his legs to the side of the bed and started to rise.

"Uh-uh. Just sit right there, Sterne. You move again and they die."

"I'm the one you seem to be after here," Alex said. "Why not let them go?"

"I've a few bones to pick with them as well. Meddling old fools—incapable of following orders. Even worse, they lack a sense of loyalty. After all I've done for them."

"Done for us?" Mullins muttered, despite the gun still against his temple. Alex admired his courage, even as his own mind worked furiously for a way out of this situation.

"Drove our sweet Letty to her death is what he did," Mrs. Mullins said, with a sob and a hand to her reddening cheek.

"Let them go," Alex said. "What is it you want? Money? Is that it? I haven't much on hand, but you can have it."

"Oh, I'll have it. But first I'll make you pay in pain for what you've done to me. I think we'll start with the right knee. What do you say, Tom? The right one?"

"Ah, I don't know, Will. They're both so purty, ain't they?" Tom was the one holding the gun at Mullins's head. He leered at Alex. "But let's get on with it, Will. You told us there's a couple of pretty little maids we could have. And there's that lovely cellar we came through."

Teague gave an evil laugh. "Right one first, then. You do it, Joe. I want to watch as he absorbs the pain."

Joe, who had been standing next to Mrs. Mullins said, "Sure thing, boss." He stepped away from her and took aim, but before he could pull the trigger, she grabbed his arm and the shot went wild.

Tom, the other gunman, moved the angle of his gun to take the shot, but Mullins thrust a sharp elbow into his ribs, knocking him off balance. Tom fell to the floor, dropping the gun as he took Mullins with him. Before any of them could recover from that surprise, the door to the hallway burst open and Michael Whitby said rather calmly, "That will be enough of that kind of fun, I think." Alex's heart jumped as he saw Hero right behind him.

Teague instantly turned his gun toward the two in the door. There was another shot. Teague uttered a cry, grabbed at his chest, and fell to the floor. Everyone stared in wonder for a split second, then looked to see who had fired the shot. All eyes centered on Mullins. Somehow, he had managed to wrest control of Tom's weapon and fired from the floor.

Stewart and Perkins burst into the room, their pistols ready. Joe, apparently seeing the futility of pursuing this venture, dropped his weapon and he and Tom raised their hands. As Michael bent to check Teague's pulse, Hero ran to the bed to enfold Alex in her arms.

"Are you all right?" she whispered. "Please tell me you are all right."

"Naked and embarrassed," he said against her chest, "but I think I am going to be fine—that is, *we* are going to be fine." He held her tightly for a moment, then pulled her down to sit beside him on the edge of the bed.

Michael stood and shook his head. "He's dead," he said.

"I wish I could say I'm sorry," Mrs. Mullins said. "He was an evil man. Handsome devil, but evil. Letty was just so taken with him."

"That was some shot, mister," Michael said to Mullins.

"I served in the colonies in the seventies," Mullins said, his tone matter-of-fact. "Haven't shot a gun since. 'Til now."

His wife went to put her arms around his waist and lay her head on his chest. "It's all right, my dear. Our nightmare is over."

"If you all will take these two miscreants down to the library and watch over them, I shall endeavor to get dressed and join you there," Alex said, reluctantly releasing Hero's hand, which he'd been holding. "I'm sure Mullins can find some rope to restrain them."

"Yes, sir," Mullins said.

Alex dressed hurriedly in the first garments that came to hand—his buckskins and a cotton shirt that he did not bother to tuck in at the waist, though he rolled up the cuffs of the sleeves. Nor did he take time to wrestle with his boots, opting for his slippers. *Well, it isn't a fashionable affair,* he told himself.

Downstairs, he found his library quite crowded. Samuel Porter had arrived with five townsmen. They were disappointed at having missed the action, but they readily took charge of the two prisoners, and the dead body as well, though not before they had learned the details of this night's sorry business. Alex knew it would be all over the town and into the countryside by midday.

As the townsmen departed, Alex, standing with Hero at his side, made a point of thanking Trevor Prentiss. "I think your father would have been proud of you for this night's work, Prentiss."

"Thank you, sir."

With that lot gone, Michael said, "My lord, if you will lend us a means of transportation, the Whitby party will leave as well."

"There is a landau and a team in the stable. You are welcome to take them. But really I must insist that you stop 'my lording' me." Alex put his arm around Hero. "I fully intend that we shall be brothers just as soon as humanly possible."

Michael grinned at them. "I suspected as much."

"And," Alex added, "I will see Hero home later, if she pleases. She and I have a few things to sort out."

* * * *

The moment the door had finally closed on everyone, Hero melted into Alex's arms for a very long, very passionate display of their mutual affection. After a while, she pulled away slightly. "How dare you make that announcement so blatantly," she said in a feeble attempt at umbrage. "You have not even asked me."

He pulled away and sank to one knee. He gripped her hand and said, "My sweet, lovable, stubborn Hero. I love you to the point of distraction. So—will you marry me?"

"I'll have to think about that," she said. She tugged at his hand to bring him to his feet and gave him a quick kiss. "There. I've thought about it. Yes. Of course I'll marry you. I've loved you ever since you showed up unconscious in our clinic."

"Ah, but you kissed me awake—remember? Just as Annabelle told you to do."

"She will be so pleased at this turn of events," Hero said.

"I know. I saw it in her note. So, my love, when?"

"When what?" she said blankly.

He gave her an impatient shake. "When will you marry me?"

"You must know these things take time. I need a dress, there are the banns, and—"

"And I have a special license."

"Wha-at?"

"In London, while my father was doing his business about a special court of the assize, I went around to Doctors' Commons and procured a special license. It is valid for three more weeks, I think."

She dropped her arms from around his neck and tried to step back. "You were certainly sure of yourself—of me—were you not?"

He refused to loosen his hold on her, and bent his head to nuzzle her neck. He murmured, "No. Just very, very hopeful."

"Oh. Well, in that case..."

"Well, in that case, let's discuss it further upstairs, shall we? There is a perfectly good bedchamber up there—the one I used my first night in the Abbey. We'll have the master chamber renovated."

"Well, in that case—" she repeated.

"We'll have to be relatively quiet," he cautioned. "Mac is sleeping right next door."

"You mean I can't scream out my delight?"

"You are not a screamer."

"I could be."

But she was not a screamer. Not that night.

Epilogue

The Duchess of Thornleigh came into the most elegant guest chamber of Weyburn Abbey to find her husband already in bed, propped up and reading a book.

"Things have gone very well while we've been here, do you not agree, my dear?" she asked as he threw aside the covers for her on the other side of the bed.

"Are you speaking of the wedding or the trial, my dear?"

"Both, actually. I am already quite fond of our new daughter-in-law."

He emitted a soft snort. "I should think you would be. The two of you are very much alike, if you ask me."

"Really? Do you think so?"

"Really. I do think so," he repeated with a great show of patience.

She snuggled closer. "That makes me feel very good, my love. They say that in the matter of choosing wives, most men judge prospective brides by their own mothers."

He looked up at the canopy over the bed. "Just as I did, eh?"

She pulled back and punched his shoulder. "I certainly hope that is not the case. You know very well your mother and I did not get along at all. I think I will get along very well with our Hero."

"Yes, dear," he said in a show of insincere contrition.

She babbled on. "And the trial went well too. Those truly dastardly sorts are off to the penal colony in New South Wales and Alex got to keep his own people where he needs them."

"Do not forget, my dear, that he had to ensure their being upright citizens for at least twenty years. They all signed on to that."

"I'm in love with our new granddaughter too. I shall have to return to Cornwall on a regular basis just to keep track of Annabelle."

"She's a pip," he agreed, then asked in a sleepy voice as he slid down in the bed, "What did you think of the way Alex dealt with Teague's family?"

"That was pure Alex, was it not?—finding the perfect solution in giving that abandoned farm to the Mullinses. Mullins apparently started life as a farm boy. The country is usually a wonderful place to rear children. And Alex promised him adequate help."

"And the new butler?"

"Well," she said, "most butlers I know of are usually close to six feet tall. Mac falls short of that by a good ten inches! But he is devoted to my son, so that is the most important factor."

"That does seem to be your basic requirement for many things," he said. "Now turn out that light, won't you? Alex told me this is a new bed, so let us make proper use of it, eh?"

She emitted an exaggerated sigh. "You're too old to be so randy." She eagerly complied with his request and slid down closer to him. "But I suppose I must take advantage of that while I may."

Meet the Author

Wilma Counts devotes her time largely to writing and reading. She loves to cook, but hates cleaning house. She has never lost her interest in literature, history, and international relations. She spends a fair amount of time yelling at the T.V. She is an active member of Lone Mountain Writers in Carson City, Nevada.

Readers can visit her website at www.wilmacounts.com.

Printed in the United States
by Baker & Taylor Publisher Services